# THE REBEL DIARIES

## AN ANTHOLOGY

### SACHA BLACK

*To the rebels out there with a spark inside them, let this be your match.*

# INTRODUCTION

*"Creativity is the greatest rebellion."*
***Osho***

**Rebel: noun**

"1. a person who refuses allegiance to, resists, or rises in arms against the government or ruler of his or her country.

2. a person who resists any authority, control, or tradition."

Rebellion has a bad rap. But I believe it's the greatest gift humanity has. Rebellion is change, it is empowerment and freedom, it's opinion and growth. Every step forward humanity takes is because one small act of rebellion sparked an idea or an invention or a revolution. Because one brave soul said "I don't think so," and found another way.

The world needs activists and revolutionaries like Emily Pankhurst and Rosa Parks but it also needs the quiet child standing up to her bullies, the employee quitting on principle, the girl shaving her head and dying the spikes blue. Sometimes we need to hear "no," or "you're not good enough," because it lights the fire for us to say "yes," and "I've always been good enough."

Rebellion is laced through creativity. Creatives think differently. We are magicians and wizards creating something from nothing. We see beyond, craft new worlds from paper dust and ink.

I have been inspired, humbled and awed at the rebellions shared in the community. Each one a reminder that we have the power to make our world the way we want it to be. This collection of stories is an examination of rebellion, of morally gray lines and deviant characters. It's meant to be fun, lighthearted. But beneath the surface lies many questions, where are moral lines? What is right and just? Is it a rebellion if the action is morally just? Are we all really the villains of our own stories?

My goal with this anthology was to make you laugh, help you escape into the minds of the dubious and irreverent all while experiencing the joy of reading exquisitely told stories. It is an honor and delight to have worked with these deeply talented authors. It would be remiss of me not to thank my critique partner, Helen Jones for helping to read through dozens of stories submitted and help me make the final selections. Thirteen stories—a fitting number, I think—that will take you on a rollercoaster of grumpy witches, literary thieves, terrifying orphans, ghosts, pirates, snarky demons, skull drinking book worms, sociopaths, superheroes, and ex-celebrities. Tales of inspiration and second chances, of empowerment and choices. Each of these stories is utterly unique in its voice, tone and shape and yet, they're all united by one glorious gift: rebellion.

In rebellion and revolution,

Sacha Black, January 2022

# PEARL'S TEA BY SCOTT WILLIAMSON

Pearl had run out of tea.

Now to any normal, healthy, old age pensioner, running out of tea isn't a huge problem, they would just pop to the shops and get some more.

Not Pearl.

Her knees creaked, her hip ached, and her tits chaffed against her thighs. And that was just standing still. Her popping to the shops days were over. She would make it to the end of the care home drive and pish herself from the effort and pain before being wheeled back inside by one of the care assistants.

She could, of course, send one of those useless bastard assistants to pick her up some tea bags. Sure. But the tea Pearl drank wasn't the standard swill drank by the pish-smelling, biscuit-chewing old goats she shared the Helping Hands care home with.

This tea was different. Special. You couldn't buy this in a shop. It wasn't meant for any normal old hag to drink. It was for witches only, and had been keeping Pearl alive for the last three hundred years.

But now she was down to her last tea bag.

This was a problem.

The flimsy off-white kettle in front of Pearl wobbled and clicked as it came to a boil, shouting for attention like a toddler having a tantrum. Hunched against the small kitchen, Pearl watched the steam cover the grubby tiles in drops of moisture. Pearl was more black shawl than woman with a thatch of gray hair framing crooked features, highlighted with an ugly wart on the end of her bent nose. The kitchen unit she used for support was shunted in the corner of the care home's lounge and supplied never-ending cups of weak tea to its residents.

Pearl hated using a kettle to make her tea. There was a patience she missed of sitting round a fire with her band of sisters waiting on the water to boil, then ladling out cupfuls of the bubbling liquid to each other. But those days were gone. As were all of her sisters. It seemed in today's society everyone had to have everything fed to them at a faster and faster rate. They wanted their tea ready now, their food pinged and ready in minutes, and their entertainment fed to them constantly. She had watched patience slowly disappear over the centuries she had been alive—along with her own for the world.

As the bubbling water settled, Pearl leaned harder on the kitchen unit, trying to take the weight off the pain in her right hip. The useless sack of bones hadn't stopped hurting since she had rationed herself to one cup of tea a day. Now she stared down her crooked nose at the last bag, the crimson red leaves inside ready to be steeped. Unless she found a replacement source of tea, the pain would only get worse until the relief of death came along and pulled her under to the waiting arms of her sisters. To find a replacement was why she was in this home—wasn't it?

Wrapping her two gnarled hands around the kettle handle, she lifted it toward her favorite black teapot. The kettle weighed like it was full of rocks and a spasm shot up her right leg and into her hip from the effort of lifting. A groan escaped her thin lips. Why did her bloody hip hurt from lifting a kettle? Old age could go fuck itself.

The boiling water caused the tea bag to fizz at the bottom of the pot. She placed the kettle back down as the familiar aroma drifted up to her nose—log fires, nutty ale, and fear. The smell of him. She could still see him now lying out on the floor of the shack they had shared, the whites of his eyes clear and his face slick with sweat. Her heart hammered in her chest at the memory of the blood covering the floor, the sound of the approaching hooves and the orange glow appearing through the window. Back in the good old days when baying mobs would hunt for the likes of her. That day she had slipped the knife into her dress after cutting him open and spoke the words under her breath to collect his blood. The last of which, hundreds of years later, she was about to drink.

"And on *Mid-Morning Today* we are going to be talking to a woman who can contact spirits through her lady parts."

Pearl flinched, almost knocking over the pot of tea. The memory of her last day with him evaporating at the sound of the voice coming from behind her in the lounge.

"Thanks, Molly, as if that's not enough, chef Dino Di Lonzo will make a lovely carbonara for you all to try at home."

"Mmm, sounds delicious, Bill."

One of the old fuckers had turned the TV on to the inane ramblings of morning entertainment. As usual, they had set the volume to ear-bleeding levels.

She frowned at the teapot in front of her. The last cup

she would drink would be while watching a woman describe summoning demons through her fanny. The sisterhood would be so proud.

"I love me a bit of Dino," came a shout from the lounge. The voice was Donna Crabbits', the care manager for Helping Hands, and its sound was as common and about as welcoming as a worrying cough in the care home.

With a shaking hand, Pearl placed the chipped lid onto the teapot, sealing the scent of the tea inside. Positioning her twisted black wooden cane into the crook of her elbow, she lifted the pot before turning in stages toward the lounge. The room was a sea of mismatched armchairs, all of them a different color of beige, all of them facing the hypnotizing glow of the television. All except one. Her throne. Black, taller, and undeniably less comfortable than the other chairs around the room, its solid, imposing frame sat off to the side, a small wooden table next to it. On the table, her favorite black cup and saucer waited. Her chair was deliberately pulled away from communicating distance with the rest of the room, but close enough for her to observe through her milky white eyes.

Pearl was constantly observing the other residents. She needed new tea bags, after all.

There were only a few bodies to scrutinize this morning. Most of the care home had been taken out for a morning walk in the garden. Pearl had refused, she wasn't a dog who needed taking outside for her morning shit.

No, she just needed to sit and have her tea—and pick her next victim.

As always, Donna had her fat arse plonked on one of the seats reserved for the old and frail. Built like a British Bulldog, top-heavy with a face that was meant for sniffing arseholes, Donna had her short stumpy legs propped up on a stool, her thick white ankles poked out from beneath her blue trousers. The matching blue t-shirt she wore had the Helping Hands logo stitched on its chest—a pair of gentle-looking hands holding the sun. Nothing like the clubs Donna had for fists. Currently, she held a mug of tea in one and a handful of biscuits in the other which were from a tin set on her stomach; a gift brought in for one of the residents no doubt.

Pearl shuffled toward her seat, the lid of the teapot rattling as she limped toward safety. She could feel Donna's beady eyes on her as she walked, a comment about her teapot no doubt on the edge of her lips. She was always dropping in comments about the pot. "We don't really allow junk like that in here as it's a safety hazard. Why don't you put it in the bin and use one of our own?"

"Oh no, dear, this is special to me. I couldn't throw it away. I've had it all my life," responded Pearl every time.

*And if you touch it, I will rake your fucking eyeballs out.*

Pearl found her seat and dumped the teapot on the table next to her, almost scattering the matching black cup and saucer set on the table. A rattling breath left her lungs as she slumped into her chair. She really couldn't go on living with this much pain. She needed to make her choice soon.

She lifted the pot and poured some of the claret liquid into her cup, the scent of burning fires thankfully overpowering the usual stench of pish wafting around the room. Or was the pishy smell coming from her after that walk? Hard to tell these days.

Puckering her wrinkled lips, Pearl took a loud slurp of the tea. Even after the thousands of cups she had drunk she hadn't grown tired of this particular flavor.

Strong. Earthy. Him.

Is this why she hadn't found someone else? The fear of replacing this taste?

Pearl was ready in some ways. Ready to cross the veil and reunite with her sisters. You didn't live all these years and not suffer. The physical pain wasn't even the worst part. And that was a persistent bitch. How many hundreds of friends, lovers and pets had she watched die out as she had carried on her march through time? All the so-called important people in her life faded away until they were nothing but a speck in her memory. It had gotten to the stage where Pearl no longer bothered building relationships as the pain of them ending was too much to bear.

Maybe now was the point where she let time win? It was always going to win, anyway. The sneaky bastard.

She slipped her hand into the pocket of the top layer of her black shawl and wrapped her hand around the rough jagged surface of a tea bag for what seemed like the hundredth time that day. The tea in her pocket was different to the crimson red tea she drank. This tea wouldn't keep her alive. The tea leaves felt almost hot beneath the mesh protection of the bag pressing into the tips of her fingers like needles. Pearl knew if she lifted the bag out and inspected the leaves inside, they would be a vicious green and give off a toxic reek. If she dropped the bag into some boiled water, the stench would disappear, replaced by whatever she desired the most to drink at that moment. But with one sip of the irresistible liquid, she would curl up on the floor of the lounge shortly after as her guts fought over which orifice to escape from.

The thought was morbidly appealing given the slow, excruciating way she was going to go anyway now she had run out of tea. Then again, the poison she held in her hand would have her shitting blood and vomiting up every inch of her insides until her body gave up. A slightly less appealing way to go, although it would give Donna something to clean up.

The poison had been in her pocket since she walked into Helping Hands care home in search of a victim to replace her source of tea. It should have been easy. A building already full of bodies close to the end, Pearl just had to pick one. But she hadn't been able to yet, put off by the thought of finding a tea which didn't mean as much to her as the one currently keeping her alive.

Pearl eyed the alternatives over the lip of her cup. Besides Donna, they were all potential victims. All of them potential bodies to keep her going. All of them saggy messes.

Slumped like a sack of potatoes in the hideous wool armchair on her right was Colin. His eyes, as always, raced his jaw to see which would droop the fastest as his false teeth slowly protruded out from behind his lips. It wouldn't be long until a stain formed on his brown chino's. Was that really who she wanted to be drinking from to keep her alive? A toothless old man with a bladder problem?

And then there was Helen. Sat perched on the edge of her seat, immaculately dressed in a tartan skirt, a cream jumper with a set of pearls around her neck and a pompous smile plastered across her face, revealing a good set of teeth. Unusual for in here.

But then she would have. Apparently, her son John was loaded, which didn't go unnoticed by Donna. He pranced in here once a month and Donna just about wet her knickers over him. Then the entire home would have to listen to Helen prattle on about her son for hours after his brief visit. "My John does this. My John does that." Blah, blah, blah. As always, a stupid grin on her face.

No matter what Helen said, her John had left his mother to live in this beige nightmare.

Pearl took another sip of tea and returned the cup and saucer to the table by her side. The warm liquid soothed her throat. The familiar effects would kick in once she finished the pot, and she would at least be able to move with less pain. Then she could pick her next victim.

But first, it was time to wipe the smile from Helen's face.

"What you smiling at?" Pearl said.

Helen kept her eyes plastered on the TV in front of her.

"So, when did you find out you could speak to the spirits, Mary?" the female presenter said. The presenter's voice was light and airy and totally inappropriate for talking to someone who thought spirits could speak to her through her front bum. If she had actually known what the spirits were like, then she would know they were more likely to make an appearance out your arsehole.

"Well, I was at the toilet one morning and just heard a voice," replied the guest.

"Isn't that lovely," Helen said from the chair opposite Pearl.

"What? The nutter is saying she can talk to spirits through her fanny," spat Pearl.

"It's always nice to have company."

"What, even in your fanny? I suppose. I bet it's been a while since you had any company down there though, Helen, eh?" Pearl let out a cackle at her joke.

Colin flinched in his sleep at the sound, returning his teeth to the safety of his mouth. Pearl looked toward Donna for recognition of the joke, but the care manager had nothing but a deep frown on her face as she stuffed another biscuit in her mouth.

"Did you not feel like a walk this morning, Pearl?" Helen said.

Pearl shifted in her seat.

"Yeah, why you not out for a walk?" grunted Donna, spraying biscuit crumbs as she spoke.

"The cold, Donna, it's not good for my leg."

"I have always found walks to be good for the circulation, Pearl," Helen said.

"I bet it doesn't unclench that arsehole of yours though, you uptight bitch."

"Right, that's it. You're going out," Donna said, pulling herself up from her seat causing the biscuit tin that had been clinging to her stomach to clatter to the floor.

"No, I'm fucking not—"

Donna's hulking body loomed over Pearl, blocking out the light in the room. Pearl lurched for her cane ready to strike the woman if she got any closer.

"Come on. Up and out."

"But I've not even finished my tea."

Donna reached and grabbed the cup and saucer.

"No!" Pearl lunged forward and swung her cane at Donna, but the care manager just turned her gorilla-sized back and the cane bounced off, causing a shuddering pain to travel down Pearl's arm.

Donna stomped away with the pot, cup, and saucer all in one shovel-sized hand, leaving Pearl to sink back into her chair, sucking at mouthfuls of air.

What had just happened? She had lost the last of her tea. Why hadn't she savored it? That last cup would have seen her through the night. How was she going to find a replacement if she could barely walk?

A tut came from across the room.

Pearl looked up to find Helen's pretentious smile aimed at her.

"You bitch!" Spital flew from Pearl's mouth as she lurched forward again and tried to get to her feet. A pain burned from the top of her right hip down to her toes stuffed inside her black slippers causing another spasm in her leg. She gasped and flopped back down in her seat.

"Donna, she is in a lot of pain. I think a walk will do her good," cooed Helen.

The gargle of liquid disappearing down the plug and dishes clattering into the sink came from the kitchen. Pearl's chest felt tight, the last of her tea gone. The last of him, gone. Only pain would follow now.

A misshapen silhouette like a dark storm cloud gathered over Pearl as Donna stepped back to her chair. Pearl looked up at the twisted smile on the woman's drooping face.

"Up."

"No, please—" Pearl hated how pathetic she sounded. Without her tea, she was nothing but a frail old woman.

Donna gripped hold of Pearl's shoulders and hoisted her to her feet like a mother handling a child. Even through the layer upon layer of shawl, Donna's fingers dug through into Pearl's paper-thin skin. She bundled Pearl toward the door who didn't even squirm or fight back, there was no point; she had to conserve her energy.

"Enjoy your walk, Pearl," came the sweet call from Helen as Donna led Pearl from the Helping Hands lounge.

Like a shuffling shadow, Pearl moved through the hall of the care home. The cane in her left hand tapped on the bare, rough carpet. A scraping followed as she pulled her slab of meat right leg reluctantly after her left. Each step caused her eyes to water and the cup and saucer she held in her hand to rattle—sloshing the cup's contents toward the rim.

The earlier walk around the garden had been hell. Even with the couple of mouthfuls of tea, each hobbling step had felt like someone driving a blunt knife through her legs. Two nurses had helped her back into her black throne after one lap outside, her whole body shaking like a shitting dog. The chair was her relief and her prison for the rest of the day. As darkness descended, Pearl watched the surrounding frail be carted off to bed. She conserved her energy for revenge.

The first part of that revenge was behind the door at the opposite end of the hall—a hall which seemed to grow longer with each fucking step. Was this the last challenge she faced to continue living? A long hallway?

Oh, how the sisterhood would be proud.

The hall was dark except for the blurred cracks of light appearing from under the doors to the Helping Hands rooms. The odd cough escaped from behind closed doors as Pearl limped past, some more worrying than others. She recognized that type of cough. Normally a pine box arrived shortly after, along with a group of relatives who had never appeared in these halls prior to the box. The relatives' faces would be etched with relief at no longer having to fund the care of whoever was being carried out in the coffin.

Pearl tried to hold the cup of tea in her hand as steady as possible to avoid letting the liquid spill over the sides. Her nose filled with the familiar bouquet of log fires, nutty ale, and fear. The smell of him.

"Take a sip," the tea called, "this will dissolve all the pain you feel."

And the tea would taste just like the half cup Donna had

thrown down the sink this morning. But there would be no relief from the pain. That familiar warm, comforting flavor would quickly sour, replaced with a burning which would have her curled up in a ball on the floor.

A hiss escaped her mouth as a sharp pain radiated down her leg into her toes. Tea spilled over the edge of the cup onto the saucer as her hand shook. She paused, her head swimming with the desire to lie down.

Through her blurred vision, she could make out a blue light under the door she struggled toward. Her intended prey was still awake. What would the poison in her hands taste like to her chosen victim? Black tea? Coffee? Whisky? They wouldn't see what was actually in the cup—a violent bubbling green. Not even Pearl could see that. All she had to do was get the poison in front of her victim's nose.

Easier said than done. She blinked away the tears and kept shuffling.

Pearl's chest heaved as she finally reached the door, her breath rattling in her lungs. Muffled voices came from the other side, no doubt from a TV. Her victim wouldn't have guests. Pearl wondered how her prey would taste once drained and made into tea leaves. She wrinkled her nose; the thought wasn't a pleasant one, but neither was carrying on in this much pain.

Lifting her walking stick from the crook of her elbow, Pearl gave the door a rap and resisted the compulsion to lean against the door. She was likely to collapse through into the room when the door opened if she did.

There was a curse and a groan from the other side of the door. Pearl took a deep breath, trying to calm her thumping heart as footsteps approached.

The door opened inward, and light spilled out from within causing Pearl to squint. The stench of stale food and musty farts followed, and Pearl pushed away the thought of that flavor of tea.

She blinked until her eyes adjusted to the light and met the eyes of her intended victim.

"Oh, it's you. What do you want? Another stroll in the garden?" Donna said, her mouth curled up in a sneer. The buttons of her Helping Hands t-shirt were open, and the collar sagged open, revealing an extra couple of chins Pearl hadn't had the pleasure of being disgusted by before.

"I thought—"

"What's that? Hot chocolate?"

Donna's gaze had already moved from glowering at Pearl, down to the cup in front of her. She licked her lips, grazing at a bit of saliva already caught in the dark hairs of her upper lip. Her normally narrow, hard eyes were wide and never left the poison Pearl held out in her hand.

"It's for you. A peace offering."

Pearl twisted her face into the most genuine warm smile she could muster. The effort hurt more than her leg.

Donna looked up from the cup to Pearl's smile and the desire had gone; replaced by a narrow-eyed mistrust. Who could blame her after all, a witch stood in front of her with a cup full of poison in her hand.

Pearl forced herself to smile harder, her heart beating inside of her chest as she tried to keep the cup steady. Before she could pass out, Pearl hoped the greed of the woman standing in front of her would take over—it normally did.

With a grunt, Donna grabbed the cup and saucer from Pearl's hands and turned back into the room, leaving her door ajar.

Pearl followed Donna into the room, pressing the door closed behind her, wondering if Donna would taste as bad as the room smelled.

～

Donna didn't taste as bad as her room had smelled. She tasted worse.

Pearl placed her teacup back on the saucer and swallowed. The tang of moldy cheese and armpits caught the back of her throat. Three cups in, and she still hadn't gotten used to the flavor of her new tea. Each mouthful stronger and more disgusting than the last.

She sat the teacup and saucer down on the side table next to her black throne and eyed the yellow liquid floating in the cup with disdain. It looked like the pish of someone whose liver had given up a while ago. And her body felt more rejuvenated with every sip.

Sunday afternoons were for visitors and around Pearl the lounge was busy with the Helping Hands residents and their guests. As usual, Pearl had no visitors, but she was happy to sit and people-watch.

The record player was on and jazz horns floated in and out of the conversations and laughter filling the room. Colin was awake and up dancing with his great granddaughter who had come to visit. She wore a tartan dress with a frilly white collar and stood on Colin's slippered feet as they danced. Every time Colin swung a leg, they both giggled, and he almost lost his teeth onto the floor.

The room felt lighter. Even the care assistants were laughing and mingling with the guests. Pearl had overheard one of them comment that Donna had taken her first day off in a long time and it was a relief to have a day off from her.

Donna would have to take a day off—considering she had been drained and folded into the suitcase under Pearl's bed.

It had been a full night's work getting her there last

night. Draining Donna's body, then carrying through what was left of her, had almost killed Pearl. Only the fuel of a never-ending stream of swearing and the thought of never having to deal with Donna again kept Pearl from collapsing on top of the shriveled carcass of the care home manager. But now she was three cups into the tea made from Donna's blood and better for it. Her leg no longer moved like a lump of dead meat, and her hip wasn't throbbing in pain. She could be up dancing by the end of this cup. If she didn't absolutely *fucking hate* dancing.

More importantly, in the next few days, she could stroll out of this waiting room for the dead and back into a world without hideous armchairs and soggy biscuits.

She just had one more life to ruin first, though.

A familiar exaggerated laugh came from across the room. It was Helen, sitting bolt upright in her chair, dressed as always in an understated jumper and skirt, pearls at her neck. Sitting to her right, his head buried in his phone, was a man in his fifties who dressed as uptight as his mother. He wore an immaculate pinstripe suit with red socks poking out from the bottom of his trousers and shiny black brogues covering his feet. His slicked-back, suspiciously black hair, failed to cover the bald spot he showed off while checking his phone.

"Oh, John, that's so funny! You get your sense of humor from me," squealed Helen over the record player. As she giggled, her gaze searched the room for others joining in. But her laughter quickly dissolved into a frown as she realized no one was paying her any attention. With Donna no longer around, everyone was having too much fun to give a flying fuck about how funny her John was.

Helen looked toward Pearl, and their eyes met. Helen's gaze suggested it was somehow Pearl's fault no one was paying her any attention. The stuck-up bint was probably right. Pearl broke into a smile with all the warmth of a polar bear's nipples.

*That's right, bitch, no one is interested in you or your John's shitty jokes now.*

Helen didn't return the smile; she turned away and inched herself closer to the edge of her seat, reaching out a hand to rub John's arm. But her son paid even less attention to her than the rest of the lounge. His eyes never left his phone, fingers flying across it constantly.

Pearl kept her eyes on them both as her hand found its way into the pocket of her shawl. The familiar rough texture of a tea bag and the sharp stab of the poisonous leaves within met her searching fingertips. Now that she had used one of the lethal tea bags on Donna, it seemed a shame not to use another. It would be easy enough to pour a cup of something deadly for Helen. She was old and frail after all. If she dropped dead, no one would bat an eyelid. That's what old people did, wasn't it? Her own son would probably be relieved, it would save him a trip on a Sunday.

Pearl thought of the call from Helen as she was being dragged from the lounge yesterday. *Enjoy your walk, Pearl.* That walk had almost killed her.

No, poisoning Helen wasn't the answer. That wouldn't cause enough pain.

Pearl leaned forward.

"John," she shouted across the din of the lounge.

John raised his eyes from his phone to meet Pearl's, his thick dark eyebrows arched in confusion at someone daring to call his name.

"What do you want?" spat Helen

"Just wanted to speak to the famous John," Pearl said with a smile.

"Ignore her, John, she causes nothing but trouble in here."

"Every group needs a rebel," Pearl said and winked at John.

A smile played at the edges of John's lips and he relaxed back in his armchair, letting his phone screen turn black.

"How can I help?" he said.

"Oh, laddie, I don't need any help. I can help you though, I see your own mother hasn't poured you a cup of something warm."

John laughed, revealing a perfect set of white teeth.

"No, she has not. Have you got something I could have?"

Pearl hopped to her feet. Thanks to the tea from Donna, her joints moved like someone had smothered them in oil. She lifted the poisonous tea bag from her shawl and smiled at Helen's son.

"I have got something special just for you. None of that standard swill you are used to."

# ABOUT SCOTT WILLIAMSON

Scott Williamson's stories have his twisted Scottish cheek, a nip of darkness and a sprinkle of hope. Scott lives in Auld Reekie Edinburgh with his wife and three kids. When he is not in his writing cage fighting with the blank page, Scott can be found curled up and broken on the couch with a book after a day parenting his tearaway children.

**Find out more about Scott at:**
www.scottwilliamsonauthor.com

 instagram.com/scott_williamson_author

## LITTLE ORPHAN AGGIE BY
## KIMBERLY GRYMES

Most people look forward to the weekends, but not me.

Then again, I ain't like most people. I'm one of those unfortunate souls—a kid without a home, parents, or even a last name.

I used to have a mom and dad, but Mom died of the fever and Dad decided he wasn't gonna come home after working the factory one day. After he didn't come home that night, I taught myself to strike a match to heat some food on the stove and light candles when it got dark. I don't remember much about our home except that the floors creaked, and it was cold at night.

One day, when the food was all gone, I remember trudging up the dirt road to our neighbor's house, Old Lady Gums. I called her that because she didn't have no teeth. She was nice and fed me a hot meal. Nothing special. Some kind of smashed meat stew with mushed up vegetables. It tasted off, but I remember devouring every bite.

Anywho, by the time I'd finished eating, the police were standing in front of me, asking all kinds of questions about my mom and dad. They weren't too happy with my answers because next thing I knew I was being dropped off to live with the nuns at the orphanage.

Seven years I've been living in this ruler-smacking hell hole. Some girls don't mind it, but other girls—like me—can't wait to leave. I'm surrounded by cranky nuns and whiny brats. I ain't complaining too much. There's a solid roof over my head and half-decent meals three times a day, but still, there's got to be something better out there. A life where others are doing gratitude chores for me. I hate scrubbing toilets, washing windows, sweeping stairs, and whatever else the nuns think we should do for what they call *gratitude-time*. What goop came up with *"thank you for taking me in and not leaving me on the street"* gratitude chores is beyond me.

For the most part, I can tolerate all that bull. Everyone, young and old, has gotta work for a living, right? What I hate the most about this orphan gig are the what-the-fuck-not-again weekends. Same thing, every weekend.

Sundays ain't too bad, they're just boring as hell. Sister Meredith and Sister Trudy, the two nuns who run this place, make us sit through hours and hours of God-babble during morning mass. After lunch, we're forced to sit and read Bible verses. Then, without a break, we're marched to the choral room where we sing hymns like angels for two hours with Sister Trudy. I was just kidding about that *singing like angels* part. But seriously, by the end of the day, I'm dog-tired from boredom.

You'd think that was the worst part of my weekend, but nope. It's Saturdays that I dread. Fucking visitation day.

You'd think a kid without a mom and dad would be excited to stand tall and look all innocent enough to hustle some new parents. Yeah, well, no one's buying what I'm selling. I ain't got the right look that any of those dolled-up wannabe parents are looking for.

"Her hair is too red. Her hair is too wiry! Doesn't she own a brush?" are the biggest complaints listed off to me. One woman tried to hide her dismay by covering her mouth with one hand as she told her husband, "Her face is awfully long."

*People with long faces still have ears that work*, was what I wanted to say, but I held back. No need to get in trouble with the sisters when I can help it.

I've gotten good at rolling my eyes and ignoring the hurtful things said to my face, except there was that one time. This one broad pushed me the wrong way and I pushed back. It was about a month ago, when this lady and her husband showed up right before Sister T was about to lock the doors. Visitation day was practically over! Yet, the sisters let this lady and her fancy husband inside. She was fancy too, in her green satin dress trimmed with lace. I swear her shoulder poofs were the poofiest I'd ever seen on an Edwardian dress.

Oh, I read those fashion magazines, all right. The gardener sneaks one in every now and then for us girls to browse. It doesn't cost her more than five cents, so no skin off my back.

Anywho, this pompous Miss Look-At-Me-I'm-So-Rich was making her way down the line. Her blonde hair pinned up with a miniature top hat set on her head, white feathers sticking out the side. The man had a white shirt, black vest, and a long matching dress coat. I couldn't help but stare at his top hat and cane as he followed his wife around the room.

I'd immediately known this lady and her gent weren't going to be my new mommy and daddy, but I stood tall and smiled anyway. I could hear her scrutinizing each girl as she moved from girl to girl, down the line. When I snuck a quick glance, I saw her looking through a monocle that hung from a chain around her neck.

*Seriously*, I thought. *She needs a magnifying glass to get an up close and personal detailed inspection. Sheesh, I kind of feel bad for the hubby. This lady screams high-maintenance.*

When her scowl and beady eyes landed on me, I was ready for the onslaught of insults. There was nothing she could say that I hadn't already heard, but to my surprise, that richey-rich bitch turned to her husband and said, "No-no, this one won't do. She'll produce the most hideous grandchildren."

Well, I sure as hell wasn't expecting that and she wasn't expecting the kick to her shin. That cost me a week in isolation, but it was worth it because I'd be locked up until the following Sunday. Meaning my ass ain't lining up for any insults come the next visitation day.

But my isolation is over, and here I am getting ready for another fucking day of being scrutinized for things I have no control over. I am who I am.

"Come, come girls. Find your best dress and put on your happy faces," I hear Sister Meredith announce. Her wooden cane bangs the stone floor with a rhythmic *thump, thump, thump* as she marches the halls of the orphanage.

"Can't they just show them our files, you know with our pictures, and let us be?" I say to Gerti, the closest person I've got to a best friend in this place.

Gerti's one good eye looks at me from across the top of her cot. "Just fix your blanket straight and play nice. Can you do that? It ain't no fun when you're locked up."

Gerti means well, and we weren't always the closest of friends. Right after I'd arrived here, somebody donated a bag full of new clothes for us girls. Sister Meredith told everyone to pick one new dress from the pile and to keep it clean for visitation day. I found a pretty red dress. It was too big, but I was determined to make it work while I grew into it. Gerti was quick to snatch my new dress from me. "Thanks, this'll look nice on me." Yeah, I was upset about my dress, but it was also the first time I'd really gotten a good look at Gerti's face, and that in itself had distracted me from wanting my dress back.

"Whatcha staring at, you little shit!" Gerti, who was a foot taller than me, shoved me hard against the stone wall.

"What the hell's wrong with your eye?" I asked. Thinking back, I probably shouldn't have been so blunt, but being subtle or polite ain't my thing.

"You talk'n to me?"

"Ah, yeah." Ten-year-old me wasn't the brightest back then either. "Why's one eye looking over there and your other eye looking at me? Is that a trick or somethin'?" The blow that came from Gerti's right fist caught me off guard and I landed on my ass, black spots speckling my vision. Before I could react, Sister Trudy, our choral teacher, rushed over and escorted Gerti away. I was taken to the infirmary.

Later that night, after everyone went to sleep, I snuck over to Gerti's cot and held a butter knife to her throat. She tried to scramble free, but I pressed the dull blade harder to her skin. "Listen here, I know I'm new and all but I ain't one of those little shits you can push around. I just want to be left alone. Maybe I'll find a new home, maybe I won't, but in the meantime, I don't need any more black eyes from you. Got me?"

The windows in the orphanage are crap. Old and dingy, they barely let in sunlight during the day let alone moonlight at night. I was close enough to Gerti's face to see her narrow her eyes. She lay silent for a long moment before nodding. "Yeah, yeah, whatever. Just get the hell off me."

"And I want my dress back," I added between gritted teeth.

"Yea, sure. Just get off me!" Gerti yelled in a hushed tone. Neither of us wanted to wake the sisters.

I shushed her while slowly lifting the butter knife from her throat. Not wanting to lose the knife, I tucked it into my belt. "That's a pretty nice right hook you got there. Maybe you could teach me one day?" It was the best peace offering I could muster.

A wry smile cracked her lips. "All right." We sat on her cot, face to face. "What's your name?"

I'd been there for days, and no one had asked me my name. The nuns don't use our names and only refer to us as "girls" or "girl," and I only know Gerti's name because one of the other girls gave me a good warning when I first arrived. "Hey, new girl. Best to stay away from Gerti. You'll know who I'm talking about when you see her."

"Agatha, but you can call me Aggie."

"All right, Aggie. Now, get off my cot and get some sleep." Gerti sounded annoyed, but through the faintest light shining in from the stained glass I could see a smile on my new friend's face.

"Right," I said, and snuck back to my cot.

Seven and a half years later, the red dress now fits me like a glove. It's been stitched in a few places over the years, but this dress has been with me through every visitation day, and I plan to make it last until the day I walk out of here. Four more months until my so-called rebirthday. The nuns don't technically know our birthdays, so they give us new birthdays based on the day we arrived at the orphanage. We call it our rebirthday. Not like we celebrate it or anything. It's just the official day they took us in and started turning us into the fine ladies we are today, or some bullshit like that. That's one of the perks when you're running an orphanage. You can do whatever the hell you want, like give out rebirthdays or change a girl's name, or tell her to clean the toilet after you've just finished exploding in it.

I stare at myself in a small, chipped mirror while running a broken brush through my hair, trying to flatten the frizz from the curls. *Their lives must be nice, delegating all the work to be done around here. Maybe one day I'll be some kind of boss lady too. Telling people to clean up after me. I like the sound of that.*

I'm about done buttoning up the front of my dress when a string of wild girls run in from the hall, screaming and chasing one another and weaving between all the cots in the room.

"Hey, stop running and get ready before Sister Mer sees you, you little brats!"

"Yes, Miss Aggie!" the lot of them yell in unison. They stop running and tend to their cots.

"And stop calling me that!"

"You ready yet?" Gerti asks from behind me. Over the years, she's gotten taller and curvier. Her brown hair is a mop of curls on top of her head.

"I thought you were going to give that dress to Bess?" I say, glancing at her midsection. We eat the same food at the same time every day, yet I've barely gained a pound and look as lanky as ever. Gerti, on the other hand, has rounded out in her hips and butt and grew a chest that could be considered a weapon if she turns and catches you the wrong way.

"I'll give it to her after today's looksies. If I can't find a family to take me in, maybe I can find a man to take me home."

We laugh because we both know our days are running low. Come our eighteenth rebirthdays, Sister Meredith will happily walk us to the orphanage gates and shove us out into the world they have not prepared us for. They teach us about how to polish silverware, make a cot, and etiquette for when guests come on visitation day, but they don't tell us shit about what to expect out there—in the real world. Secretly, I think they like keeping us in the dark. That way, we'll want to stay and pledge our devotion and loyalty to their Lord above. Recruit us into their world and dress us up in their black-and-white getups. Fuck that. There's got to be something better out there, and I intend to find a way to be in charge of it all.

"What's today's number?" I ask Gerti, slipping on an old pair of brown shoes. One of the laces is broken and I make do with knotting them instead of tying a neat bow.

Gerti pulls out a worn piece of paper and a stubby pencil from under her pillow. She scribbles over something before writing something else in its place. Her hand grips the pencil like a five-year-old trying to hold a fork for the first time. "Forty-nine."

Forty-nine days and then my friend will be pushed out through the front gates. I'm not too far behind her, with only ninety-three days left. Gerti slowly slips the paper and pencil under her pillow. Her hand lingers there for a long moment before pulling it back out. The silence between us speaks louder than all the ruckus around us. She's afraid.

"Come on, Gerti. Sister Mer is waiting."

Gerti gets up. She plasters a fake smile between her two plump cheeks, as the nuns instruct us to do. We hear Sister Meredith's cane banging in the hall, coming our way. "Don't forget to wash your faces, brush your teeth, and for the love of all that's holy, BRUSH YOUR HAIR!"

We stand at attention at the doorway of our room. Sister Meredith stops and glances us over with narrowed eyes. Well, she's not really looking at me, but more focused on Gerti's tight dress. Sister Mer's never one to address us as individuals, never has. But we can always tell from her glares which girls she favors and which ones she's coined bad seeds.

When Sister Meredith continues down the hall and up the back stairwell to the nursery, I relax, leaning one shoulder against the wall, and ask, "What's up her ass today?"

Gerti shrugs, and then with a giggle, she says, "Well, I did overhear someone say she'd misplaced her rosary."

"Misplaced!" I say, and we burst out laughing. I'm bowed over, hands on my knees. The image of Sister Mer's prayer beads sticking out of her ass has my insides rolling. "Oh, that was good," I say, wiping a tear from my eye. "I thought I was going to have to change my underwear!"

In the foyer, ten girls line up on one side of the room and eight girls on the other. Sister Meredith and Sister Trudy stand at the front, waiting patiently for all the girls to get into place.

"Nice of you to join us, girls," Sister Meredith says and points the tip of her cane to the two empty spots.

"Apologies, Sister," we say in unison and scurry to our spots.

After a long pause, Sister Meredith slowly walks the aisle between our lines. We stare up at the cracks in the plaster ceiling as she inspects us.

"Where are your socks?" she berates, while smacking her cane against the leg of a young girl. The girl looks to be no older than six. Her eyes are as big as doorknobs, glassy and trembling.

"Should we say something?" Gertie whispers out of the crook of her mouth. "Draw her attention away from the girl?"

"What? No. That girl's on her own. Now, shush. Sister T's opening the doors."

Bright sunlight pours into the foyer, like God has opened the doors himself and shines a spotlight on Sister Meredith and the lovely girls she's raised. Only to me, it's more like we're opening the front doors for the big guy to get a better laugh at the shit show that's about to go down in here.

"Welcome, welcome!" Sister Meredith greets the few couples that stroll into the orphanage. "My name is Sister Meredith, and this is Sister Trudy. We're so pleased to have you on this fine Saturday afternoon." She turns and gestures for everyone to come in with a wide sweep of her hand. "Come, come and meet our precious girls."

The two couples part, each pair starting at the beginning of a different line of girls.

*It'll all be over soon, and Gerti and I can get back to our card game. Hopefully, before dinner.*

As usual, it's the women who do all the shopping, and so far, neither of these women see anything worth taking home.

One couple politely thanks the sisters and heads out the door, probably thinking how they wasted their Saturday afternoon. While the doors are open, I catch sight of an old woman outside, older than Sister Mer, shuffling her way up the front steps.

My attention is drawn to my right, toward the back of the room, where Sister Trudy is talking to the second couple. I catch the end of their hushed conversation as they move toward the back stairwell.

"The nursery, you say? Ah, yes, of course. Our older girls

are all good and ready for new homes, but yes, I see your point. The little babies have yet to be corrupted. Come, come."

I can't help but stare at the woman following Sister T. She's so young, maybe a year or two older than me, with the softest skin and silkiest hair I've ever seen. She's like something straight out of one of those hoity-toity high-end fashion magazines. Even her rump is impressive and makes Gerti's curves look flat as a board, though it could be one of those bustles I read about lifting her butt from underneath her dress.

I elbow Gerti and she turns to look at me. "Ow, what was that for?"

"Look. Look at that lady." I point with one finger barely raised, because heaven forbid Sister Meredith catches one of us moving.

"What about her?" Gerti asks, mouth hanging open. Gerti's nose is often stuffy, so she breathes through her mouth. It's an acquired trait of hers that I've come to accept. "She's pretty, but I don't think she'd make a good mom for either of us. She'd be more like a sister—"

"Are you talking?" Sister Meredith seethes, inches from Gerti's face. "That's one hour of gratitude."

"Yes, Sister," Gerti says. Her eyes dart to the ceiling and she clasps her hands behind her back, making her chest stick out.

Sister Meredith doesn't drop her gaze as Gerti's chest pushes out and bumps her. Instead, Sister Meredith rolls her eyes and says with an annoyed groan, "Keep your hands to your sides, and shrug your shoulders for heaven's sake."

"Yes, Sister." My friend lowers her hands to her sides and drops her shoulders into a sag.

I can't help but giggle, and Sister Mer shoots me a look

that says, *Do you want to join your friend in an hour of gratitude chores?* I clear my throat and return to my statuesque form. When I hear the banging of her cane on the stone floor, I risk a glance. She's gone to greet the old woman who's finally made it into the entryway of the orphanage. Hopefully, the lady's here to see Sister Mer and we'll get dismissed early.

No such luck. I can't hear their words, but I become wildly suspicious when Sister Meredith turns and gestures for the old woman to have a look at all the assembled girls. Everyone straightens, and I prepare myself for the criticism to come. I can only imagine what bitter words she'll use to describe my gaunt features, untamed red hair, and the length of my jawline.

One by one, the old woman moves in silence from one girl to the next. She's wearing some kind of animal wrap over a satin dress the color of a tomato. She's not a large woman, but rather quite short and frail-looking. When she reaches me, she stares up at me from beneath white hair that has been styled into an impressive pompadour. "What's your name, girl?"

"Agatha," I say, as instructed by the sisters. They always tell us: *respond to every question with a smile and an answer that'll make us proud.* Translation: lie if you must, and more importantly don't make us look bad.

The old woman nods in approval while I note the layers of expensive pearls wrapping her neck.

"And tell me, Agatha, what is your age?"

"Seventeen. I'll be eighteen in a few months, ma'am."

"Interesting." She turns to Sister Meredith, and says, "Yes, I like this one."

*What. The. Fuck? Is she pointing to me?*

I drop my gaze and stare at the old woman.

*It's got to be some kind of cruel joke. There's no way this old bitty is looking to adopt a kid!*

Sister Meredith approaches, offers an arm to the old woman, and leads her across the foyer to the main office. "Excellent choice, ma'am." Sister Meredith congratulates the old woman like she's just purchased a new sofa or curtains for her home—soon to be my home!

"What just happened?" Gerti turns and faces me. With Sister Mer out of the room, everyone relaxes. Gerti's lazy eye is staring off in one direction while her good eye is locked onto me. "You can't go. Not before me! And-and with that old lady? How does that work? She's too old to be your mom!"

"Something's not right," I whisper, while shifting my gaze over to the main office. My future was being decided behind that closed door.

"She looked rich," Bess says. Her voice is both sweet and excited from across the line. "That's a plus, right?"

"Maybe she needs someone to wipe her ass," Faye snickers from the other side of Gerti.

"You're gonna need someone to wipe your ass if you don't—"

Sister Trudy and the couple from earlier emerge from the back stairwell and we all take our positions again. The young woman is beaming, cautiously walking down each step, a baby swaddled in her arms with her husband walking close behind. His smile's as wide and elated as the woman's. They follow Sister Trudy and disappear into the main office to sign the paperwork for their new bundle of joy.

"Why anyone would want to purposely adopt a baby that only cries, eats, and shits all the time is beyond me," Faye says.

"Shut up, Faye," Gerti says and holds up a fist. "Or I swear I'll shut you up."

Faye smirks in amusement, and says, "Give me a black eye and you'll be doing more than an hour of gratitude chores for Sister Meredith."

"Seriously, Faye. Shut it," I snap at her.

We stand there for thirty minutes before the door to the main office opens. "Girls, you can return to your rooms." Everyone takes flight. Even I try to escape, but Sister Meredith calls me out, "Except you." She points and stares at me. "Come here." I cringe and take a few calming breaths before trudging over to the two women.

"Yes, Sister."

"This is Mrs. Han—"

"Never mind the formalities." The old woman waves a hand, cutting off Sister Meredith. "Please, call me Dottie."

"Are you sure?" Sister Meredith's expression is a mixture of shock and confusion twisting on her face. It's not proper to address people by their given name, but it makes me like this old bat a bit more.

Dottie nods, and I can't help but ask, "You're looking for a daughter?"

"Where are your manners?" Sister Meredith exclaims, swooping over to my side. She drapes one arm along my back and digs her nails into my shoulder. I swear she's gouging bone. "My apologies. I assure you we've—"

"Never mind. And there'll be no need for that," Dottie narrows her eyes at Sister Meredith. It's as if she knows what Sister Mer is doing. "Let go of the girl."

Sister Meredith releases her claws from my body, and I shake off the lingering sting and stand tall. I'm so impressed with Dottie's boldness that I decided to give her the benefit of the doubt. "So, when do we leave?"

"If you think you can hastily get your things, then now. But if you need the night, I can send a driver with the carriage in the morning. Your choice."

"Now is fine," I say.

"Excellent!" Wrinkles appear, creasing on the outskirts of Dottie's gray eyes.

"Run along and get your trunk," Sister Meredith instructs me, and I don't hesitate, dashing off down the hall to our sleeping room. I have no idea why I'm smiling, because I have no idea what awaits me at Dottie's house. Will there be other kids to play with? Would she make me do gratitude chores? There are so many unknowns that my mind is a twirling whirlwind.

I race between cots and over to where mine is pushed against the wall. Across from my cot, Gerti sits on the edge of her bed with her head low, staring at her shoes.

I pull out my trunk from under my cot and stuff all my belongings in it. The trunk was mine to keep, they told me the first day I'd arrived, like they tell every girl on day one. They were all identical, except mine. My trunk is missing one of the metal decals from the top right corner. I pried it off a few years ago, flattened it with my shoe, and then used a pair of shears from the gardening shed to trim it to look like a coin. After polishing and stamping it with an old nail I'd found, I'd told one of the new kids it was a priceless coin. Convinced her so well that she traded me two pairs of thick socks for it.

"You really leaving? Like, right now?" Gerti asks, her eyes puffy and red.

"Yup."

"Then that's it. I'll never see you again?"

"Probably not, but maybe." I stop packing and look over at Gerti. "Oh, come on. You knew this day was coming. That we'd be leaving this hellhole and making a new life out in the real world. You'll be doing the same in less than two months. Now, stop crying."

"But—"

"No buts. It is what it is, Gerti. It's time to grow up."

Bess comes over and sits next to Gerti, who drops her head on Bess's shoulder. It looks awkward because Gerti is twice the size of Bess. "Well ... good luck and stay in touch."

With my trunk in my arms, I give a wink to Gerti and Bess, and then walk out of this dank, dingy room for the last time. I'm excited, scared, nervous, and elated all at the same time. The only thing I know for sure is that my orphanage days are finally over.

"Come on, dear. The carriage is waiting." Sister Trudy stands at the front door. Outside I see the happy couple walking off with their new baby while a large black carriage with two giant horses waits for me outside the orphanage's gates. "You'll be fine, just remember your manners." She hands me a Bible and adds, "Don't forget to practice your hymns, and I do hope we'll get to see you at mass tomorrow."

*Mass. I'd completely forgotten all about mass. I'd see Gerti and Bess on Sundays during mass.*

A man approaches. He's dressed in an overcoat, and the hems of his pantlegs are cinched around his knees. Bright white stockings cover his chicken legs all the way down to the black buckle shoes. He looks ridiculous, but I ain't one to say what a carriage driver should be wearing.

I nod and take the Bible. I won't be reading it anytime soon, but it's the only way I can think to thank her. She pulls me in for a hug, which catches me off guard. We stand there, awkwardly, until she's done, before scooting me along. Down by the carriage, Sister Meredith waits for me. Dottie's already inside the carriage.

"Got everything?"

"Yes, Sister."

"Good. Now, get in and be a good girl for Mrs.—I mean, Dottie," she corrects herself with an annoyed trail of her words. Dottie stares at her with a raised eyebrow.

"Thank you for your help today, Sister," Dottie says before leaning back in her seat.

"Yes, well, be good, Agatha."

My foot freezes mid-step as I go to climb the carriage steps. I face Sister with narrowed eyes. She's never said my name before, and I swear she looks pleased beneath her scowl. Like she's hiding something.

"Yes, Sister," I say, my jaw clenched, and without another glance, I climb the steps into the carriage. The inside smells like old cheese and moth balls. The door shuts and we're off.

Dottie doesn't speak the entire ride to her home. Actually, I think the old lady fell asleep two minutes into the ride. Hours later, when the driver finally stops the horses and the door opens, we step outside. It's nearly dusk, and we're in a—a city! I've never been to a city before. I can see tall buildings, the tallest I'd ever seen, off beyond the houses. My gaze dips to the tall homes, squeezed together, lining both sides of the street. Gas lamps are blazing bright along the sidewalks. The cobblestone street seems to stretch forever in both directions. My heart is fluttering with all the possibilities in a big city like this!

"Come this way," she beckons, and I follow her up a set of stairs to one of the narrow, four-story homes. My new home.

The driver behind me unstraps my trunk from the back of the carriage and follows us. At the top of the stoop, the door opens, and a young girl stands there with a satin-trimmed blanket in one hand.

"What are you doing out of bed?" Dottie scolds. "Go on, get!"

I watch the child run inside and disappear up the stairs. Another child runs past the front door. And another. Then two more. *What the fuck?*

Dottie turns and tells me, "Welcome to my home. To your new home. You, my darling, are exactly what this place needs, as I'm a dying woman."

I tilt my head up to the sky, and let out a sigh—a long, exhausted sigh. "What exactly is it you need from me before you die?" I lower my gaze after asking, waiting for her to explain.

The woman's gray eyes narrow. "You are a Hannigan now. Miss Hannigan to these girls. You will love them and take care of them as I have."

Shock zings through me. I crane my neck to look behind the woman. Next to the front door, welded to the exterior brick wall, is a tarnished copper plaque. It reads: Miss Hannigan's Orphanage for Young Girls.

"You've got to be shitting me." It's probably something I should've said inside my head, but oh well. Too late.

"I am not shitting you. I need someone to take over and oversee the business, and you my dear have been living the business for most of your life."

My blood boils. My hands clench into tight fists. I'm ready to pound this old lady right here on her front steps. "This is not the life I want."

"None of us get the life we wanted." Her friendly voice has gone cold. "You are a Hannigan now. I need someone with thick skin and likes a good challenge. Your Sister Meredith recommended you during a *private* visit I made the other day."

"This was all prearranged? Sister Meredith knew you were going to take me home today?" *That conniving old— Ugh! That's why she was looking at me all sly-like before I left. What a bitch!*

Dottie nods. "Don't dwell on the details. Come inside and let's get you situated. You've got a lot to learn about running an orphanage."

I hesitantly follow Dottie inside where girls of all ages are sitting on the floor in the hall, along the steps of the stairs, and up on the second floor looking down at us. I don't see any over ten and they're all wearing the same white nightgowns. Just my luck that I ended up in a dingy old orphanage run by cranky nuns instead of a homey place like this; all warm and cozy with ornate furniture, pretty wallpaper, and a big city just outside the front door. I swear these kids with their brushed hair, clean faces, and hole-free garments look as if they were ready for visitation day.

A woman in a brown dress emerges from within a dark hall ahead of us. She's untying her white apron as she approaches the front door. "You're home, good. There's dough rising in the cupboard for tomorrow morning, and clean rags for Miss Porter. The girls have been fed, and they're supposed to be in bed, but they insisted on waiting up for you."

"Your time is much appreciated, Mrs. Whittle. I can take things from here. Plus," Dottie turns and nods in my direction, "I have full-time help now."

*I knew it was too good to be true! I'm here as* help.

Mrs. Whittle glances me up and down. "Yes, I can see

that." She shrugs on her coat and shakes off her questioning expression while saying, "I'll stop over Tuesday after lunch."

"Thank you, dear. See you Tuesday." We part, allowing Mrs. Whittle to hurry out the door. The driver carrying my trunk also steps aside, letting the woman pass. He then continues inside while the path is clear and heads off to our right, into a small parlor-looking room. If I remember correctly, Old Lady Gums had a similar sitting room in her house.

I step closer to Dottie and ask, "Who's that lady?"

"Oh, that was our neighbor, two houses down. She's a delight, and often comes over to help out here and there."

"And Miss Porter, who's she?"

A small girl with long brown hair tied up with a white ribbon tugs on Dottie's dress. When she turns her attention to the child, she asks, "Are you feeling any better, Mrs. Hannigan?"

The old woman's warm smile returns and pats the girl on the head. "Nothing for you to worry about but thank you for asking. Now, please sit with the others while I finish talking." When the girl sits between two other children, our conversation continues. "Miss Porter is our housemaid. She comes to help cook meals and clean up around the house."

*Housemaid?* I scan over the children staring back at me. *How ridiculous to hire a housemaid when you've got over ten pairs of little hands sitting right here. Money wasted in my opinion.*

Dottie takes off her fur shawl and hangs it on a tall wooden coat rack. She then faces the girls, waving for me to come closer, and says, "I want you to welcome the newest member of our family."

As if rehearsed, they say in perfect harmony, "Welcome, Miss Hannigan."

I have a decision to make. This might be my new hell, or an opportunity. It sounds like when the old lady dies, I'll be running things around here. Then, I can turn this place into my own haven and be their boss lady. These little brats will be doing gratitude chores for *me*. I definitely like the sound of that.

The corner of my lip curls up and I've decided haven over hell.

"Hello, girls."

# ABOUT KIMBERLY GRYMES

Kimberly Grymes is a debuting YA science-fiction and fantasy author. Her debut novel, ISOLDESSE is book one in The Aevo Compendium duology series. She and her family reside in the outskirts of Wichita, Kansas with their two crazy min pins. In addition to writing, she enjoys baking, crafting, graphic designing (amateur style), and hanging out with her three kids. Her favorite time of day is TV time with her husband every night while the dogs snuggle up between them.

**Find out more about Kimberly at:**
kimberlygrymes.com

 instagram.com/kgrymes.writes

# FIFTEEN MINUTES OF FAME BY
## SACHA BLACK

Caleb Prior was broke, horny, and about to lose his minimum wage radio station job. Two of the three were problems, though which two he couldn't quite settle on. He could, however, solve one of them.

He whipped out his phone and sent a text. Denise said they were dating and had been for six months. But Caleb was a lifelong bachelor and was insistent it was just sex. Denise, however, was equally insistent that if Caleb wanted to continue receiving blowjobs while she wore the lip-tingling gloss, then they were dating.

Caleb rather rapidly agreed they were, in fact, dating—though out of earshot, he continued to claim his bachelor status, anyway.

It's safe to say Caleb's best days were long gone. Despite his reality TV fame in the noughties, twenty years on the frequent B, C and ultimately Z-list parties filled with copious amounts of free booze, bad sex, and lines of coke had taken their toll.

His nasal septum was decaying, and he needed to see a specialist, but that cost money and according to the bank balance blinking at him from the cashpoint, the two million he'd scratched together during his fifteen minutes of fame was now just £626. Barely enough for his coke habit, let alone his booze habit or his more recent whore habit, although Denise had seen that off. Caleb stared at the screen, a brief malaise itching at his insides. He knew his post-reality TV modeling gigs were over too, thanks to the beer-rounded belly he'd developed. Keeping the six-pack had been easier in the noughties.

He also hadn't had a TV presenting gig in six years, and now his executive producers were getting irritated with his waning listeners at Three Hearts Radio station and they barely had two listeners to rub together as it was.

"You done, mate? I got a meeting at nine."

Caleb glanced over his shoulder. A young man dressed in a high-vis jacket stood behind him.

It took everything Caleb had to suppress a "don't you know who I am." He pulled his card and cash from the machine, and left, muttering, "Wanker," as he went.

Caleb needed two things: coffee and a plan.

He used to get TwinkleCoffee for free. Seven glorious years they had sponsored him. Every geek, jock, and forty-year-old virgin still living at home and working there knew his name. They used to pander and fluster around him, ushering him to the front of the queue. Didn't matter what London store he went to. In fact, most of the baristas across the U.K. knew him.

When he was in his twenties and at the height of his fame, he especially liked the baristas with big tits and bigger asses, though when bored by tits, he'd often found himself in bed with abs like mountain ranges and cock for days. Tits and dicks were all the same, really. He didn't care as long as he got to fill someone's orifice.

But those days were long gone. Caleb hadn't been propositioned in years. Denise was one of those swipe up... swipe left? Swipe something connections, and it'd seen him right for the last six months.

He sloped inside the store. No one greeted him or ushered him anywhere. He simply joined the back of the queue like a normal person.

But Caleb wasn't normal.

He was a fucking god, damn it. He'd earned fame. He'd earned the worship. Fuck fifteen minutes. Caleb wanted a lifetime of it.

He opened his front door a short while later, greeted by a pile of bills. Bills he didn't want to pay. He kicked the pile across the hall and stepped over what remained into his kitchen.

Something needed to be done.

Something big.

Something extraordinary.

Caleb had his coffee. All he needed now was a plan.

But first, Denise.

Sexting wasn't cool, but then nothing about Caleb had been cool since 2010. He had no idea what kids did these days. They probably TikSnapped their sex texts or whatever social media nonsense was popular now.

Caleb decided he preferred it old skool. A solid picture of a set of tits and some explicit messages about where Denise was going to rub her lips—either set—he wasn't fussy.

It hadn't started that way, of course. A few "what you up to?" texts, but it rapidly turned into "what you wearing?"

And then "what are you *not* wearing?" It appeared Denise had a high sex drive, and that was something Caleb didn't mind one bit. If she wanted to nosh him off while they watched TV, who was he to complain?

A message pinged up from Denise. A tit pic no less. The resulting boner required two vigorous handshakes to get rid of it.

If he was honest, her boobs had seen better days. They were on the saggy side and her decolletage had that dappled appearance of middle-aged skin overexposed to sun. That said, she had a banging set of nipples. Real squeezable. Aside from Denise, Caleb couldn't remember the last time he'd seen a pair of breasts he hadn't paid for. So, as far as he was concerned, he was winning. After he'd finished satisfying himself, another message arrived.

Wanna meet up?

Caleb stopped scratching his balls and froze. Was she for real? Did he want to meet up? Obviously. But this posed a problem. She clearly wanted sex. And he'd just expended his testosterone supply for the day in a bout of aggressive wanking over Denise's text-titties.

That, however, would not stop Caleb—he supposed he could always pop a Viagra. A booty call was exactly the sort of thing a bachelor did, after all.

Pop over, babe.

〰

The following evening, Caleb had resolved his horn, but he still had the thorny issue of being broke and barely clinging to his radio gig. But alas, no strike of divine inspiration had arrived, which is why Caleb found himself approaching his local pub. Divine inspiration—he'd discovered—tended to be at the bottom of a beer or during the height of fornication. The latter hadn't produced any ideas the previous night, so it was time to try the former.

An email popped up on Caleb's phone. Another invite to some god-awful local fete. The organizers wanted him to open the event for a whopping £150—like he had time to judge who's grown the biggest pumpkin. It was a fucking insult. Local fetes were beneath him. If that's the level of requests he was getting, he really must have slipped from fame.

The days of being begged to open the Miss U.K. events with half-naked women fawning all over him were distant memories. Caleb used to command five figures and a sumptuous rider for basic ribbon cutting and hosting events. He was partial to a baggie of coke mixed with edible glitter, three Twixs drizzled in Peruvian white chocolate served by a set of leather-clad women (and men) in G-strings and studs. And god forbid the venues forgot the blanched, minted broccoli specifically shipped from Mexico, over steamed lamb rump. He used to command a fortune. Now he couldn't even command Denise to be a friend with benefits.

He hit delete on the email and entered the pub.

"Usual?" Harv the landlord nodded.

Caleb tipped his head. A few of the locals sat up straighter as they spotted him. Some waved, a few smiled.

Caleb appreciated the fact they—in his mind—still respected his fame. Sadly for Caleb, the smiles and waves were because he was just another regular in the local boozer. In fact, Little John, the farmer from the next village, was the only local who actually recalled Caleb's days on TV, and that was only because Little John's cousin was in the same season of the show.

Harv passed Caleb his G&T and a slip of paper. His bar tab had surpassed £300 and needed paying. Now. Caleb slurped a gulp of gin down and tried to suppress the discomfort writhing in his gut.

He'd arranged a meeting with one of his remaining producer friends at Filmflix earlier that day.

It had not gone well. He took another slurp of gin. It gave him indigestion. Fucksake, he'd have to buy that rancid chalk-shit medicine again. He never used to get indigestion.

Apparently they—Filmflix—didn't need, and he quoted, "some aging, Z-list celebrity alcoholic no one remembered to present the latest season of Romance Island."

Caleb thought that was harsh. Forty-three wasn't old. It was barely scratching middle-aged these days, what with the likes of new medical interventions and such. Granted, his thinning hair, increasing wrinkles and slightly booze-induced red tinge weren't on brand for current presenters. But who cared? Most of the presenters they had were hair-less, brainless, personality-less coke heads with gaping legs and a thirst for cameras, anyway.

The fact that's precisely what Caleb had been for more than a decade was beside the point.

He wasn't that anymore. No. He'd matured, seasoned— like the silver fox presenter TV was missing. That's the pitch he'd gone with.

"Listen, Phil, you're missing a trick," Caleb said.

Phil raised a manicured eyebrow and returned to chewing his pen. "This should be good."

"No. No, bear with me. The middle-aged population isn't represented on TV. Your presenters are all anorexic waifs, tanned to within an inch of skin cancer and jacked off their tits on drugs."

Phil nodded aggressively.

"What happened to representing the people?" Caleb said.

"The people? Have you lost your fucking mind?"

"I'm just saying you could reel in advertising spend. Think about it. It's a whole new section of society you can target."

Phil leaned forward, his eyebrow still at peak curvature. "With what? Viagra pills and vagina tucks? That's hardly marketable at prime time. Think of the kids, Caleb."

"The specifics of advertising aren't the point."

"Okay. Enlighten me." Phil waved a lazy hand at Caleb. "What point are you trying to make?"

"You're missing out on targeting millions of viewers. The aging population wants to be represented. They want to see people like them hosting these shows. They're the ones with money in the banks. Not the ignorant tweens."

Phil snorted. "If you think that, then you've truly lost your edge. The only thing middle-aged people want when they watch TV is escapism. Wishing they were still as young, fun, and fuckable as the presenters. Sex has always and will always sell. And you, mate, are not fuckable."

To drive the point home, Phil poked Caleb's belly and said, "Listen, pal, I like you. I do. You're funny when you're high, you're generous at parties, but I can't help you. No one wants to watch some aging Z-list celebrity alcoholic no one remembers present the latest season of *Romance Island*. You don't get second chances in this industry."

It was a gut punch, literally and figuratively. But Caleb wouldn't be defeated. He hadn't spent a decade at the top of the game just to be relegated to the dusty corners of society's mind.

Times had changed and so should what society wanted from their celebrities. He wasn't going to be deterred just because some jumped-up Filmflix exec had rejected him. Well fuck Phil, and fuck Filmflix.

He picked up his gin and slumped down at the end of the bar to consider his options. If Phil wasn't willing to hear him out, he was out of contacts and out of ideas. An email pinged in. It was his tween-looking manager at Three Hearts Radio:

Do not be late on Thursday, Caleb, you're on your final warning and I don't want to lose you. You're good at what you do. But I will if I have to. Don't force my hand.

Caleb's esophagus burned, how dare the jumped-up little cu—

Denise appeared in the pub doorway. She was wearing some lacy black thing that, if Caleb strained, he was pretty sure he could spot a hint of nip through. He shoved his phone down and adjusted himself as she bent down and kissed his cheek.

Oh yes, he could confirm that from this angle it was definitely a bit of nipple he'd seen.

"Hey, honey," she said.

Caleb shifted in his seat. Hey, honey? That was a bit too "committed" of a hello. Caleb wasn't sure how he felt about that. He and Denise weren't a thing. Were they? They were just doing that Tiksnapping thing. He only agreed to say they were dating, so she kept blowing him. Obviously.

Except Caleb knew damn well that Denise was the last thing he'd thought about at night, every night, since they'd met. And she was definitely the first person he'd text in the morning.

No. It wasn't possible. Caleb was a bachelor.

He didn't fall for women, especially not mediocre specimens like Denise. Even if she was quite literally the best cook he'd ever met, and she did that thing with her tongue, and he also quite liked the way her skin smelled before a shower.

But they were trivial things. And irrelevant because Caleb Prior was 100% a bachelor. He knew that right down to his bone... r.

"How did the meeting go with Phil?" Denise asked.

"Phil's a useless son of a whore. Complete waste of oxygen."

"Oh, dear."

Caleb slurped some gin and his esophagus protested with a burning rumble. Christ, he needed some Gaviscon.

"What's the plan?" Denise said. "You always have a plan."

"God, I don't know. I've got all these ideas of cracking shows aimed at the underserved middle-aged population, and I can't seem to get anyone to listen."

"That's a shame, honey, shall I get us some drinks?"

Caleb grunted. She didn't get it. He had ideas. Good ones. Big ones. Ones the world needed to see.

"Yeah, love. Get me a JD and coke, please."

Denise raised an eyebrow. "You want a JD?"

"That's what I said, yeah."

"But that makes you"—she leaned in—"frisky."

Caleb's eyes glimmered in the pub's dim lighting. He grinned, licked his lips. If he couldn't win a Filmflix contract, he was damn sure he could get his leg over.

"Guess it's your lucky night, then. Are you ready to invite me to yours?"

She hesitated, her shoulders slumped. But then she

popped a kiss on Caleb's cheek. "Only if you do that thing when I sit on you."

"Sit... on... me... naked?"

"Naked," she winked.

Caleb's trousers tightened.

"Deal."

Denise wiggled her way to the bar. Caleb was sure she was swinging those sumptuous hips a little bit more than usual. Denise flicked her head over her shoulder and pouted.

He really did like her arse. It was bigger than was polite, but my god did she know how to make it jiggle when he bent her over. Yeah, she was gonna get it tonight alright.

"Make it a double," he bellowed.

And this time, Denise's eyes glimmered.

Stinking of cheap booze, quick fumbles and back alleys, Caleb and Denise staggered into her two up, two down house. Caleb—drunk as he was—had amorous eyes and amorous hands and he was slathering hungry kisses down Denise's chest and over those lace-covered boobies.

"Oh, just rip it off," Denise gasped as she slammed the door shut behind them.

"But it's your favorite," Caleb said between mouthfuls of lace.

Denise gripped his fingers and yanked. The lace parted with a satisfying shred. Almost as satisfying as the pop and pout her nipple made as it fell between the lacy remains.

"God, you drive me wild," Caleb said as he pressed his swelling crotch against her thigh.

And she did.

He wanted her more than he'd ever wanted those pin-waisted models from the noughties. Sure he'd wanted to stick his wang in them for the badge of honor. Same way he had the boys with bulging... well, bulging everything. But they were just badges to be lorded over the other celebrity presenters at the time—it was always a competition: who'd gotten the most, the biggest bum, the best breasts, the most holes.

Denise was different. And yet, she was nothing special; he didn't understand why she affected him the way she did. But she had these teasing eyes and slightly wonky boobs that made his balls ache, his chest throb and his brain hysterical.

Every. Single. Time.

She was a paradox. A mediocre ecstasy pill pulling off the greatest high he'd ever had. He wanted to touch all of her, hold her, keep her overnight just as much as he wanted to shove and thrust all night long.

He didn't understand. What was this voodoo witching?

They stumbled their way through the dark. His fingers locked in hers. If he hadn't been so consumed trying to unzip his trousers while helping her up the stairs, he might've realized he wasn't supposed to hand hold—that's what couples did and Caleb was a bachelor, thank you very much.

Together they inched their way toward the bedroom, exchanging kisses and strokes and occasional dry humps. She pulled his nob out and gave him a few kisses—just enough to make him groan.

"I can't take it, Denise, get your arse in the bedroom," Caleb said as he gave her backside a little smack.

Denise giggled in response as she sauntered off. It was the kind of giggle that made his best bits clench. He pulled himself up off the stairs, both knees crunching under his portly belly.

"Fucking Christ," he flinched. "I'm too old to chase you."

Denise was already naked by the time Caleb made it to her bedroom doorway. He took three steps before suddenly he was on the ground, staring up at her very bald vagina. Caleb was too busy silently determining how much of a filthy slut Denise was for having waxed her vajajay to notice what had toppled him.

"Fuck, honey. You okay? Sorry. Sorry. It's all my bloody books," Denise said.

But Caleb wasn't paying attention because as she was scurrying around, she was also bending over and picking up who-gave-a-fuck what. The view consumed him.

"You missed one," he said, grinning.

Denise, having realized what Caleb was distracted by, said, "Oops. What... This one?"

She turned, bent over, spread her legs just enough to give him a delicious view. He stood so fast his knees didn't have time to protest. Dropped his pants and, well...

She gasped.

He moaned.

She cried out some strange sound that was a mix of whale birth and pig grunt. Whatever it was, Caleb liked it. He pumped harder. It was all going so well...

And then he caught sight of the pile of books.

Fucking romances.

All of them.

All with middle-aged men and women on the covers. To be fair, some of them had two women on the front, others two men and others still had these oddly blue creatures on them. But every one shared the same two things: the words "second chance" on the cover, and a look between the cover couple that stopped Caleb in his thrusting tracks.

He was limp. The, it's-the-end-of-the-fun-tonight kind of limp.

Caleb's face was feverish.

Denise arched around, looking up from her down dog position—she'd been practicing that after her yoga classes. Especially because Caleb had this bend in his—well, anyway.

"Babe?" she said.

But Caleb wasn't listening. He slumped down against the end of her bed, his eyes stinging. He picked up one of her books. Then another. It was one of those time-stands-still moments. A pathetic montage flashing past his eyes. He was a complete failure. He'd fallen from fame, never been in love, failed to pitch a decent show to Filmflix and couldn't even keep his penis stiff.

But what hurt was the look the couples were giving each other. That's what surprised him.

The problem was, that was how Caleb looked at Denise. *Exactly* how Caleb looked at Denise. Did that mean? Was Caleb in—?

No. He couldn't be. Caleb was a bachelor. But as she lifted the books out of his hands and cradled her legs around his back, peppering soft kisses over his wet cheeks, he couldn't deny it.

Caleb Prior was in love.

He was also, miraculously, hard. So he pulled her mouth to his and on the floor of Denise's second-chance-romance-covered bedroom, Caleb did something he'd never done before. He made love.

～

Making love wasn't the only "first" that night. He also stayed over at Denise's. Kept her wrapped in his arms all night long. And then smiled when he woke up. But strangest of all, is the fact he didn't mind one bit. In fact, Caleb discovered he rather enjoyed waking up to Denise's nipples staring at him and the smell of last night's love in his nostrils.

"Breakfast?" Denise said.

"I'd kill a coffee."

She rolled out of bed and disappeared downstairs. Caleb sat up, his eyes scanned her room. It was littered with those fucking books. Hundreds of longing looks filled with come fuck me eyes. It made his insides itch. There was something to this, he was sure of it. The niggle he'd felt last night hadn't gone away. He got out of bed and scooped up a handful of paperbacks.

Denise reappeared carrying a tray of toast and two mugs of steaming black coffee. Caleb took a mug and wafted a book at her.

"What's with all the stories?"

"Escapism, mostly. You know?"

Caleb did not know. But Phil had said the same thing.

"So... umm. What are they all about, then?"

"Mostly, middle-aged people. Lonely hearts looking for a second chance at happiness. Divorcees, widows, parents with grown-up kids. That sort of stuff. But the thing I love is that all the stories are full of drama and tension, but despite that, they always end up together. It's like binge-worthy TV. I can't get enough of it."

And there it was.

The idea.

Caleb put his mug of coffee down. Slid his hand into Denise's and pulled her toward him. He kissed her deeper than he'd ever kissed anyone. Wrapping his fingers through the back of her locks.

Denise pulled away, breathless. "Ooh, Caleb, you are naughty. I've got work this morning."

Not yet, she didn't.

He slid his tongue down her neck and over her chest. It elicited a moan so raw he had to concentrate on not ending things prematurely.

And to think he'd considered Viagra the other day. Who needed Viagra when you had a Denise? She was his own personal brand of cock-crack. He continued sliding his tongue down her body, over her stomach, thighs and delightfully smooth... Oh dear, he couldn't stay down here for long, and his stamina wasn't the best this morning—he was far too excited about his idea.

He flipped her over.

She giggled.

He considered briefly whether they'd reached the point in their relationship where she'd let him stick it in her—no.

No, not yet.

There was time for that now he was in love.

He managed exactly eight thrusts before it was all over. He dutifully finished Denise off—it was only polite after all. She'd given him a cracking idea.

Three days later, he sat in the headquarters of Filmflix. Fuck telling Phil his concept. No, he'd had his chance, and he'd knifed Caleb in the back. So this time, Caleb had gone right to the top. Phil would hate that.

Correction, as Phil walked past the glass cubed exec's office, he dropped his bottom lip into a delightful "O" shape that said it all. Phil was furious, and his outrage was almost enough to make Caleb horny. Truly, there was no sweeter thrill than victory.

Caleb leaned back in his seat and winked. As it happened, he couldn't lip-read, but "mother fucker" seemed to have a particular mouth shape that he was more than capable of distinguishing.

"So let me get this right," Max said.

Max was the top dog at Filmflix and Phil's boss's boss. He was also unacceptably young, slick and smeared in a dangerous amount of wet-look hair gel. Fucking millennials. Along with his hair, Max sported a slick-looking watch which also matched his slick-looking suit, and likely came with a very fucking slick pay check.

"This will be a reality TV show aimed at the middle-aged?" Max asked.

Caleb nodded, a streak of his own slick sweat appearing on his brow. Max's expression was blank. This was either going to be the prime-time TV idea he'd been looking for, or he was going to be laughed out of TV forever.

"I see. And tell me again how it works."

"*Second Chance Island.* You take a bunch of lonely hearts, middle-aged of course, you can pick the dramatic ones, the ones still clinging to their looks or whatever will make it sell, and you get them to 'blind' date. Literally blind. They'll meet each other through opaque windows, never seeing each other. Only falling for their voice and whatever they learn about each other. Then you get them to commit to marrying someone. There's bound to be fights over who wants who. You can gamify it, obviously. We get to film them walking down the aisle, having never *seen* each other. Then we follow the first few months of their second chance marriage. It'll be a new drug for the middle-aged. It's what they all want. Who doesn't want love or a second chance? Think of the escapism, the advertising revenue. It could be big, Max. Really big."

Max was silent. The air was thick. Caleb was sweating. He wanted to twitch in his seat, but he didn't dare move.

One minute passed.

Then another.

Then, "Fuck, Caleb."

Caleb froze, Max's face still completely unreadable. Whatever happened, whichever way this went, Caleb had decided Denise was his second chance. He loved her. He knew that now, even though he didn't really know what that meant for the future. Hell, it had taken him forty-three years just to fall in love.

Max pulled out a leather notebook and looked Caleb in the eyes.

"Two million. Exclusive rights. And I want you on the executive producer board."

Caleb grinned. It appeared Denise wasn't his only second chance. He held out his hand.

"Deal."

# ABOUT SACHA BLACK

Sacha Black is a bestselling and competition winning author, rebel podcaster, and professional speaker. She has five obsessions; words, expensive shoes, conspiracy theories, self-improvement, and breaking the rules. Sacha writes books about people with magical powers and other books about the art of writing. When she's not writing, she can be found laughing inappropriately loud, sniffing musty old books, fangirling film and TV soundtracks, or thinking up new ways to break the rules. She lives in Cambridgeshire, England, with her wife and genius, giant of a son.

**Find out more about Sacha at:**

www.sachablack.co.uk

pod.link/rebelauthor

# A BIT OF BOTH BY HELEN GLYNN JONES

Black Anvil rose through the smoke and swirling sparks, his arms wide, his cloak billowing dramatically. His back was killing him, but he knew how important it was to leave his enemies with a memory of darkness and shadows and fear, not of an old supervillain who struggled to do up his costume.

"I'll be back," he roared, shooting a last couple of thunderbolts from his wrist. They hit their targets, one of which was one of those ridiculous winged monkeys Iron Maiden insisted on using. He felt a surge of pleasure as it dissolved with a squeal, a puff of purple-blue smoke all that remained.

Iron Maiden turned mid-strike, her sharp-penciled brows drawing together, ruby lips dropping open. "Sorry," he mouthed, shrugging. Inside he was laughing, though. If only he could do it to all of them.

Flying monkeys. He snorted as he lifted higher into the clouds. Back in his day, all a good villain needed was a superweapon, an excellently evil laugh and a devious plan. None of these stupid accessories and pets and special effects nonsense, half of them designed just to look flashy on social media.

Down below the fight continued, Iron Maiden cleaning up the remaining two superheroes, her monkeys already feeding on the body of a third. The fact that the rotten little vermin had fangs was something, he supposed. But he'd done the lion's share of the work down there, Iron Maiden showing up late and too busy taking selfies and making sure she was streaming the whole thing to her millions of fans to actually be of much help.

Lord, he was tired.

Being a supervillain wasn't easy, not when new heroes seemed to appear every week. There was the upkeep of a lair, for starters. All those locks and secret chambers and traps, not to mention how tough it was to keep sharks. And don't even mention the time the hyenas fell in the shark tank... He closed his eyes, shaking his head. The assistant who'd left the gate open had followed the hyenas into the water, he'd seen to that. At least the sharks had been well fed that day. But then he'd had to get a new assistant and a new pack of hyenas, and the government tended to be a lot stricter about importing animals now, all paperwork this and do they have enough food and water that. He'd thought of feeding the pompous official to the creatures, but he'd needed that rubber stamp.

He rolled his eyes, floating higher. The clouds wreathed around him, cold fingers of mist caressing his skin, curling along the purple velvet (expensive but worth it) of his cloak, reminding him of how things used to be.

Iron Maiden had arrived at his lair one night, a young brash villain-in-the-making. Well, not so much arrived as evaded all his traps, waking him with a knife to his throat and a sensational pair of tits pressed against him. He still wasn't sure what had excited him more. And she'd more than proven her prowess, both in and out of bed, her outrageously curved body able to contort itself in new and... stimulating ways, seeming to disappear like smoke during battle, then reappear, their enemies never sure what she might do next.

But she didn't seem as interested in him anymore, the ungrateful wretch, not since that new villain, Scarlet PimpONell, had come on the scene, all red glitter and high heels and cut glass cheekbones. Black Anvil quite fancied him himself, to be honest.

He drifted through the clouds, lost in dreams of a threesome where, somehow, he ended up on top and everyone else had a bad day. Just as he was envisioning Iron Maiden's lush curves trussed up like a turkey, his phone pinged, causing him to lose his train of thought.

He frowned. Whoever it was could wait. He closed his eyes again, imagining Scarlet PimpONell, still in those damn heels, his buttocks as red as his ridiculous sequined costume, a whip in his hand, and...

Another ping. Then another. Then a whole flurry of them.

He sighed, his fantasy dissolving in a puff of red-tinged candy-scented smoke.

He looked at his phone.

His eyes bulged.

How.

Dare.

She.

He threw his head back and roared, his body curving like a bow, his arms rigid.

Who in sweet fuck did she think she was?

He looked at his phone again, at the notifications

pouring in. And at the short video Iron Maiden had posted in her stories. If she hadn't been using all that bloody billowing smoke he would have seen the rock. But he hadn't.

```
Black Anvil takes a trip #oldschool
```

The words danced across the screen as he fell, and got back up, and fell again, and again, and again, his humiliation replicated like a funhouse of endless mirrors, each of them showing the world what he really was.

#Oldschool

He knew what that meant.

And, worse, he thought she might know it, too. It wasn't a great angle in the video, the strain in his suit showing, the stomach he held in using triple Spanx bulging, the skin on his face rippling like sand underwater.

"Fuuuuuckkk!" He roared again, his muscles vibrating with the effort, as though he might be able to turn back time itself through the sheer force of his rage. But only Superman had that power, and he wasn't even real. The real heroes, the ones who were an endless scourge on his existence, were nowhere near as powerful.

But there were Just. So. Many. Of. Them.

He sank down slowly, his head back, eyes closed. He didn't care where he landed. In fact, he hoped it was somewhere painful. Like an incinerator. Or a nuclear power plant intake pipe.

But when his feet touched the ground it was soft and slightly yielding. There was a smell of paint and lollipops. And a squeak. He wondered whether he'd landed on a mouse, or perhaps one of those awful yappy little dogs. But when he opened his eyes, lifting his feet one after the other, he realized where he was.

It was a playground.

A normal child's playground, with the usual array of wooden and brightly-painted metal structures, and a rubbery ground surface installed so the little brats bounced instead of breaking. Black Anvil curled his lip.

Not really his scene.

He was about to take off again when there was another squeak. He turned, his cape swirling, eyes narrowed beneath his helmet.

"Oh, please don't hurt me!"

The words were spoken with a slight lisp, the voice breathy, and unmistakably that of a child.

He squinted. The playground was deserted, or so he thought. But then his eyesight wasn't what it had been, and he would be damned before he would wear glasses out in public. He wished he could get some sort of laser sight thing added to his helmet, but it was hard to know who to trust these days to make it. His assistant, the one he'd fed to the sharks, had been remarkably good at building gadgets and costume upgrades – in fact, he'd never found anyone as talented to replace him. But sharks didn't tend to give back those they'd taken, and so it was a mild regret in a life that didn't have many. He couldn't turn back the clock, though.

What he could do, however, was be menacing.

"Show yourself," he growled. "Or else."

"Or else what?" the little voice squealed. "You're so scary."

"Yes, I am, aren't I?" Black Anvil smoothed down the front of his costume, his head turning as he sought the source of the voice.

There. Underneath the slide.

He marched over, his cape billowing behind him. It was worth every penny to get the extra meter of fabric added, it really was. He let sparks fly from his wristbands, snapping and crackling, and drew his eyebrows together in what he knew was a rather threatening frown.

A little girl was huddled beneath the slide, clutching a large yellow teddy bear. She looked about seven, or maybe eight – who could tell, children were just blobs until they reached their teens anyway.

"Y-you're B-black Anvil, aren't you?" She stared at him with big blue eyes, her bottom lip trembling.

"That's right," he said, still frowning.

"You're the worst!"

"I am?" His frown deepened.

"The worst of all the villains!" She hugged her teddy bear closer, her frown matching his.

"Who says?"

"My daddy. He told me all about you!"

Black Anvil raised an eyebrow. "If I'm the worst villain there is, doesn't it make me the best?"

The little girl's eyes widened. "I guess," she said. "My daddy said you were very good at being evil."

Black Anvil smiled. "I am, aren't I?" He let out a menacing laugh, one he knew always made people shudder.

But the little girl didn't shudder. She just cuddled her damn bear, her small face screwed up like she was figuring something out.

"What is it?" he snapped.

The little girl put one finger to her lips, which were pursed like a fat rosebud. "If you're the best, why are you so sad?"

"Sad?"

"When you landed. I saw you. You looked sad. Like you were going to cry. Did you hurt yourself?"

"No. I'm a supervillain. We don't get hurt."

"But you were making a face like, I don't know, like my friend Marcie made when she fell and scraped her knee. Like you were about to cry."

"I. Do. Not. Cry," Black Anvil said, through gritted teeth. He turned, swirling his cape with one hand. It was time to go. Inane conversations with small children were really not what he needed.

"Don't go, please."

"What?" He paused mid-swirl.

"Please don't go. I want to ask you something."

Black Anvil ignored her. He bent his knees, looking up. But before he could launch into the sky, the little girl shouted, "HOWDOIBECOMEAVILLAIN?"

The words were all smushed together, and it took Black Anvil a moment to work out what she was saying. When he did, his eyebrows shot up.

"You want to be a villain?"

The little girl nodded. "Yes. And you're the best villain ever, so I was hoping, maybe, you could help me."

It had been a while since he'd been really, truly surprised. The last time, in fact, had been waking to Iron Maiden in all her lush glory. But he was surprised now.

"Are you sure that's what you want?" He walked back to the slide, sitting down on the end, his cloak tucked around him. "You're still very young."

"I just know that it's something I've always wanted to do, even though you are very scary. I want to be scary, too. My daddy said all the best villains are, especially you."

Black Anvil blinked. "Your father sounds like a very smart man."

"Oh yes," the little girl said. "The smartest. He told me that some villains are born, and some are made." For a moment her eyes looked different, older and wiser, as though a woman was peering out through her childish gaze. "I think I might be both, but I need help with the making bit. How about you?"

"Well," Black Anvil said, crossing his legs, his hands on his knee. "I'm also a bit of both, I guess. I knew when I was a kid what I wanted to be. Started off small, pulling the wings off flies, that sort of thing."

The little girl giggled. "And now you pull the wings off superheroes."

Black Anvil laughed. "I do, don't I?"

"It was so funny! I saw it on YouTube. You were awesome." Her fear seemingly gone, the little girl came out from under the slide, sitting down next to Black Anvil.

"I suppose I was, wasn't I?" It had been a fun day, he remembered. One of his best. But it didn't matter how many superheroes he crushed or fried or tore into small pieces. There were always more.

"But if you're so awesome, why are you sad? I know you are." The little girl's voice cut across his thoughts.

"I told you, I'm not sad." Ugh. Children with their endless questions. He'd never had a child, not that he knew about, anyway, and he was happy to keep it that way. He frowned. "I just..." He blew out a breath. "I just want to get rid of all the superheroes. Is that too much to ask?"

Why had he said that? He really must be tired.

"I don't think you can, though," said the little girl, sounding thoughtful. "There are loads of them. They're in space and all over the world and under the sea and just everywhere. No wonder you're sad." She patted his arm with her small hand.

"I'm really not s—"

"What you need is some help. I could help you, when I get older. I can already do some stuff."

"You can?" Black Anvil was intrigued. This was not how he'd imagined his day would turn out. Maybe it was time to cut Iron Maiden loose and train a new apprentice. This kid was the most promising he'd met in a long while. "Like what?"

The little girl screwed up her face, her nose crinkling. Her fists clenched, then she opened her hands. Two little blasts of blue light shot out, pinging from the metal post opposite, the swings shaking.

Another jolt of surprise. "Well," he said, "that's pretty impressive."

"Oh, I'm never going to be as good as you are," she said. "But I'm glad you liked it."

"I really did," he said. "Maybe you can come and work with me, when you get a bit older." Not that he was sure how old she was, but parents tended to get annoyed when you just flew off with their kids, unless you were a super-hero. His mood darkened again.

"OhmygoodnessIwouldlovethat!" The little girl clasped her hands together. "So I can come to your lair? And see all the stuff you have there? I bet you have the best stuff! And we can make more villains – my daddy said you even had a machine that could do it, it was on the news once!"

Black Anvil blinked. "What?"

"You need to make lots more villains, to make it fair, so all the superheroes can go away."

It was like being hit by a lightning bolt. How could he have forgotten?

She was right. She was so very right. About everything.

He did have a machine. A cloning machine. Oh, he wasn't supposed to use it, proper permits, free will, blah blah whatever nonsense the government had said when they found out about it. But why did he care what they or anyone else thought? It was time to reclaim his crown. Iron Maiden might have her monkeys, but soon he could have a whole new army of villains, made in his mold. The Purple Posse, he thought, or maybe the Black Knights. Whatever. They would be unstoppable.

"Thank you," he said to the little girl.

She smiled and hugged her teddy. "You're welcome." Her smooth brow crinkled in a frown. "I'm not sure what for, though."

"Don't worry," he said, standing up. "You've helped me, that's all. So keep practicing, and make sure you come and see me when you're old enough." He held out his hand.

The little girl, her mouth an "o" of surprise, took it. Black Anvil shook her hand, once, resisting the urge to take her with him. There would be time enough for that.

He rose into the sky once more, his cape swirling majestically, his chest puffed out with pride.

It was time for a new wave of villainy, and he was going to ride it.

Down in the playground, the little girl watched Black Anvil go until he was nothing more than a speck among the clouds.

Her features blurred, her body swelling and undulating, the bear in her arms dropping to the ground.

"Well, that was fun." Iron Maiden stretched, her back popping. Those curves of hers hid more secrets than Black Anvil ever knew. Shapeshifting had been her talent since she was a child. But it was revenge that had turned her into the villain she was now. Some villains were born, others made. Just like Black Anvil, she was a little bit of both.

"I'll miss the old bastard, I suppose."

She hadn't been lying about her father. He had told her about Black Anvil, including how to bypass all those traps and gadgets he'd built at the supervillain's lair. "Just in case, kitten," he'd always said. "Just in case." He'd taught her everything he knew.

Right up to the day he was fed to the sharks for leaving a gate open.

She held out her arms, and the creature on the ground, a bear no more, leapt into them. "There, there, my darling," she crooned. "There, there." The flying monkey curled and hissed, baring its tiny fangs. How dare he kill one of her monkeys! Black Anvil deserved whatever he got, just for doing that. But he'd signed his death warrant the day he'd pushed her father to a gruesome, watery fate.

And so, last time she was at the lair, she'd made a small modification to the cloning machine. A couple of wires swapped, a chip moved from one spot to another. No one would ever notice, unless they knew the machine really well. And Black Anvil didn't.

So he would have no idea it wasn't so much a cloning machine anymore as it was... a liquefying machine.

Revenge really did taste so very, very sweet.

She pulled out her phone, wondering what Scarlet PimpONell was up to. Might be time to film another video together, something spicy for their OnlyFans account. But now she had endorsement deals to chase and fans to talk to.

After all, she was the best villain of them all.

"Hello, darlings," she said, pouting into the lens. "Today has been a Very. Good. Day."

# ABOUT HELEN GLYNN JONES

Helen Glynn Jones is an author of seven novels. She's been published in magazines and anthologies, written for the Writers & Artists website and The Guardian, and created regular content for a variety of businesses and publications in Australia and the UK.

She writes for middle-grade, young adult and adult audiences, and lives in Hertfordshire with her husband, daughter and wonderfully chaotic cockapoo.

**Find out more about Helen at:**
www.helenglynnjones.co.uk

[f] facebook.com/authorhelenglynnjones
[𝕏] twitter.com/AuthorHelenJ
[◎] instagram.com/helenglynnjones
[BB] bookbub.com/authors/helen-jones
[a] amazon.com/author/helenjones

## THE DEMON, THE HERO, AND THE FOREST OF ARDEN BY A.E. KINCAID

It's been five hundred years since a hero petitioned a demon. Five hundred years since the Summoning Bell rang out in the Underworld Suburb of Artifice-on-Lethe. Demons live...well, basically forever. But five hundred years is still a long time. We were beginning to get a bit twitchy.

But what's that, you ask? Why would a hero summon a demon?

Let me take you back five hundred and some years...

Once upon a time, the self-proclaimed "Glorious Land of Widdershins," experienced a golden age of heroism. Damsels were rescued, jewels recovered, honors restored... the usual stuff. But the more heroes there were in the game, the harder it became to play. The challenges became more challenging; the heroing more harrowing. The valiant heroes began to suffer a previously unknown sensation: desperation. They grasped at any opportunity that would set them apart and help them achieve their noble ends.

And that's when one very clever hero by the name of Quill Valor remembered *us*.

Yes, Valor was the first to outsource his problems to the Underworld, but he wasn't the last. We became independent contractors in the hero business, and the future never looked more wicked. For though Valor might have been clever to think of us—we were clever too. For every quest whose success we ensured, a dam would burst, destroying a town. For every ancient artifact whose recovery we guaranteed, a kingdom would be cursed to darkness. The amount of evil we were licensed to unleash was directly proportional to the good deed in question. In other words—the greater the good, the more mayhem we could sow.

It was truly the best of times.

That is, until the nonhero population of Widdershins got wise to what was going on and shut it down.

They formed a committee and—I won't go into specifics here—decided that from now on, heroes must be properly vetted. Not by any measure of physical prowess or derring-do, but through a résumé, an interview, and 127 pages of paperwork signed in triplicate. And it was all to safeguard against us somehow weaseling our way into heroing again.

We demons were almost impressed. Paperwork? It was diabolical.

But we weren't ready to be cut out of the deal completely. So I, Malgon Belroth Kirranith, Fifteenth of His Name, Giver of Paper Cuts, Collapser of Soufflés, Inventor of the Humblebrag, Lord of the Underworld Suburb of Artifice-on-Lethe, snuck in during the night to make a little revision. To the third footnote on the seventy-third page, I added a magical addendum that stated:

*On page ninety-four, under the heading "Methods of Heroing, Unacceptable," there sits a lone checkbox. If said checkbox*

*remains unchecked and the paperwork is properly filed, a Demon*
*will be automatically summoned to aid the new hero.*

Checkmate, you fuckers.

But, alas, the joke was on me. While they could do
nothing to change the addendum, there was still a loophole:
they simply *told* their hero candidates of my little deception
and insisted that they check the box.

And they kept it up for five hundred years.

So imagine my elation when I heard the bell toll once
more. Its deafening clang was music to my ears. I jumped
up, grabbed my ebony morning coat, and sprinted to the
town square; my black leather boots slapping against the
broken cobbles as I ran. I needed to be the first to touch the
Summoning Bell. Somewhere up above there was a hero so
crafty as to have fooled the committee into overlooking the
barren checkbox. Here was the partner in crime I'd been
dreaming of—we might do some real damage together.

And save some lives or jewels or whatever.

The point is—I would be back in business.

I could see other demons racing forward in my periph-
ery, but it didn't matter. I was already there. After calmly
donning my coat, I bid the smell of brimstone adieu and
placed my hand on the bell. The darkness squeezed around
me as it transported me up, up, up...

"Fucking, shitpants, damnation, I forgot how bright it is
up here," I hissed as I popped into the shining world above.
I shielded my eyes as best I could, but after five hundred
years in the shadows, I suspected it would take a while to get
used to again.

"Oh no..." came a wobbly-sounding voice beside me.

"Ah, and you must be my hero," I said, turning toward
the voice, still covering my eyes with one hand. With my
other arm I swept my morning coat back and bowed

dramatically. "I apologize for my rather uncouth entrance just now. Please don't think it a reflection on my level of professionalism. I assure you that I am well qualified and up to whatever task you have set before us. I merely...haven't seen the sun in five centuries."

"Oh no, no, no," whined the voice again.

"You keep saying that. Is that your name? Well, I am pleased to make your acquaintance, and..."

"It's not my name. Aw, geez, my gran is gonna *kill* me."

I tried to drop my hand, but it was too soon. Hissing in discomfort at the blinding light, I said, "I don't understand. You deviously left the checkbox unchecked. You should be celebrating your success!"

"What? No, I just forgot! How did it get through the committee? What am I going to do?"

My elation evaporated and was replaced by bewilderment.

"So...you *didn't* summon a demon?"

"Not on purpose!"

"Well...fuck."

I dropped my arm and slumped my shoulders. Sunlight be damned. Literally, for all I cared. For the first time, I got a good look at my hero companion. He looked like a flaming willow branch: tall, lanky, and pasty, with red hair. And, if I may be permitted to say so, he wore a rather dull expression. His posture was abominable, and it seemed to me that a stiff wind would blow him over. To top it off, he was cleaning out his ear with the end of his pinky. Disgusting.

"So you're a demon, then?" he asked. The tone of his voice implied that he was hoping I would deny it.

"Malgon Belroth Kirranith, Fifteenth of His Name, Lord of the Underworld Suburb of Artifice-on-Lethe, at your service," I recited, bowing deeply.

My hero's eyebrows rose. "Impressive."

"Thank you," I said, dipping my head slightly.

The boy's brow furrowed. "But where's your tail? You just look like a fine gentleman to me."

I pursed my lips. "I don't have one."

"Why not?"

"*Because*, okay?" It was a sore subject for me as it reflected a deficit in my overall level of evilness compared to other demons; something I hoped to change during this visit. I didn't like talking about it with anyone and certainly wasn't going to discuss it with this idiot, so I changed the subject.

"So...you're...a capital-H Hero, then?"

He looked skyward as if the answer were written in the clouds.

"Well...yeah. As of like an hour ago. My name's Reginald. *Sir* Reginald P. Asstradle, now."

I blinked.

"Asstradle."

"Yeah."

"Your surname is *Asstradle*?"

"What of it?"

I squinted at him. Then I made a box with my fingers and peered through it. Still unsatisfied with what I saw, I began to circle him. He must have some ancient, magical blade upon his back that would make up for his general stature and *painfully* average intelligence?

"What're you doing?" he asked, taking up his auricular hygiene in the other ear.

I'd come around front again and seen nothing to improve my opinion of him.

"What am I doing? What are you doing?" I cried, gesturing with both my arms to all of him. "What is this?

You're no hero. Heroes are strong! Gallant! Carry large swords!"

He gaped at me for a moment, then burst out laughing.

"Yeah...maybe five hundred years ago. A lot has changed since then. The title is the same, but we're not so much *heroes* anymore. We're more like glorified delivery people."

I sighed and uncrossed my arms. "So, what are we going to do?"

"What do you mean?"

I pinched the bridge of my nose in an effort to squeeze out any remaining patience I might possess. I don't possess a lot. I am a demon, after all.

"I mean, what is your quest? Maybe we can just make a quick deal, get it done, and that will be that. Like this never happened." It was not my ideal scenario. Truthfully, I was crushed. But I was determined to make at least *some* mischief before tunneling back down to Artifice-on-Lethe.

"No, no, no..." said Reginald, waving his hands in front of his body. "I don't want to make a deal. I want to get rid of you."

"You can't 'get rid' of me. I go away when our deal is concluded."

"But I don't want to do that."

"Then why did you summon me?"

"I didn't *mean* to summon you."

My eye twitched. "You are an *irksome* individual. Did you know that?"

He started grinning again. "My gran says that. A *lot*."

"Your gran sounds like my kind of human. Anyway," I held up one long finger, "I think we need a recap. You don't want to make a deal with me because then I'll do something evil in exchange for your noble deed. But I can't leave your side until you've concluded a deal with me."

Reginald scratched the end of his bulbous nose. "Yeah, that sounds right."

"So we are at an impasse."

Reginald looked around. "We are at a park."

"Fucking tar-dipped shit balls, Reginald! I know we're at a..." I closed my eyes and took a calming breath. "What I mean to say is, until you make a deal with me, I can't go away. So why not think of something small we can do together? The amount of evil I can inflict on the world is proportional to the good that you do. So what small things will ease your conscience and allow me to return to my infernal home with demonic dignity?"

Reginald nodded slowly. "Yeah, okay. I get it. Well, I guess the thing I was going to do isn't that big of a deal, anyway."

"And what was that?"

"I'm just returning this rock to its owners."

He opened a canvas sack that I'd neglected to catalog in my earlier appraisal. I peered inside, and in the place where a heart would be in a human, I felt a flip-flopping sensation. It was not a rock. It was a magical connection stone. The Stone of Eno. Created in the Forest of Arden, it was stolen during the Golden Age of Heroes by none other than Valor himself. The rightful owners were a troupe of human-abhorring dryads. Reginald would be eaten alive. Possibly literally.

I opened my mouth to explain to him that this would be a mammoth quest and that the level of evil I would be authorized to unleash would be nearly unparalleled in all of history. But then I shut it again.

"Sure. Yeah. Good idea, Reginald."

Reginald grinned his silly grin, and I almost felt bad for him.

"Great. So how do we do this?"

"Ah," I said and reached into an inside pocket in my coat. I extracted a pin and a stoppered vial. "I'll just poke you like this—"

"Ow!"

"And collect a little blood like this..."

"Is that..."

And down went Reginald. Fainted at the sight of his own blood. We were off to a terrific start.

~

"Merrugh..."

"You coming around, slugger?"

I was perched on a low stone wall next to Reginald's prone form as he sluggishly ascended back into consciousness.

"What happened?"

"You fainted."

"I did? Why?"

I hopped down from the wall. "No idea. Can you stand? Time to get started."

Reginald got shakily to his feet, one hand cradling his head. "I've got a headache."

"Ah, yes. You hit the rock-in-a-bag on the way down."

Reginald's eyes crossed and uncrossed several times as he tried to focus on the bag. "I think I have a concussion."

We did not have time for this. There was evil to be done.

"Nonsense!" I cried, taking his arm in mine and hoisting the canvas bag up onto my other shoulder. "Heroes don't get concussed. You're *Sir* Reginald P. Asstradle now."

This seemed to perk him up. "Yeah. I am, aren't I?" He immediately tripped over his overlarge feet and nearly took me down with him. With monstrous effort, I held my ground and kept us both upright. "Sorry 'bout that," he mumbled. I forced a smile.

"Think nothing of it, Reg."

We were walking alongside the low park wall. Spring had sprung. Flowers were blooming. There was a hint of gardenia in the air. It made me want to vomit.

"So, while you were snoozing..."

"Unconscious..."

"Whatever. I mapped out our route to the Forest of Arden."

Even in his concussed condition he managed to look grateful. "Wow. Thanks for doing that."

I flashed him the least evil grin in my arsenal. "What are partners for if not to help each other out?"

He frowned in concentration. "Three-legged races?"

At this point I started to wonder if I was being punished for something. How was I paired up with this imbecile?

"Yes, Reg. Those two things. Helping each other in times of need...and bureaucratic picnic activities. Anyway, the route. I think if we head northwest, we can cross the Stone Rot Mountains and then circle back to the Forest of Arden."

"Aren't the Stone Rot Mountains a bit dangerous? I mean—they're rotting," he said. "I thought we'd go through Squishy Bottom."

"First, that swamp's actual name is the Marais. And second," I shivered, "we're going to stay as far away from there as possible."

"Oh wait," he said, stopping short and almost causing us to topple over again.

"What?"

"Before we do any of that, we have to go see my gran."

"Your... gran? Why?"

"Because when you're near your gran's house, you visit your gran. That's just manners. Plus... I'm hungry."

I wanted to be accommodating, but I had an evil agenda to attend to. Plus, everyone knows that stopping at a gran's house always takes eight hundred times longer than expected.

"We can't," I said.

"Why not?" he asked.

"I..." I tried to think of a reason beyond *I don't want to.* "I can only eat foods prepared in anger. Or sorrow."

Reginald huffed a laugh. "Then you're gonna eat like a king at my gran's. Come on."

The prospect of a home-cooked meal must have made him feel better because he released my arm and strode ahead of me. I scowled at his back and stalked after him.

~

"Gran? You here? I brought company!"

Banging and muttering sounded from down the hallway, and Grandmother Asstradle shuffled into view. She had approximately twenty-four strands of wispy gray hair, a body like a professional boxer, and what I assumed was a permanent scowl on her face.

"Company? That's not *company*! You brought a flipping demon to my house, Reginald!"

Reginald looked over at me, paying special attention to my backside. "How could you tell?"

"He's got *yellow eyes.* And poise and grace. Compared to him, you look like a wet noodle."

"She's not wrong, Reg. Though I prefer to think of my eyes as more goldenrod."

She clucked in disgust and turned on her heel. Halfway

down the hall, she paused and called, "Well, you're here and that's that. You'd best come in. I've got some leftover pasties, lamb stew, poached salmon, banana bread, peach cobbler, brownies, saltines…"

Her voice faded away as she continued to tally off comestibles. Reginald turned to me, his eyes alight, and rubbed his hands together. I sighed and motioned into the house.

"After you, Sir Asstradle."

~

"Well, invert my ass and call me the Archfiend—this is *delicious*."

I was licking the tips of my fingers after ingesting a slimy log of forcemeat. Gran was watching me with what she claimed was disgust but I could tell was growing admiration.

"Oh, I have the approval of a demon, do I? Maybe they'll put that on my tombstone."

I leaned over to Reg and, with my hand up to my mouth, whispered, "I like her."

Reginald, who was digging into a chicken leg, nodded. "Yeah. She's terrifying."

She growled and—I'm being honest here—it made me jump. "So, when am I going to hear the story? How'd you two get hooked up and all?"

Reginald stopped eating and hung his head. "I forgot to check the box."

"On your hero application?"

"Yeah."

She stood up abruptly. Grabbing a pamphlet from a nearby counter, she rolled it up and bopped him on the head. "You. Don't. Pay. Enough. Attention."

"Okay, Gran! I know, I know." Reginald was cowering, arms above his head.

"It's not all his fault you know," I said, daintily dabbing at the corners of my mouth with a napkin. "The committee didn't catch it either."

"Am I talking to you, Demon?"

"Hey—he has a name. He's Malgon Batshit Kir-some-thing-or-other..."

"Just 'Mal' is fine," I interrupted before he could butcher my name further.

"Fine," said Gran. "But I'm still not talking to you." She turned back to Reginald. "What deal have you made?"

He smiled and tapped his forehead. "I was clever, Gran. We're going to return this rock to the Forest of Arden, he'll give someone a nosebleed or something, and then he goes away."

"The Forest of Arden?" Her eyes narrowed suspiciously. "Give me that sack."

I lunged for the bag, but too late. Her eyes nearly bugged out of her head when she saw the contents.

"This isn't a rock, you dolt. This is the Stone of Eno!"

"The magic one?"

"Of course the magic one. And there is no way that *he*," she thrust a finger in my direction, "didn't know that."

"Hey," Reginald turned toward me, frowning. "You lied to me."

I shrugged, palms up. "Sorry?"

This time I got the bop on the head.

"Hey!" I cried. "What did you expect? I'm a *demon*."

Gran smacked me once more, then sat back down. "How much damage are we talking here?" she asked me.

I tried to pull my mouth into a serious, straight line, but it was no use. It popped back out into a grin as I said, "An epic amount. I've never been able to wield this kind of power. Do you know what my designations are? Officially I am Malgon Belroth Kirranith, Fifteenth of his Name, Giver of Paper Cuts, Collapser of Soufflés, Inventor of the Humblebrag."

"Ha!" barked Gran in spite of herself.

I squinted at her. "Laugh if you will, Reginald's gran. But soon I will be the Collapser of Worlds."

She cocked an eyebrow at me and smirked. "We'll see."

"What's that supposed to mean?"

"Just what I said. Now, come on. It's high time you two were on your way and out of my hair."

I looked out the window. The sun was already halfway to setting.

"You're right." I stood up. "Time to go, Sir Asstradle." I pulled him forcefully away from the chicken legs.

"But..." he whimpered, reaching back toward the table.

"Nope."

I dragged him out of the kitchen, down the hall, and out the door. On the doorstep, we paused. "Thank you for your hospitality, Reginald's gran. And if you ever find yourself in the Underworld," I produced a card from an interior pocket, "I'd be delighted if you looked me up."

She spat in my face, retreated into the house, and slammed the door.

"That actually went better than I'd anticipated," I said, wiping my cheek.

"Mal—" said Reginald, and it was as serious as I'd ever heard him.

"Hm?"

"What do you have planned for your big evil...thing?"

I tilted my head, considering. "I haven't settled on anything for certain yet. Maybe opening up a gaping hole to the Underworld. Would make my commute easier. Or gifting every household with a toddler who can only say the word *why*. But I'm open to suggestions."

He gaped at me. "You wouldn't."

"I really would."

"But that's so *mean*."

I rubbed my forehead. "You do know what a *demon* is, don't you?"

Reginald looked uncomfortable. "Yeah, well, whatever you do... Just don't hurt my gran, okay?"

I was shocked. Hand to my chest, I said, "I swear to you on my honor as a demon that I would sooner cuddle a litter of puppies than harm a specimen such as your gran."

Mollified, Reginald relaxed.

"Right, then. What's next?"

"Off to the Stone Rot Mountains."

Reginald groaned. "I think I have a tummy ache."

"Then it's a good thing that walking aids digestion. Now come along, Reginald."

We walked for a few hours, with Reginald spewing out a litany of complaints at top speed. One in particular—that we should be going through the Marais, or "Squishy Bottom," as he called it—made me feel a bit guilty. Technically, he was right. The Marias was the fastest way to the Forest of Arden. We were actually skirting its borders now. But I had my reasons for not wanting to go.

"You're being a child about this, Asstradle. Just deal with it."

"But I don't wannaaa," he cried.

There was a shift in the air and my body tensed.

Reaching back, I clamped a hand over Reginald's mouth.

"Mhfhgmffhu," he mumbled.

"Because I said so. Now quiet." I hissed back.

We stood there for a few more seconds before Reg pulled my hand away, shrieking, "What is that awful *smell*?"

It was like low tide had taken a shit in a pigsty. And worse—it was depressingly familiar.

"Shit! Fuck! This can't be happening." I squatted down and tried to hide behind some tall grass.

Reginald smirked at me. "Are you...flustered?"

"Don't be ridiculous," I whispered. "I am unflappable. I cannot be flapped."

His smirk widened into a full-on grin. "You *are*. This is amazing. What is happening right now?"

I was about to say, "Nothing," but that we should probably run away as fast as we can anyway, when I heard a deep, gurgling voice behind me.

"Hello, *Lover*."

I sighed, shoulders sagging, and stood up. "Hello, Ob," I said reluctantly.

"I wondered if I'd be seeing you again, *mon cher*."

I turned, forcing a smile. "Here I am."

If humans could unhinge their jaws, Reginald's would have been on the ground. "He's...he's a...that's an ogre."

Ob bent his head in acknowledgement. "I am indeed. Ob the ogre, at your disposal."

Reginald was moving his mouth, but no words were coming out. Ob turned to me. "Is he quite all right?"

I waved my hand dismissively. "He's fine. He'll snap out of it soon."

Ob shook his head and turned back to me. "Where did you find this one?" he asked and cocked his head at Reginald.

"He found me."

"Didn't check the box?"

"Didn't check the box."

Ob nodded his understanding. But then he thrust out his bottom lip and pouted. "And you are only now coming to find me?"

"Actually," said Reginald, regaining the power of speech and coming up beside us, "Mal said we should avoid the swamp at all costs."

If we ever got to the Stone Rot Mountains, I was going to find a particularly precarious boulder and squash him with it.

Ob put one mired hand to his chest and staggered backward. "*Mon amour,* you cut me deeply."

"No, no it was nothing like that. It's just that we have this quest and all. I was going to circle back. But you know how it goes. You have to, er...do the things you have to do before the things you want to do?"

It came out as a question, but Ob didn't seem to notice. His eyes shone with happy tears. He leapt at me and threw his arms around my neck. "Ah, I knew you could not have forgotten our love so soon."

"Well," I wheezed as he wrung the air from my lungs, "it has been five hundred years."

Ob pulled back, shaking his head vigorously. "Love knows nothing of time."

Reginald was watching us with gleeful fascination. "I wish I had some popped corn," he said. "This is amazing."

I glared at him, then turned back to Ob. "So...unfortunately we must be going. Quest things. You know how it is. We've got to get to the Forest of Arden by tomorrow, so... It's been great seeing you again..."

"The Forest of Arden? That's right on the other side of *Le*

*Marais*. Come, come. You will stay the night with me, then I will lead you through in the morning. It will take half the time."

"I don't think..."

"Yes, please!" exclaimed Reginald. "I've never seen an ogre's house before."

"*Magnifique*. Follow me." Ob tucked my arm in his, and Reginald trotted after us like a needy puppy.

"Huh," said Reginald, when we'd reached Ob's abode. "I was not expecting this."

People often think that because ogres are disgusting, filthy half-monsters, they would make their homes in dank caves or rotting tree stumps. But ogres are some of the most cultured creatures in all of Widdershins. While it's true that they stink like wet dog, look like a cross between a troll and a clump of seaweed, and live on a diet that would be poisonous to your average human, they really are remarkably chic in their own way.

"You can take the guest quarters in the east wing," said Ob, gesturing to the left side of the two-story swamp oak house. Still holding my arm, he looked deeply into my eyes. "I want this one all to myself tonight."

I shivered in horror and changed the subject. "I see you've added on since last time. Looks lovely."

"It was meant to be a nursery for our little adopted demons," he mewled.

"Oh, for fuck's sake," I breathed.

"What was that, *mon petite monstre*?"

I ran my hand down my face with a groan. "I can't take it anymore. Look, Ob, you're a wonderful...um...creature. But we have been *over* this. I didn't know I was standing on the Stump of Destiny. I'd never even heard of such a thing. I wasn't hanging out in a swamp looking for a life mate. I was simply standing on a stump looking for an *alligator* with which I could torment a nearby village, okay? It wasn't destiny. It was..." I cast around for the right words, "...bad luck."

One of Ob's hands was on his chest, the back of the other against his giant forehead. "*L'amour de ma vie!* Five hundred years you let me believe our love was true?"

I waved my hands in front of me as if that would turn back the tides of time and let me rephrase my answer. "Luck is the wrong word. And it's not that we didn't have our fun–I had a lovely time...er..." I cast a glance at Reginald. "... getting to know you."

"You got to know him? Like *know* him?" asked Reginald, face screwing up in disgust.

"Oh, for Lucifer's sake–this is the moment you choose to understand nuance? Yes, Asstradle. I got to *know* him. Ogres happen to be extremely generous lovers," I barked before pivoting toward Ob. But in doing so, I realized that I should have already been backing away. Ob's face was contorted in rage. His cold stare bore into me so deeply I thought my insides might actually be coated with frost. In a dangerously quiet voice he said,

"There are only two reasons why a couple is called to the Stump of Destiny. The first, and most common is to be lovers. But if you were not there to be my lover, you were there to be my enemy."

At that, he ran at me full speed, arms outstretched as if to throttle me. Admittedly, ogres are not exactly spritely and so full speed wasn't that swift. But when a massive, angry ogre starts running in your direction, you get out of the way.

"I don't think he means to hug you, Mal," said Reginald, moving clear of Ob's current course.

"I figured that out, thanks," I said as I grabbed Reg by

the arm and the two of us sprinted past the house, back into the swamp proper. Vines slapped our faces; roots clawed their way up to snag on our clothes and pull us down into the murky water but we kept moving until the crashing, lumbering, wheezing noises of a pursuing ogre ceased. Only then did I slow our pace.

"Can't we stop and rest?" Reginald asked.

"No," I said as I pushed aside a vine as thick as a python.

"Why not?"

"Because we are lost, without food, and on a mission."

"There must be *something* in here we can eat."

"Not if you want to continue living. Now come on, Reginald. You can pick some berries in the Forest of Arden."

Reginald's face darkened, and I heard him mumble something about roast chicken, but he followed after.

"Looks like Gran was right about one thing," he said as he nearly lost his balance on a mossy log.

"What do you mean?" I asked, ignoring his plight and moving past him.

"Things aren't exactly going as you intended."

I pursed my lips. "And whose fault is that?"

"Me? What did I have to do with it?"

"Oh, I don't know. How about, 'What's that awful *smell*?'" I mimicked.

"I think you're remembering that scene differently than I am. We were already in trouble before that."

I hopped nimbly across a line of stones peeking their heads out of the water. He was right, of course, but I would never admit that. "Look, if we can't agree, let's just walk in silence."

"Yeah, okay," he said, slipping off the first stone and falling knee-deep into the swamp.

But apparently Sir Asstradle was incapable of silence.

He spent the next hour acquainting me with the names, physical descriptions, and dispositions of every teacher he'd ever had since he started school. *At the age of six*. At some point I tuned him out and my thoughts drifted back to Reginald's gran. So far she was spot-on in her assessment of how this would go. And while I knew we were less than a day's walk from our ultimate goal, only a fool would ignore the wisdom of a cantankerous matriarch.

By the time we exited the Marais and saw the eaves of the Forest of Arden in front of us, we were covered in midge bites and soggy to our knees. Reginald had thrown up twice during our journey: The first time because he broke his toe tripping over a hidden tree root in the water. The second time because, "Sometimes when I think about throwing up, it makes me throw up."

I was eager to be rid of the lad.

We stood gazing across the clearing to the forest beyond.

"There it is, Asstradle. Our final destination. Let's get this over with."

But Reginald didn't move. He held the canvas sack against his chest and shook his head.

"What's the matter, Reg?"

"I can't do it."

"You can't do what?"

"Return the Stone of Eno. I had a lot of time to think about it in the swamp, and it's not right. I won't let you unleash... What did you call it?"

"An epic amount of evil?"

"Yes! That."

I smiled at Reginald as if he were a petulant child. I inclined my head and rested my hands on his shoulders. "I understand that you're feeling apprehensive, Reg. But a deal is a deal. You took a blood oath."

"You stole my blood."

"Technically, yes. But you were going to take the deal, and you know it."

Reginald shuffled his feet. "Okay, sure. But I've changed my mind."

"Reg, if you change your mind, you forfeit your life."

Sir Reginald P. Asstradle, Hero of Widdershins, turned so pale he was nearly translucent. But, damn him, he stood his ground.

"Then I forfeit my life."

I removed my hands from his shoulders. My pretense of fatherly affection was spent. I was starting to get peeved.

"For fuck's sake, you brainless walking migraine! Now is not the time to grow a backbone. The forest is right there. We bring the stone to the dryads, you go home to your gran, and I get to reduce that steaming turd of a swamp to an empty crater in the ground!"

"You wouldn't. You're not really as mean as you say."

I cackled my highest, most evil cackle.

"Of course I would, Asstradle. It's what I was spawned for. Now give me that bag."

"No!"

And Reginald took off at a run. But, being a bit dim-witted, he ran directly into the forest.

"Well, that's step one, done," I said aloud to myself. Then I dashed after him.

"Stop following me!" Reginald called back.

"I could if you would stop running!" I shouted forward. I was gaining on him, but I had to hand it to the kid, he was fast.

"I'll never give it to yooooo…"

The last vowel hung in the air as Reginald disappeared from view. I'd been almost upon him when he lost his footing and started rolling down an embankment in front of us. I threw myself over it as well and, bouncing and tumbling, we grappled with the bag and each other.

"Give me the—"

"It's mine!"

"It's not..."

"I'll never..."

*Crack.*

We stopped rolling and hit the bottom, which turned out to be the base of a long-dry riverbed. The Stone of Eno had come loose from the sack and sailed through the air as if in slow motion. We both watched it arc, fall, and crash down to the stony ground. It split into three pieces and began steaming and oozing a whitish, sparkly goo.

"Oh no," said Reginald.

"Oh fuck," I groaned.

We raced over to the rock and picked up the pieces. We tried to put it back together before it was too late, but the shards were slick with supernatural runoff.

I was frantic. Magical contracts were quite specific. We weren't returning just any stone to the dryads. We needed to return the Stone of Eno. If the stone was no longer magical, it was no longer the Stone of Eno, and we would have failed in our task.

So consumed were we with trying to smash the thing back together that we didn't notice them arrive until it was too late.

"A demon and a hero walk into the Forest of Arden. Sounds like the beginning of a joke. But how does it end?"

We were surrounded by arrow-wielding dryads, but the question came from one in the middle of the circle. She was taller and broader than the rest, with a crown of oak leaves at her temples.

"Actually...we didn't walk. We ran in," Reginald corrected.

"*Silence*," spat the dryad queen.

"My dear lady," I said, bowing my head respectfully. "We are only here to restore to you the long lost Stone of Eno. Once you have taken possession, we will be on our way forthwith and will cause you no more trouble."

The dryad narrowed her eyes at the object—well, objects—in our hands. She signaled the other dryads to lower their weapons, and moved closer. "Let me see that."

"Ah, well, first," I said, shifting the stone away from her, "would you agree that it has been rightfully restored to its owner?" If she agreed, we might get by on a technicality.

Her flat gaze was all the answer I really needed, but she still said, "No."

I deflated, defeated.

"Then there's something you should know," I said, as Reginald and I handed over the broken pieces of the stone.

A storm brewed in her eyes. "The stone is *broken*?"

The ice in her voice nearly froze me to the bone. I wasn't sure how Reginald was still standing when a broken toe could make him toss his lunch.

"It is, your Dryadness," said Reginald seriously.

"You people are unbelievable! First you steal it, then you lose it, then you break it? We should kill you where you stand."

"Please," said Reginald. "My partner and I here were trying to fix it, but it was just so gooey and slippery that we couldn't do it right."

The dryad queen turned each of the pieces over in her hands. "The magic just left the stone? Now?"

I stared down at my sodden, mucky boots and nodded shamefully. "Yes. It is gone."

Then, to my astonishment, she began to laugh. At first it was just a rumble in her chest, but it crescendoed to a loud, manic howl. "You fools," she gasped, still laughing. "The magic isn't gone. You said you had it on your hands? It's inside you now. You..." she began laughing again, and now all the dryads were chuckling. "You two are bonded for eternity!"

My stomach twisted unpleasantly. "What?"

She wiped at her eyes and sighed. "You broke a connection stone. The magic seeped out of it and looked for the next strongest bond in the vicinity to bolster. There is only one reason for a human and a demon to be traveling together. And what is stronger than a blood oath?"

"You mean," said Reginald doubtfully, "that we can't leave each other's side...ever again?"

The dryad queen crossed her arms. "Try it."

Needing no further encouragement, we faced opposite directions and ran as fast as we could. We'd nearly crossed the dryad circle when I felt a zinging sensation, and Reg and I got pulled forcefully back to each other's sides.

"Oof!" I yelled as we were rammed into one another.

"See?" said the dryad queen with a sly smile.

"But...but..." I started. "I can't stay attached to this buffoon forever!"

"Hey, that hurts my feelings," frowned Reginald.

"Shut it, Asstradle," I snapped. "Isn't there any way to reverse it?"

She shrugged a shoulder. "I don't know of a way. Maybe the wizards know," she said as she returned the broken stone to the canvas bag. "But I'll tell you this..." She leaned in close to the two of us, and we could feel her warm breath on our faces. "You will fix this. And you will not set foot in these woods again until you do. Right now I'm amused by the unfortunate situation in which you find yourselves. But my amusement will not last long. So take your sack, take your posteriors, and run like hell."

An arrow whooshed past us, and I could see Reginald's eyes starting to roll back in his head.

"No time for that now, Reg. Got to go!"

I slapped him hard across the face and grabbed the bag, and we sprinted as fast as we could out, out, out of the forest.

As we cleared the edge of the trees, I finally had the courage to look behind us. The dryads formed a forbidding line just under the cover of the leaves. Slowly and silently, they retreated back to the heart of the forest. But the message was clear: you're not welcome here.

"First the swamp. Now the forest. Pretty soon we're not going to be able to go anywhere."

Reginald's breath was coming in gasps. "Whose...fault... is that?"

I growled at him, but he ignored me and continued.

"Just to be totally clear here... We're stuck together for the rest of time?"

I flopped down onto the grass. "Apparently," I said glumly.

Reginald looked up at the sky. "Even for bathroom stuff?"

"Ugh."

I cradled my head in my hands, and Reginald dropped down next to me with a thump.

"Gosh, I wonder what my gran's going to say about this?"

"Nothing good, I imagine."

We sat in silence for a few minutes. Then Reginald said, "So...what do we do now?"

My mind was sluggish. It was hard to put together

productive thoughts. But one piece of helpful information managed to worm its way into my consciousness. "The wizards. The dryad queen said the wizards might know."

Reginald considered this. "Do you know where they are?"

I nodded. "Yes. But they are a long way from here."

Reginald stood up and held out a hand to me. "We've got nothing but time."

I looked up at his overbite and elephantine ears and sighed. Shackled? To him? Forever? The thought lit a fire in me.

"Okay, Asstradle," I said, taking his hand and standing once more. "We're off to see the wizards."

"Great. But we're getting lunch first, right?"

I glared at him. "How can you think of your stomach at a time like this?"

"What? We're gonna need our strength."

I balled my hands into fists. "Fine. But no detours to grandmothers." I stalked away only to be thrust back into his orbit after a few yards. "This is going to take some getting used to."

Reg helped me to my feet again and we set off together. "You know, we may not have fulfilled the contract exactly. But I think the spirit of it is intact."

"What do you mean?"

"I stood my ground against a demon—a pretty obviously good deed if you ask me. And the bad consequence is—now we are shackled together forever."

I slapped my palm against my forehead. The wizards better have the answers we needed. Otherwise this was going to be the longest eternity of all time.

# ABOUT A.E. KINCAID

A.E. Kincaid is a creative director by day and fiction writer by night. She is originally from the east coast of the United States but currently lives in Iowa with her husband, young son, and the nosiest cat that's ever lived.

**Find out more about A.E. at:**
aekincaid.com

facebook.com/authoraekincaid

twitter.com/authoraekincaid

instagram.com/a.e.kincaid

tiktok.com/@authoraekincaid

# THE BOOK THIEVES BY L.F. WHAM

Becca crouched low on the slated roof, surveying the handsome building beyond. Drizzle irritated her eyes, like a fly she couldn't swat. The coolness of the slates soaked into her knees, but she stayed still, leaning into the sloping roof in front of her.

She thought of Jamie, tucked up in bed, warm, the nightlight offering him protection from all imagined evils. The ghouls under the bed, the monsters in the wardrobe. Becca was left protecting him from the real evils of the world; hunger, cold, homelessness.

He'd been her responsibility since their mother died. Not quite the university experience she'd envisioned for herself, being the primary caregiver of a seven-year-old and the sole breadwinner.

Which is what brought her here, muscles cramping, shoulders aching, eyes trained on the University Library.

A glass domed roof covered the front of the building. Through it Becca could see into one of the many study rooms and beyond it into the main stairwell. Below the stairs, she could glimpse the foyer. Or at least, she could see light and she knew it was coming from the foyer. She tracked the shadows that blocked the light; security guards making their rounds. She needed to get a sense of their pattern so she could slip inside and move about unseen.

The library was usually full of arts students looking like they'd stepped off the Ralph Lauren webpages. It was a place of illegal seat saving, dark corner canoodling and many stress-induced breakdowns. Now it sat quiet, a comforting glow from the lower floor windows.

Becca examined her mind's map of the building. She knew it well. Had even paced around the length of the shelves earlier that day, under the pretense of checking out books for her business class. Well, it wasn't really a pretense; she did have that fifteen hundred word essay to write for her economics class, so she supposed the books would come in useful.

She focused back on the eclipsing light, pushing the tip of her tongue through her teeth, running over their edge. Her pulse kept a steady beat. The individual streaks of drizzle sharpened in her vision. The smell of moisture, of summer rain, filled her nose. She flexed her fingers, anticipating her next move.

Beyond the domed glass roof of the library, guarded by security, was something Becca wanted. A first edition of Nero's Veleno e Prosa, worth two and a half grand; or six months' rent, or five months' and full bellies. She wanted that book.

A flash of movement made her still. Meters away, the silhouette of a man climbed onto her roof. Despite his size, he glided down the steep slant of the slates, landing gracefully on his feet. Becca's heart quickened as the stranger approached the glass dome.

What was he doing? He'll ruin the plan.

Becca pushed off her perch and prowled between shadows, keeping her eyes on the man now crouched by the glass.

He was fiddling with something. Was he here for the book too? The first edition had only arrived at the library last night. It seemed like too much of a coincidence that he'd be skulking on this rooftop tonight.

Becca was a meter behind him now. She stood, silent, as he fiddled with the latch at the window.

She leaned back on her heels, cocked her hip and, raising her hand as if to examine her nails, she asked in a bored voice, "Need a hand?"

He whipped around. Becca was face to face, not with a man, but a woman. From across the roof, she'd mistaken her broad shoulders as belonging to a man, but it was definitely a woman staring at her now. A pretty woman. Her mouth parted in shock. Long earrings dangled from her lobes. Her hair was buzzed short. On her feet were a shiny pair of thick-treaded boots.

The woman recovered her surprise. Leaning back, she stuffed her hands into her pockets. "Didn't expect to meet anybody up here tonight."

Becca didn't reply. The woman had a rucksack at her feet; the top rolled down, revealing rope. It was clear she was planning on breaking into the library. To steal the book?

The woman followed her gaze. "I know they're overpriced, but I couldn't resist. You have one?"

It took Becca a minute to realize she was talking about the bag. She shook her head and nodded at the rope. "You're breaking in." It wasn't a question.

"Yes," the girl admitted, no hint of remorse or chagrin on her face. "And you? Up here for a quiet stroll or simply to admire the view?"

Becca shifted on her feet and didn't answer. Was this woman here for the book? How would she get past her? Becca was slighter, probably quicker on her feet, but if it came to a fight, she had no skills. The woman was obviously stronger. She'd win if it came to blows and Becca might be sucking her food through a straw.

"You're not the most talkative thief I've met."

Becca's head jerked up. She'd met other thieves? She cleared her face. "Who says I'm a thief?"

*That's right, you'd be a winning poker player.*

The woman looked at her. "You're on a roof in the dark wearing tight, black clothing. It doesn't exactly take Sherlock."

She cast around for a realistic cover story: a nighttime window cleaner; roof surveyor; security tester?

The woman didn't wait for a rebuttal, rummaging around in her pack until she pulled out a piece of wire that may have once been a coat hook. Stepping back to the glass dome, she fiddled with the wire and one of the window panes. She called back to her, "You here for the book?"

Dread enveloped Becca like she'd stepped into ice water. "Book?" She asked, unable to keep her voice smooth.

"I know our trade kid."

Becca jutted her chin up. "I'm not a kid."

The woman looked back at her, eyes roaming up her body, falling on her face. Becca grew hot and her treacherous heart fluttered in her chest.

The woman shrugged. "Figure of speech." Then winked before returning to her work.

The time between seconds stretched out like pulled toffee, before there was a click and she pulled open the window. Becca stilled, watching the woman closely. She had to get to that book before her.

The woman turned to give Becca a broad grin, gently swinging the window closed. Becca's heart skipped a beat.

The woman straightened, sliding her hands into the baggy pockets of the dungarees she was wearing. She was taller than Becca, by maybe half a foot. She stuck out her hand. "I'm Mel."

Becca looked at her palm, then back at her smiling face. "Becca," she took the outstretched hand and shook once. Electricity shot through her and into her gut. She dropped Mel's hand, drawing her arm back to safety. Her skin tingled where they'd touched and her cheeks grew warm. She was glad for the darkness.

*What is with you?*

Mel smiled, "So, Becca, what are we going to do?"

"What do you mean?"

"Well, I'm here for this book. You won't admit it, but you're here for this book. Two thieves after the same trinket isn't the ideal situation. I'm all for some healthy competition but on the same job? More potential for mistakes. Clumsiness."

Becca didn't answer, though she agreed.

"See, I'm thinking our options are that one of us concedes and goes home." Mel leaned forward, examining her.

Becca's cheeks rose from warm to hot, but she refused to look away.

"But something tells me you're not one to back down and I'm certainly not. Option two, we both carry on with our plans to steal the book, winner takes all. But as I said, that doesn't tend to end well. So that leaves us with option three."

Becca expected her to continue. When she didn't, she was forced to ask, "What's option three?"

Mel beamed. "I am so glad you asked. Option three," Mel leaned forward conspiratorially, "we work together."

"You mean, we both break in and get the book?"

"Yes." Mel confirmed, her expression alight with amusement.

Becca's eyes narrowed. "Do you not see a problem with that?"

Mel cocked her head, enquiring, like a puppy hearing a high-pitched noise.

"We can't exactly split the book," Becca explained.

Mel's eyebrows knit together. "Are you stealing the book, so that you have the book?"

"No." Becca said, sounding like a toddler, her face now at extreme temperatures.

"You mean to sell it?" Mel looked at her, eyebrows raised.

"Yes," Becca hissed through gritted teeth.

"Perfect. We'll split the takings." Mel grinned.

Share the profits? Two thieves splitting an investment amicably? Becca shifted on her feet.

If she trusted Mel, best-case scenario, which wasn't something Becca usually dabbled in, was half the worth of the book: three months' rent. Meaning, Becca would need to take extra hours at the cafe or do another job before the money ran out, which would be right at the beginning of exam period.

It was more likely that Mel would double-cross her and take the book and it's worth all for herself.

But what if she got the slip on Mel? Six months' rent was too good an opportunity not to go for. She could help Mel get the book then, once they had it, she could grab it, fence it off and keep everything.

Mel knew nothing about her; it would be easy to vanish in this city. It wasn't like they'd bump into each other on a job a second time. Lightning didn't strike in the same place twice.

"What do you think?" Mel asked, her pale eyes shining.

Becca paused. If it came to blows, Mel would win, but Becca was willing to bet, well, six months' rent, that she was faster. Much faster. As soon as she had the book, she'd slip down one of the city's winding streets and vanish into the darkness.

She gave a tight-lipped smile. "Sure, why not."

"Great." Mel threw her arms up in triumph. "Now, this is what I was thinking."

Becca lowered herself from the open window, stretching out the cobwebs in her arms. Carrying trays laden with plates all day had made them stiff. Her toes found a shelf of books, gaining purchase on the edge.

She let go with one hand to grab hold of the bookcase below, the muscles in her right arm screamed in protest. She made it and climbed down. On touching the floor, she ducked behind a table.

The air in the library was stuffy. Other than the glass roof, there were no windows to open and let in a fresh breeze. The smell of hundreds of books lay stagnant across the room.

Ahead of her, Mel crouched by another table, gazing up at the bookshelves stretched along the walls, as if she were admiring great works of art.

Becca scurried over to join her. Mel smiled at her. "Isn't this place mad? Look at all these books! You think anyone ever reads this many?"

Becca huffed. "I think many pretend to." She thought of

the last party she'd made it to. She'd been stuck talking to some pretentious wazzock whose ego was so fragile, he constantly felt the need to quote eminent philosophers and classic literature. A complete waste of a night off.

Mel nodded, squinting at the book covers in the low light. "You're probably right." Then Mel swiveled around to face her. Her face was inches away from Becca's. She could make out every one of Mel's eyelashes. Her top lip was elegant, a neat "M" shape, her lower lip plump. They parted. "Which way do you think this book is?"

Becca blinked. "You." She frowned. "You didn't stake the place? Familiarize yourself with the building?"

Mel shrugged. "No," she said, her voice light. "I prefer to follow my nose. Got a good instinct for this work." She looked around the room. "I'd say, that way."

Becca's jaw set. Anger pulsing inside of her at the fact that Mel had just pointed in the exact right direction.

But to rely on instinct? Was this a game to her? She called it work, but maybe it was more of a fun hobby to pass the time. Probably has a rich parent that could make any charges disappear if she got caught.

For Becca, this wasn't fun. This was necessity. The difference between empty bellies and a full fridge. A roof over their heads or using one of these books to research squatters' rights.

Becca's eyes narrowed, but Mel didn't seem to notice as she smiled, and with an encouraging nod, moved across the room, keeping low and hugging the bookcase to avoid patches of moonlight.

Becca stalked after her, keeping an ear out for security.

She expected Mel to move awkwardly, but she was efficient, keeping her body tucked in, only making necessary movements. Still, Becca was confident she could outrun her.

If she was the one to take the book and she made her way back up to the roof first, she could lose Mel across the rooftops. No one knew those rooftops better than her.

They were meters from the doorway to the next room when the light from the hall shifted. Someone was coming.

Becca shrank into the shadows, freezing herself against the wall of books. To her side, Mel was a coiled spring; ducked behind a desk, leaning forward on one knee, her shoulders bunched toward her ears.

Footsteps echoed along the tiles in the hall. A silhouette formed in the doorway.

Mel's breathing quickened. Becca had the feeling she was more comfortable taking action than taking her time.

The guard stepped away and light from the hall was visible once more.

Mel let out a breath.

"This way," Becca whispered, stepping away from the bookcase and gliding past Mel to the next room; a smaller, darker room, not immediately connected to the hall and full of social science books.

Anytime Becca walked through here she glanced at the titles wishing she could study from books titled "Passions and Pleasures" and the "Sociology of Emotions." Instead, she had to press her nose to tomes on business management and economic theory. At the end of her degree she needed a job that paid.

"Sex. This book is on sex. Hetero-normative sex, but still!" Becca glanced back to find Mel had only made it a few feet into the room. She was studying a page from a book she'd pulled off the shelf. "I might have done a bit better at school if I'd known you could study this stuff. Imagine getting to go to university and study sex. Exams wouldn't be so bad, huh?"

She couldn't see Mel's face, but Becca knew Mel was waggling her eyebrows at her. She rolled her eyes. "Come on."

They moved through a series of small rooms, all crammed with lines of books. Mel paused, examining titles and commenting. "This author's eyes are open—" "Typical, a man writing about the female orgasm—" "Oh my, this one has pictures." They were lucky her whispers didn't draw any unwanted attention.

"You have got to lighten up," Mel said after she read out another wild book title and didn't get so much as a smile from Becca.

"I'm here 'cause I have to be, not for fun," Becca retorted.

"Really? You're telling me you don't get any pleasure from this. No rush of adrenaline? No smug satisfaction of outsmarting others?"

Becca stuck out her chin. "I need the money."

"You could get a job," Mel suggested.

"I have a job, pay barely fills our bellies."

"You know you're not meant to eat the money, right?" Mel grinned.

Becca ignored her.

"Come on," Mel coaxed, catching up to her and slipping past. "I don't know a thief that doesn't get a buzz from stealing. You telling me you're immune to that? A regular Florence Nightingale, only steals because of the circumstances of life?"

Becca sidestepped her. Of course she only stole because she needed to. She'd love to put it behind her. Love to have one job that paid enough for rent, for food, for books. Thank god tuition was covered.

Of course, there were aspects to stealing she was good at,

even liked. But that was true of all things. There's always some good that can be found.

But if her situation were different, she wouldn't even think of stealing. There'd be no reason to. No need. As soon as she had a decent job all of this would be behind her.

"Who's our?" Mel asked.

"What?" Becca asked, distracted.

"You said, 'Barely fills our bellies.'" Mel brought up her hands to make quotation marks. "Who are you doing this for?"

She hadn't meant to say that, to reveal the presence of another person in her life. "I meant the other workers." Becca explained. "No one gets paid well."

"Right." Mel dragged out the word.

"You know if you'd checked the place out during the day," Becca snapped, "you could have taken your time looking at all these books."

"I'm not a student, they wouldn't let me in."

"It's card access. You telling me you couldn't swipe a card from someone? Surely pickpocketing is thievery 101."

"You know I bet they have a book titled that somewhere here," Mel said, looking around, a smile in her voice.

Becca huffed. "Is that why you want Veleno e Prosa? You've got a thing for books?"

"Goodness no. What would I want with a book? I've never had much cause for them. Of course, Jack would say that I just don't have the attention span. But I'm finding what people come here to study..." she ran her fingers along the spines of the nearest bookshelf, "...enlightening."

"Jack?"

"Jack, grandmaster of thievery 101. You never met him at the thieve's conference?" Mel jested.

"Not one for networking I guess." She hadn't given much

thought to the existence of other thieves. It was a bit unnerving to imagine them all working across the city. She did what she needed to do and that was that. Until tonight, she'd not met anyone else who did the same.

"Well, Jack's always reading those stories about space and time travel. At least that's what I think they're about, judging by the cover."

"You don't ask him?"

Mel shrugged. "I've learned Jack's best left alone when he's reading."

There was a light up ahead. They were coming up to the reading room, a fancy room on the other side of the library with leather-bound books, armchairs, and plinths displaying figureheads of who cares who, some old white dude that used to have money once upon a time, whose family probably still did. The room was usually filled with pretty arts students in their checked "got out of a charity shop" shirts, their leather book bags at their crossed ankles, a cup of coffee from the cafe on the table next to them.

Becca was looking forward to seeing the room empty. She might just sit in a few seats for the novelty. There was never one free by the time she got to the library after her shift at the cafe.

"You should come by and meet them sometime."

Becca blinked at Mel. Pulling herself from her student reverie of an available seat and a quiet place to read. "Who?"

"Jack and the others."

"Others?"

"Other thieves."

Becca reeled at the idea that Mel knew not just one other thief, but a few of them. What would that mean if she double-crossed her? Would they all be out to get her?

"You all hang out?" She asked.

"Yeah. Sometimes a job takes more than one, you know?"

She didn't, but Becca nodded anyway.

"Plus, lots of us don't exactly do this because we have a plush house in the countryside and need to get our kicks. We're a fair ways off from the Thomas Crown Affair — you seen it?"

Becca shook her head. She'd read the book version.

"Ach, the original's great. But most of us need a place to crash so we crash together."

An image of a crowd of sleeping bags on a concrete floor flashed through Becca's mind.

*Don't be judgmental.* "There are a few of you?"

Mel shrugged. "People come and go. Some have their own digs or lives going on, like you and your 'our.'" Mel looked at her, but the smile on her face was kind, understanding rather than suspicious. "There's, maybe...a dozen who stay."

A dozen thieves all in one room? "Sounds like carnage."

Mel laughed. "Only if you try to talk to Jack when he's reading." She winked, then her eyes went wide, taking in the surroundings of the room they just entered. "Fuck me."

They were in the reading room.

Blue light dappled the floor from the tall stained glass windows. Slim bookcases of dark wood were placed around the walls, a shining brass bar allowing a matching wooden ladder to move along connected bookcases. Marble busts stood regally around the room, a line of soldiers ready for inspection.

In the center of the room were curved leather seats, shiny and worn through use, some missing the metal rivets that bolted the leather together along the back.

A quiet feeling of calm always settled over Becca when

she came here. It was disconnected from the outside world, almost like it was frozen in time. A sanctuary where all that mattered were the pages in your hand.

Mel reached out as she passed one of the chairs, running her hand across the leather, her neck stretching round as she gazed at the stained glass and the busts. "This is very different to my idea of a library."

Becca put on a tone of disgust. "It's a uni library, for posh people."

Mel glanced over at her, her eyes flicking up and down her. "Right," she said, looking back at the room and moving to inspect one of the statues more closely.

Becca walked between the chairs and was in the center of the room. Exposed. The hairs on the back of her neck pricked. There were no bookcases to duck behind. No dark alcoves. If someone came through that door at the end of the room, they could try to hide behind the seats in time, but Mel would struggle to get her whole body behind a chair.

What were they doing admiring the scenery? They had a job to do; they needed to move on.

Becca prowled toward the door in the middle of the far wall. The door that would lead to the room that housed the Veleno e Prosa. Ahead, Mel peered at one of the old-white-men busts. As she passed, Becca gripped Mel's arm to tug her forward.

Her hand wrapped around taught muscle, sliding over skin. Her fingers tingled, her heartbeat quickened, and heat rushed into her cheeks. She stared at her hand, at skin on skin.

Mel turned her head toward her.

Becca cleared her throat lightly. "We should move on." She looked up at Mel.

Her face was inches from hers, her skin bright pink.

Mel smiled. "Okay, lead the way, maestro."

Becca dropped her hand and stepped back. The tingling stopped.

She nodded at Mel, then slipped into the next room.

Little light got into the small room. There were no windows, in order to protect the pages of the open books under the display cabinets.

Becca took a torch out of the side pocket of her bag. It illuminated the snug space, the edge of the beam falling on the walls of books that pressed in around them.

Becca and Mel stepped inside, moving toward the middle display cabinet. The one Becca knew held the book she was after.

Light spilled over the glass, revealing a book inside. This one was closed and looked pretty good for a four-hundred-year-old book. The worn cover, shiny in places from where the oils from people's hands had hydrated the leather. Becca's fingertips grew itchy, and she rocked forward onto the balls of her feet, hovering over the glass.

"That's it? It's smaller than I was expecting," Mel said from behind her.

Becca rolled her eyes. "Hold this." She thrust the torch into Mel's grasp, then slid her bag from her shoulders and pulled out lock picks from another side pocket.

The itch of her fingers faded as she clasped them. They were cool to the touch. Her heart beat firmer, her vision grew sharper. She breathed in the unique scent of old books, a mix of leather and dust and whatever scents had been absorbed into the pages over the years. Behind her, Mel's breathing was a steady rhythm.

She kneeled down by the cabinet; Mel shined the light at the silver lock and Becca got to work. In a few clicks, the lock gave way. They were cheap things really. She supposed they weren't a security device so much as to protect the items inside from damage.

She replaced the picks into her bag and pulled out a scarf, white with light blue flowers. The material was thin and soft. It had been her mother's.

Becca unfolded the scarf, laying it across her knees, then slid open the display case. The book was cool in her hands, which trembled as she lifted it out of the case. She placed it on her knees and wrapped it up in the scarf before storing it in her bag.

She had it. And Mel hadn't even suggested she be the one to carry it. She reached up to slide the cabinet closed.

"Wait."

Becca's hands froze. But Mel didn't say anything more. The light beam swung over to the books on the walls. Mel walked over to them, pulled a couple out by their top corner to look at the covers before pushing them back onto the shelf. After a minute, she came back with one. Becca moved over for her and Mel placed it into the cabinet where the Veleno e Prosa had been.

Looking at it, Becca could see it was similar. If security came in to do the rounds, they wouldn't notice the book was missing unless they looked properly and she doubted they'd do more than cast a quick glance for signs of a disturbance.

Mel clicked the cabinet shut.

"I wouldn't have thought of that," Becca admitted.

"*You* didn't think of that." Mel smiled.

Becca's gut twisted.

She gave a quick smile back, then concentrated on checking the bag was secure.

Now she needed to focus on being first back out to the roof.

Becca and Mel crept out of the room, Veleno e Prosa secure in Becca's bag. They scurried back through the beautiful reading room. The library was quiet.

Becca's heartbeat quickened the closer they got to their exit. She needed to be the first to climb out onto the roof so she could disappear with the book. But she had to be careful not to raise Mel's suspicions.

If Mel made it to the rooftop first, Becca would just have to try and give her the slip.

The rooms in the library were a dark tunnel stretched out before them. Their footsteps sounded loud to Becca. She looked around for signs of security while scrunching in on herself, trying to become as small as possible. They were so close.

There was a thud.

Mel righted herself after she stumbled over the doorway. She gave Mel an exasperated look and Mel mouthed back, "Sorry."

A light appeared in the corridor. Becca dove behind a set of shelves and crouched low in the shadows. A beam of light swung across the room, illuminating the spot where she'd stood seconds before.

Sweat broke out across her palms.

Across the room she could make out Mel, backed into the shadows between two bookcases.

The security guard stepped into the room, moving the

light beam from right to left.

This was Becca's chance. The guard would find Mel. She'd be detained and questioned. The police would be called.

Becca should turn and run. She'd be back at her flat with the book before the police even got here.

The guard headed left, taking steps toward Mel's hiding place.

Mel didn't know her real name, where she lived. She'd find somewhere to fence the book and then she wouldn't have to worry about rent for another six months. She could think about her exams, get As.

The guard continued to step closer to Mel.

Why wasn't she running? She should be halfway to the window by now.

*Damn your conscience. Or is it your fricking libido?*

She slumped her shoulder forward, slipping off her bag strap. Removing her arm, she let the bag slip to her elbow.

She reached inside, her hand scrabbling around. Not her flat keys, she'd need them. Not her purse that would have ID. Not her penknife, she couldn't afford a new one. Her hands clasped around a small tin. Vaseline; the answer to squeaky hinges. She clasped it in her hand and pulled it from her bag before aiming for the doorway and launching it across the room.

Seconds ticked by before.

*Clank.* The tin hit the banister in the hallway, then skirted across the floor. The torchlight swung toward the sound, the guard already moving back to the door.

"Come on." Becca hissed at Mel's outline as the guard disappeared into the hall. She hadn't exactly been subtle and if the guard found that tin, they'd know someone was here.

The dark shape of Mel moved toward her. Hands clasped around her own and Mel pulled her out from behind the bookcase and through the remaining tunnel of rooms.

They ran through the library, throwing caution to the wind, aiming for the moonlight ahead.

Reaching the room with the glass ceiling, Becca lunged for the bookcase and climbed.

She clambered through the window at the top, then reached down for Mel, who grabbed her outstretched hand. With effort, Becca pulled her up before they collapsed onto the roof, panting.

Staring up at the sky, Mel said, "I thought you were going to let me get caught."

The moon shone above them along with a few stars, but the light of the city blocked out most. "So did I."

"I thought you were gonna take off with the book."

"So did I."

The sound of labored breaths filled Becca's ears.

Mel turned toward her. "Why didn't you?"

Good question. She'd fully intended to whisk away with the book, leaving Mel with nothing. But leaving Mel alone on the rooftop with no book was different to leaving Mel inside to be caught and arrested. It turned out she just wasn't *that* villainous. It certainly had nothing to do with Mel's smile. Or that tingly feeling.

"Figured we're on the same side of things." She shrugged, meeting Mel's gaze. "Besides, I've no real idea about where we can flog this thing." She held up her bag above them.

Mel laughed. She stood up and brushed herself off, then reached out a hand to Becca. "Probably best not to hang around here too long."

Mel's hands were warm and enveloped her own. With little effort, Mel pulled her to her feet.

They were nose to nose.

Mel's smile faded, her gaze flicking down to Becca's lips, then back to her eyes.

Warmth flooded through Becca. Their hands were still clasped. Becca didn't dare to breathe as she glided her thumb over Mel's smooth skin. Mel leaned forward.

Becca pulled back.

The atmosphere broke. Disappointment was vinegar in her mouth.

*Why did she do that?*

Squeezing Becca's hand, Mel gave a small smile. "You should come by the flat and meet the others sometime. You never know when you might need the skills of another thief." Then she dropped her hold.

Becca immediately felt the loss of the contact. She stared at her empty hand before taking a breath and nodding her acceptance of the invitation. She couldn't quite find her voice.

Mel was still smiling at her. Her eyes shining with something Becca didn't quite understand.

Sympathy? Pity?

"See you later, Becks." She turned around and sloped across the roof.

Becca gazed after her.

Her bag was heavy on her shoulder.

"Wait!" She called out to Mel's back, "What about the book?"

Without stopping, Mel faced her, "Meet me at Vinnies on Shandwick street at ten tomorrow night. I've already got a fence lined up." With a last smile, she climbed up and over the roof before disappearing into the night.

# ABOUT L.F. WHAM

L.F. Wham is a new author working on her debut fantasy novel. A feminist activist, she wants to write stories that show healthy relationships and condemn misogyny. In the summer months she's found soaking up the sun and as the nights draw in, she enjoys making mulled wine and watching really bad romance films. L. F. Wham is a quine living in 'Auld Reekie' and continues to be surprised when the cannon goes off at 1pm.

**Find out more about L.F. at:**
lfwham.com

 instagram.com/lfwhamauthor

## INSATIABLE BY VAL NEIL

The heavenly scent of freshly baked bread lured Nikolai down the corridor. His stomach grumbled as he weaved through the crowd, instinct driving him as much as hunger. In all his meals at the Academy, he'd never smelled anything so tantalizing. Students hurried past, their foot-steps echoing off the cave walls, oblivious to the smell's siren call in their hurry to get to class.

The cavern narrowed into one of its many pinch points. Students ducked to avoid the low ceiling and Nikolai felt a pang of jealousy. He'd stopped growing completely during the war. Years of starvation did that to a person. It wasn't until he arrived at the Academy and received regular meals that he'd started growing again, albeit slowly. He pocketed whatever extra food he could and stored it in his room. His roommate whined that he'd attract mice; he didn't stop, just hid his treasures better. You always had to plan for the future. If necessary, mice were food too.

The first time he saw someone scrape their unfinished meal into the trash he could scarcely believe his eyes.

"What hell you do?" he'd asked. The boy had been

confused—they were all still learning English back then—so Nikolai had retrieved the food from the bin, slapped it on a plate, and shoved it in the boy's face. "No waste!"

The boy wrinkled his nose at the offering, now covered with bits of debris, and pushed Nikolai aside, muttering unintelligible insults in his native tongue. Nikolai cracked him over the head with the tray and got him in a headlock. He jammed the food into the boy's mouth, holding his nose shut until he swallowed. The act earned him a caning, an unfortunate experience that taught him nothing except to be more discreet.

Even with the extra calories, he hadn't grown as quickly as the boys who'd lived through the war in relative comfort. The Academy physician said he was fine, that puberty would take care of his height soon enough, but he couldn't help being irritated at his body for failing to respond to its current good fortune.

Nikolai inhaled deeply. The scent of bread was getting stronger. Unfortunately, the students ahead of him were taking their sweet time moving through the passageway and it was too narrow for him to squeeze by. The Academy really ought to widen some of the tunnels, but they'd been carved centuries ago and no one wanted to risk breaking whatever enchantments had been worked into the stone.

A student ahead clipped the low ceiling. He paused to let out a string of expletives while his friends laughed and teased. Nikolai leaned against the coarse granite and waited for them to get out of the way. The dining hall was agonizingly close—he could almost taste the bread. Damnit, this was taking too long.

"Hurry up," he called to the boys ahead.

The laughing stopped and the students craned their

necks to see around one another. "Why?" said the one
closest to him. "You got someplace important to be?"

"Yeah, your girlfriend asked me to meet her. Seems
you're not getting the job done."

The boy scoffed. "You're what, thirteen? Probably never
even been with a girl."

"Fifteen, and you're right, but as your girlfriend's asking
me for help, that says more about your skill than mine."

There was a chorus of *ooohs* and guffaws, and soon the
boys farther up the chamber were pulling their sour-faced
friend through the gap. Finally the cavern widened. Doors
lined either side, leading to administrative offices, the
terrace, and dining hall. The terrace was the Academy's only
outdoor area. A gigantic dome illusion made it appear as
just another part of the Turkish mountain in which the
school was hidden. Students were required to spend an
hour outside each day to help prevent rickets, though many
spent far more, often taking their meals with them.

A gaggle of girls passed with their trays laden. Nikolai
glanced at the food, but the bread was standard Academy
fare, not at all the exquisite food the scent had promised. He
made a beeline for the dining hall, but a quick peek inside
revealed it wasn't the source of the smell. He paced the
length of the chamber until he found it again, wafting from
a corridor leading only to classrooms. Were students trying
their hand at baking, or was one of the professors treating
their pupils? Either way, he'd talk himself into joining them.

Nikolai worked his way through the warren of tunnels. A
savory smell joined that of the bread and he quickened his pace.
Butter, sugar, meat—all were still in short supply after the war,
and the Academy wasn't exactly easy to get to. Their supplies
arrived by pack mule; the meat tended to be dried and required

softening in stew to make it palatable. This scent spoke of dripping fat and crisp skin, meat so tender it fell off the bone. Nikolai salivated as he rushed down the corridor, poking his head into every door, disappointment greeting him each time.

Only one hallway left to try. It was home to Mr. Couture's classroom, one of *his* classrooms. He could definitely talk his way in there. Nikolai whirled around the last corner and slammed into someone, rebounding off their chest. He looked up to find Klaus glaring down at him. Great, it *would* be him.

You'd think the Academy would refuse to admit Hitler Youth, given how many students had been orphaned or otherwise traumatized by the war, but the Collective didn't care about Mundane affairs so long as Magi society remained hidden. Any Magi child born to Mundane parents was scooped up and sent to the Academy to learn control of their powers. If they succeeded, they'd join Magi society. If they failed, well, no one talked about what happened if they failed. Nikolai suspected a quiet disposal. They couldn't have uncontrolled Magi bringing attention to the rest of them. He would've preferred they skip right to disposal with Klaus.

The older boy snarled, "Watch where you're going, *Untermensch*."

Klaus had been tossing the word at him since they'd taken the Academy's entrance trial together in Istanbul. Russians were Slavic and fell into the same category as Jews, Roma, and Blacks—*subhuman*. The Nazis had invaded the Soviet Union not to capture, but to exterminate to make room for their own people. Dissenters, intelligentsia, and Jews were killed outright. Everyone else was left to starve. Whatever grain couldn't be carted back went to feed the military horses or was torched. And that was just the countryside. Nikolai had been trapped in a city.

The scent of bread beckoned and Nikolai's stomach knotted. He made to step around Klaus—the corridor was wide enough here—but the boy blocked him. There was a poetic cruelty in the fact that, once again, a Nazi was preventing him from eating.

"Apologize," said Klaus.

"Sorry." Nikolai moved and once again Klaus blocked him.

"Sorry for *what*?"

"I'm sorry I bumped into you." Blocked again. Motherfucker.

"You don't *sound* sorry."

"That's because I'm not."

Klaus glanced over his shoulder. "You're going to Mr. Couture's class, *ja*?"

It was a stupid question, given that Mr. Couture's room was the only one down this way, so Nikolai didn't answer.

Klaus inhaled deeply, a smile on his face. "Smells wonderful, doesn't it? You would not believe what Mr. Couture has prepared for today. But this is not your time to be here." Klaus took a step forward, jostling Nikolai back the way he'd come. "You are in his afternoon class. This is not for you."

Nikolai tried to get some traction, but the floor was worn smooth from centuries of passing students. The walls were too far apart to grip. The scent of cooking meat receded, replaced with the earthy scent of the cavern and whatever passed for Klaus' soap.

"What do you want?"

"I *want* you to apologize." Klaus gave him another push. *"Properly."*

Nikolai studied his opponent, desire to attack warring with the desire to eat. Klaus was seventeen and had the advantage of height and muscle, but Nikolai knew how to fight dirty and wouldn't stop until he'd won. It was amazing how fast people gave up if you took a bite out of them. Even grown men. They'd clutch their wound and step back in abject horror. But that wasn't a normal scuffle, the kind the Academy ignored. How much time would he really gain? No, there were other ways to handle Klaus, ways that wouldn't draw attention to himself. Although ... Klaus had pushed him all the way into the next corridor. Students were passing in both directions.

Nikolai flung himself to his knees. "I'm SORRY! Klaus, handsome, strong, *powerful*, Klaus."

Several students paused, their heads swiveling toward the commotion.

"I can't *believe* I wronged you, *you* of all people. That hair, those eyes, the cut of your jaw—you're the perfect Aryan specimen. Forgive me! FORGIVE *MEEE*!"

There was snickering from the audience.

Klaus glanced nervously at the growing crowd. "That's enough."

"Enough? It can never be enough! I have to make it up to you. Let me shine your shoes." Nikolai started vigorously wiping a shoe with his sleeve. The crowd was laughing in earnest now.

Klaus took a step back. "I said that's enough!"

"No shoeshine? You're right, I'm not worthy to lick the dust from your feet. I know! There's something else I can lick." He made a grab for Klaus' belt buckle.

Klaus' eyes widened and he jerked back with a roar. "YOU STAY AWAY FROM ME!" He stared for a moment in disbelief, then stormed toward the main corridor, laughter pelting his back.

Nikolai stood and made his way to Mr. Couture's classroom.

Fucking *finally*.

A divine sight greeted him beyond the door—a feast beyond compare. Every lesson table groaned under the weight of food. There was roast pig, prime rib, pheasant, and a fish so big it took up half a table by itself. Fruit and cream, pies and pudding, bread and cheese. There were dozens of things he didn't recognize, but it didn't matter, it all looked delicious.

"Nikolai," said Mr. Couture. "I wasn't expecting to see you so soon. Aren't you in my afternoon class?"

"I promised to help someone with a spell that's giving them trouble. I was hoping to catch an early lecture, if that's alright."

Mr. Couture smiled. "Of course. There's enough for everybody. Please have a seat, but don't touch, not yet."

Nikolai scanned the tables. Where should he sit? It all looked so good. A few more students filed in, oohing and aahing at the sight. On closer inspection, each table had a theme, with dishes according to varying regions. Nikolai chose the one with the heartiest dishes, taking a seat by a prime rib encrusted with spices. He inhaled deeply, as though he could taste the meat by smell alone. The other students couldn't arrive fast enough.

Mr. Couture greeted each new arrival and instructed them to wait. Students chatted excitedly about their favorite foods. Nikolai listened, marking which came up repeatedly so he could try them. When everyone was seated and accounted for, Mr. Couture began.

"Today we're going to learn a new branch of magic. For

those of you who want a profession you can use in a Mundane city, this is one of the best. Not only does it seem immune to the effects of Mundane technology, but if you get good enough, you can also have a very lucrative career."

Nikolai barely heard the spiel. The prime rib was brown and crispy on the edges with a nice bloody center. He'd grab that first, then a chicken leg—no, a whole chicken—then perhaps some of those pastries. There were tarts near the end of the table, and something frosted with a cherry on top. Sweet was good, but meat and starches were more filling. He'd take as much as he could grab, piling it high on his plate. That was the thing about food, you had to eat as much as you could whenever you could. Tomorrow there might be nothing. Tomorrow you might be eating bread cut with sawdust and boiling leather shoes to make soup.

Mr. Couture seemed to enjoy making them wait. He droned on and on about the Collective, which spells they were allowed to cast around Mundanes, and how the Enforcers would come get them for breaking the rules. If he talked for much longer, the food would get cold, though cold food was better than none.

After what seemed like ages, Mr. Couture appeared to be winding down, and the students sat up straighter. Nikolai poised himself to strike.

"But I've made you wait long enough." Mr. Couture smiled and opened his arms. "Go ahead and—"

Nikolai didn't wait for him to finish. His hand dove for the prime rib. Instead of warm meat, his hand thumped what felt like wood. What? He tried again and his hand passed through the meat. He moved down the table, a rising tide of fury and disappointment, trying to grab fistfuls of food and coming back with nothing.

Disappointed groans filled the classroom. Some

students laughed. A few swore, but none so much as Nikolai. His hands continued to move of their own volition, long after his brain registered the problem. It couldn't be fake. It couldn't be. He could *smell* it. Maybe if he tried another table ...

"That's enough," said Mr. Couture. He waved his wand and the food vanished.

Nikolai stared at the empty table. Gone. All of it. Even the scent of bread. Only the stale, earthy aroma of the cave remained.

"Today we start learning my specialty—illusions." Mr. Couture conjured a vase of yellow tulips. Nikolai wanted to smash it over his head, but that, too, was fake. "As you can see, they can be very realistic. The best illusions appeal to multiple senses. Sight alone won't do." He plucked an imaginary flower from the vase and held it toward a girl in the front row.

"I can smell it!" she exclaimed.

"Touch is the hardest to get right, but if you feel here— uh, Nikolai, you need to sit down."

Nikolai glared at Mr. Couture with pure loathing. "Fuck you."

There were gasps from around the room.

"*Excuse* me?" said Mr. Couture.

"I *said*"—Nikolai slammed his fists against the table; fire bloomed around them and his tablemates fled—"fuck *YOOOU!*" With a telekinetic heave, he flipped the table across the room. It crashed into the far wall and shattered, sending charred fragments flying in all directions. Students screamed and bolted from the room.

Mr. Couture removed his jacket and ran to smother the flames. "Out! Out! Everybody out!"

Nikolai stood, deadly calm, willing the flames to lick up

a tapestry and set fire to Mr. Couture's desk. Burn it. Burn it all. As if in response, the fire bloomed, bursting forth and scorching Mr. Couture's jacket out of his hands.

Mr. Couture yelped and leapt back. "You!" He pointed at Nikolai. "Office. *NOW*." He didn't wait to see if Nikolai would obey.

The fire was spreading to other tables now. Acrid black smoke billowed from where someone had spilled lamp oil the previous week. Between that and the tapestries lining the walls, the room would soon be filled with smoke. Mr. Couture continued trying to smother the flames. Maybe if he'd specialized in something besides fucking *illusions* he'd have a spell worth a damn that could put out fire. His loss.

Nikolai moved casually toward the door, scanning the room as he went. Ah, there we go, a bit of broken table. He stooped to pick up the splinter. It was large and tapered, with a nice point at the end. Nikolai hid it against his arm, though he needn't have bothered—Mr. Couture was too preoccupied with the flames to notice.

Nikolai stepped into the empty corridor and closed the thick wooden door. He wedged the splinter underneath, kicking to ensure it was tight, then waited at the next junction with an air of mock concern.

"Sorry, you can't come down this way. There's been a fire. Don't worry, Mr. Couture has everything well in hand."

～

Nikolai exited the office. Harper waited for him in the hallway, worry creasing his usually affable face.

"How are you?" Harper asked. Anyone else might have asked him to recount what happened, confirm the rumors, but something was wrong with Harper that made him care about others, even when there was no benefit to himself.

"Fine. They can't very well get mad at me for a magical outburst, not when the point of the Academy is to teach us how to control that kind of thing. They even thanked me for trying to keep the corridor clear." He'd waited until Mr. Couture's frantic beating on the door had slowed before removing the wedge and jogging toward the office.

"Thank goodness you're here!" he'd exclaimed upon sighting the cavalry. "I think Mr. Couture's trapped. I heard him pounding, but I couldn't get the door open. I think the heat's warped it."

They'd returned to find the hallway filled with smoke. The door had been splintered off its hinges. Mr. Couture lay atop it, one pant leg smoldering, wand clutched in his lax hand. Nikolai had paced in mock nervousness repeating, "Is he alright? Please let him be alright."

Unfortunately, he was. Just smoke inhalation and a few minor burns. He'd have to try again—Mr. Couture and Klaus both.

"So that's it?" asked Harper. "Did they give you any punishment at all?"

"Meditation exercises." Nikolai grinned. As if he was going to do *that*. "And I promised to leave the classroom if I feel myself getting upset. I'm going to use it to ditch every illusion lecture from now on."

"You can't do that! Illusion is important."

"To you maybe. Not to me. You can't eat an illusion." Or douse a fire with it.

Harper's shoulders slumped. "It's all my fault. I should have warned you Mr. Couture introduces the topic like that. He does it every year, though the illusion is never the same. In my class, he made it look as though the ceiling had caved in over the door, trapping everyone inside. I was scared. We all were. But this girl from London—she started *screaming*. Probably reminded her of the Blitz. Even after he lifted the illusion she was inconsolable."

"Who was it?" He'd have to collect the names of everyone else Mr. Couture had fucked with over the years. Maybe they could be turned against him, or be set up as scapegoats. He couldn't target Mr. Couture again so soon without arousing suspicion. Better to wait and make the man think he was in the clear.

"Lucy. Mr. Couture used her as an example of how powerful illusions could be. That to make them really work, you have to appeal to multiple senses and evoke an—an emotional response."

"And you said nothing to me, knowing what could happen?" That wasn't at all like Harper. He'd do anything he could to ensure people were having a good time. There was no animosity in the question, only curiosity, but Harper turned to him with a pained expression.

"I'm *so* sorry. No one talks about it. And you didn't go through the war." Harper shot him a speculative glance and paused just long enough to allow a potential interjection. Nikolai refused the bait. As far as anyone knew, he'd spent the war in Turkey with his mother's family. Denied, Harper continued. "It didn't occur to me that—"

"Why doesn't anyone talk about it?"

"I don't know. It's like a rite of passage or something. We all had to go through it." Harper ran a hand through his hair —a nervous tell. The incident bothered him far more than he was letting on, but why?

"Can I look inside your head?"

"Uh, yeah."

Harper stopped and put his back against the wall, as

though he thought Nikolai needed a motionless target. Nikolai did nothing to dispel the misconception. The less people knew about how telepathy worked the better. He rarely had opportunity to use it these days. The Academy sternly warned him that such magic would not be tolerated, and Magi could sense his intrusions anyway. Harper was the first person to ever willingly give him access, and Nikolai made frequent requests since. It was good to test the boundaries of a relationship, see how much power people would grant you.

Harper shivered as Nikolai slid into his mind. As always, the forefront contained a stirring of physical attraction. Embarrassed, Harper tried to hide it, not realizing that doing so only pushed it further into the spotlight. Sometimes Nikolai wallowed in the adoration; today he ignored his friend's feelings and focused on the memory Harper recalled.

Lucy wept at the table in front of him. Harper desperately wanted to comfort her, but Mr. Couture was lecturing and getting up now would be disrespectful. Plenty of time to speak with her after class, except she'd excused herself and left early. As much as he wanted to go after her, Harper didn't want Mr. Couture to think he disapproved. Of all the schools of magic, illusion would let him live the life that he wanted, and Mr. Couture was the only one who taught advanced illusions. Confronting the man could ruin his chances of earning a slot. Harper tried to ignore the twisting in his gut and focus on the lecture.

The silence popped like a bubble once everyone filed into the corridor after class.

"You should've seen Abdul. He was cowering under the table!"

"You're one to talk. You were dodging rocks like everyone else."

Harper said nothing. What if it got back to Mr. Couture? To his relief, Paulette brought it up first.

"Well I thought it was awful. Did you see Lucy? Someone ought to report Mr. Couture."

"Oh, come on," said Marcello. "It's not like he *really* caved in the classroom." He glanced at Abdul, who stood up straighter in a vain attempt to appear less shaken.

"That's right—no one got hurt. It's all in good fun." Despite the proclamation, the body language of the group said it had been anything but fun.

Paulette shook her head. "I still think he went too far. What do you think, Harper?"

Suddenly all eyes were upon him. "I, uh ... Well, I'm sure Mr. Couture had his reasons."

"Hey, guys. Good class today?"

The group froze and exchanged looks. In front of them was a student from the next class, headed to Mr. Couture's room. Nikolai could almost see the rationalizations unfold on their faces. They'd all gone through it, and everything had been okay. Was it really their place to dispel the boy's ignorance? The shared experience somehow bound the group together and made the boy an outsider, one who'd not yet earned the right to know. Warning him meant admitting that their own experience had been cruel and meritless.

Harper—sweet, empathetic Harper—stared at his feet, willing someone else to speak.

"Class was great!" one of them finally answered, slapping the boy on the back. "You're going to love it." Others quickly chimed in. After all, no one had warned them. Who were they to break tradition?

Harper slumped against the wall, guilt and shame radiating off him like heat. "I should've said something."

Nikolai could never understand why people shackled themselves to such useless emotions. "You were only being pragmatic."

"You know what's even worse? When I heard Mr. Couture had been in a fire, my first thought was—I mean it wasn't my *only* thought, and it went away immediately—"

"You thought if he was dead there'd be no one to teach you illusions."

Harper nodded morosely. "It's awful. How could I even *think* something like that, right? It makes me feel like, like deep down I'm not a good person."

Nikolai laughed. He couldn't help it. The idea was so incredibly stupid. "I've been in lots of minds. Trust me, you're about as good as they come."

"I'm not. I should have said something. I didn't because I'm a coward." He ran a shaky hand through his blond hair. In his mind, screams and gunshots echoed in the distance. "People need to speak up when they see wrongdoing. I of all people know this! But when I was put to the test—a *small* test—I failed. I put my own desire above the welfare of another person. How could I *do* that?"

Unbidden, a memory vaulted itself to the surface of Harper's mind—Nazis dragging people from their homes, Mother shouting, little Liza crying, Harper crouching in the corner. The officers barged in and swept their home, collecting every family member, though they looked in puzzlement at Harper. So did Father and Liza. Mother grabbed his arm and pulled him toward the door.

"Go home, boy! This is no time for a visit. Go home to your father." She looked meaningfully across the street, at the home of an English expatriate, unmolested by the

Germans. Why was she pretending he wasn't her son? And why was everyone looking at him like that?

"You daft, boy?" said one of the officers. "Get out of here before I give you a lashing for playing with Jews."

Harper took a tentative step outside. The Englishman's home seemed miles away, across a great chasm. He took a furtive glance at the other homes. One of his neighbors lay slumped over in a puddle of mud tinged red. Others were being jammed into transport vehicles. With every step he knew the Nazis would laughingly call him back with taunts about how they'd made him think he could escape.

It wasn't until he reached the house that he saw why they hadn't. His reflection in the window showed a different boy—one with blond hair and blue eyes. He had no time to process why, not then. He raised his hand and knocked on the door. If the neighbor didn't take him in, if he turned him aside ...

A middle-aged gentleman in a tweed suit opened the door. He frowned at Harper in puzzlement, as though he couldn't quite place him.

"Can I please come in, Mr. Lewis?" Harper glanced furtively down the street. One of his friends—Emil—was making a break for it. The boy got half a block before collapsing, the gunshot echoing after he fell. Bullets must travel faster than the speed of sound. Harper's mind latched onto the fact, as though the concrete detail could somehow bring logic and reason to the horror he'd just witnessed.

"Please," he said again. "My mo—I mean, Mrs. Rosenberg sent me home. She said I can't come over to play with Liza anymore."

Mr. Lewis stared at him with dawning comprehension. "*Jiří?*"

He gave a slight nod. Mr. Lewis glanced around the

street, then hurriedly gestured him inside. The memory took on an almost frantic quality. Harper standing at the window. Mr. Lewis shooing him away, telling him not to look. "We'll have to give you my son's name. He died years ago in England, but they don't know that. I have pictures of him when he was younger that should do—" Harper waking up to find his hair and eyes had gone dark overnight. Crying in front of the mirror, desperately willing the illusion to come back. Crossing a train station with their bags, worrying incessantly that the illusion might drop. His face was still the same. Would they know? *Would they know?*

Harper lurched away from Nikolai, as though physical distance could break the telepathic contact. The memories had come and gone in a flash, perhaps only a few seconds. How much had Nikolai seen? Oh God, he was still there. Harper bent over and dry heaved.

"Jiří, eh?"

"Don't call me that!" Harper scanned the corridor, wide-eyed. Had anyone heard? "*Never* call me that," he said more quietly. "It's Harper. Harper Lewis. And please get out of my head now."

"Certainly." Nikolai left his mind. "You don't have to keep hiding, though. War's over."

"Not to people like Klaus, it isn't. It'll never be over for him."

"Fuck Klaus. He'll get what's coming to him. I guarantee it."

A new quarter arrived and with it, new classes. The Academy regularly evaluated their progress and bumped students up or down according to ability. Nikolai had rapidly progressed beyond his peers and was now able to take advanced classes. He even had a few with Harper, though unfortunately, more with Klaus.

Nikolai entered Ms. Hasan's class—now there was a real instructor. She taught them *useful* things, like how to conjure fire, enlarge the volume of a container, or get a sewing needle to dance through fabric with a flick of your wand. Her classes were in Turkish, making attendance comparatively low and, oddly enough, mostly female. When Nikolai first signed up he took some heat from the other boys, as if being in a classroom full of girls was a *bad* thing.

Fucking idiots.

He chose a seat next to Bisma, a raven-haired goddess three years his senior. She turned to him with a warm smile.

"Got any lokum?"

"You know I do." He'd taken to carrying candy specifically for this class. Painful as it was to watch his stash dwindle, food was a good way to make friends, doubly so when it was the rationed kind. He took out a small pouch and set it on the bench between them. Bisma withdrew a small confectionery square and popped it in her mouth.

"Mmmm, pistachios."

"There's some with dates in there too."

"You always get the best stuff."

He grinned. "I know."

"Good morning, class," said Ms. Hasan. "Please take out your wands. Nikolai, put the snacks away. Don't think I can't see you and Bisma chewing over there. You'll have something else to eat soon enough."

Nikolai stowed the pouch and sat at attention. Unlike Mr. Couture, Ms. Hasan meant it if she said there'd be food.

"Today we'll be learning to conjure bread. Hold out your

wand and make a circular motion like so. The incantation is *Panem*."

Nikolai watched in horrified fascination as a loaf of bread appeared below her wand.

Bread.

From nothing.

As if in a dream, he picked up his wand and went through the motions. It took a few tries, but eventually he had a loaf of hearty bread in front of him. Tentatively, he poked it with his finger. Still warm. He gripped the loaf and broke it in half, releasing a puff of steam.

"Hey, how did you make yours warm?" Bisma leaned over and sniffed his bread. "Oh, that smells amazing! Can I have some? All I got was this." She clacked her bread against the table.

He nodded, not really paying attention.

Bread.

Anytime he wanted.

He broke off a small piece and put it in his mouth. It tasted heavenly. Exactly how he'd imagined. Yet he took no pleasure in its consumption. He swallowed the bite hastily and raised his hand.

"Yes, Nikolai?"

"Is there a limit to how often we can cast this spell?"

"Excellent question. Collective law prohibits you from conjuring bread more than once a day, or twice a day in cases of extreme need."

"Will it run out then, if you cast it too often?" It had to be a finite resource. It *had* to be.

"I don't think so. The restriction is to keep people from taking advantage and disrupting the local economy." She wagged a finger at the class. "So no one get any ideas about opening up a bakery. The spell is meant to tide you over in times of crisis, until you can get something better."

Nikolai laughed—a bitter, hollow sound—and several classmates turned in his direction.

Bread.

Anytime he wanted.

He scarcely paid attention the rest of class. Since they were practicing, Ms. Hasan gave them permission to cast as many times as they needed to get the spell down. He'd somehow mastered it on the first try and sat with his hands folded in his lap, observing the loaf in quiet contemplation. He left it there at the end of class—it seemed tainted somehow—and returned to his shared room. He locked the door and stood in front of his desk.

*"Panem."*

It couldn't be this easy.

*"Panem."*

It had to run out. It *had* to. That's why they only let you cast it once a day, because if you did it too often, you'd run out.

*"Panem."*

You'd run out.

*"Panem."*

You'd run out.

*"Panem."*

Would it ever run out?

*"Panem."*

He could've fed himself with this. He could have fed Mother.

*"Panem. Panem."*

They could have lived on this. No more boiled shoe soles. No more stripping the wallpaper to eat the glue.

*"Panem. Panem. Panem."*

Hell, he could've fed his *brothers*, and then Mother wouldn't hate him.

*"Panem. Panem. Panem. Panem. Panem."*

She wouldn't have looked at him with that dead-eyed expression that said he was no longer welcome. Because she survived. She survived instead of his brothers, and it was his fault for putting her life ahead of theirs.

"Hey, who locked the door? Nikolai, are you in there?"

*"Panem. Panem. Panem ..."*

It wasn't fucking possible. Was this a joke? It felt like the universe was laughing at him. Was this how Mrs. Grebenshchikov had survived? She'd vanished when the blockade started and hadn't opened her door until it was over. Everyone thought she was dead, but when she came out she was a healthy weight. They'd questioned her alongside Nikolai, who was skeletal, but far better off than most. After the questioning, she'd patted him on the head and told him what he was, and to seek out the Academy.

"Open the damned door!"

He was only vaguely aware of his roommate's banging. The lock snicked—he must've found someone who knew the Unlock spell. Nikolai darted to his feet and slammed the door just as it opened, crushing his roommate's fingers. The boy screamed. Nikolai opened the door just enough for the fingers to vanish, then closed it again and dragged the desk in front of it.

He had no idea how long he sat there, but when he came to he was shaking from magical exhaustion and surrounded by a mountain of loaves.

"Nikolai?" Harper's voice now. Calm, concerned. "Are you alright in there?"

Nothing was alright. Or rather, it was, but far too late to be of use.

"Can you open the door?"

As if he'd let anyone see him this way.

"Okay. You don't have to open the door. Just know that I'm right outside if you need me. Whatever's going on, you'll get through this."

His wand hand twitched. Part of him wanted to knock Harper unconscious. How dare he be so condescending. How dare he trap him here. There were murmurs on the other side of the door, including adult voices. So Harper was colluding with the staff then. They'd lure him out and steal his food. He'd take care of the lot of them once his mana regenerated.

Except he didn't. As soon as he had the mana, he conjured more bread and hated himself for it. This compulsion, born from the need to survive, had become a weakness.

"I told your roommate he could have my bed for tonight."

Harper had passed the time telling stories through the door. Nikolai had been mostly ignoring them, but this last remark made him check the clock—midnight. He'd been at this all day and then some. If that wasn't weakness, he didn't know what was. He had to regain control.

Where to start? Nikolai shelved the problem. First he needed to deal with Harper. He rose and started hiding the loaves—in drawers, the chest, under both beds—but it was no use. There were simply too many. Even if he got rid of Harper, his roommate would still see them when he returned. The only way to deal with weakness was to squash it. He braced himself and opened the door.

Harper tentatively stepped inside, inadvertently kicking a loaf. It skidded across the floor and joined a pile under the desk. His eyes swept the room. "Do you need help cleaning up?"

The question threw him. He'd been expecting laughter, admonishment, maybe even pity—anything but the simple offer of aid without strings attached. He studied Harper's face. There *was* something in his eyes, but he couldn't identify what. Like pity, but without the implicit superiority inherent in the emotion.

"I ..." He wanted to keep them. If he slept on a mountain of bread from this day forward, at least he'd die knowing he'd never starve again. That if the spell failed, he at least had his stash. "I don't know."

"Do you want to keep some in your room?"

Relief flooded through him. "Yes."

"Okay, well, you can't work with that many on your desk. And you can't sleep with them on your bed. How about we fill up your trunk and take the extra to the dining hall? As many trips as it takes. That way they won't go to waste. And you can keep a couple loaves in your room. Does that sound alright?"

It did.

Moving the bread took the better part of the night. The dining hall was far, and they had to make countless trips. Thankfully the corridors were blessedly quiet. When they finally finished it was four a.m.

Harper flopped onto the vacant bed with a sigh and kicked off his shoes. They pattered haphazardly to the floor. Within an instant, he was asleep.

Nikolai carefully wrapped two loaves in cloth and stored them in his chest before getting into bed. He lay awake watching Harper's gentle breathing. A crown of blond hair splayed against the pillow. The war was over—had been for a few years—yet Harper maintained his illusion even in sleep. It seemed weak and illogical, but was he any better, conjuring mountains of bread?

Food controlled every aspect of his life. In class, it was impossible not to silently count down the minutes until the next meal. He could now watch others throw food away, but never did so himself. Everything on his tray had to be finished. If a fellow student showed signs of slowing down, he'd offer to clear their plate rather than watch it be wasted. He had to master food, or it would forever hold mastery over him. Getting the bread out of his room was a start, but it didn't go far enough.

When the murmur of voices and footsteps echoed in the corridor, he shook Harper awake and dragged him to the dining hall. He left Harper at the table and went to get their breakfast. Today it was menemen, a Turkish dish comprised mainly of eggs, tomatoes, and green chili peppers. There were also olives, cheese, and simit, a circular bread encrusted with sesame seeds. He took a bit of everything and returned to the table to find Harper flopped over his arms, gently snoring. He set the trays down and poked Harper awake.

"Watch." Nikolai scooped up a bit of menemen and plopped it on the corner of his tray. He broke off a piece each of the simit and the cheese, adding them to the pile, along with a single olive. Harper watched in confusion. Nikolai pointed to the food he'd set aside. "I'm not going to eat that. If I try, call me a weakling. Because that's what I'll be."

Harper flushed. "I can't do that!"

"Then get someone else who can. The whole dining hall if you have to. Promise me."

Harper had the same expression as when he'd seen the mountains of bread, only now it *was* tinged with pity. "I know you said you didn't experience the war, but we've all been through things. If you ever need to talk—"

"What I *need* is for you to tell me how weak I am if I fail at this."

Softly, "Okay."

It seemed easy enough at first, but the more he ate, the more often he glanced to the pile of food at the corner of his tray. One olive, and a couple bites of the rest. Not much, really. He might as well eat it. What if war broke out and they could no longer get shipments from Istanbul? What if there was a mountain slide tomorrow, trapping them all? He had the bread conjuring spell, but still ...

Nikolai hurriedly finished his plate, all but the sacrificial pile, and roughly shoved the tray at Harper, sloshing his water. "Take it. Take it now."

Harper pulled the tray closer but didn't get up.

"The trash! Throw it away!" Fuck. It had to be done before he reached over and grabbed it back. Harper seemed to detect this, for he picked up the food and shoved it in his mouth.

"No!" Nikolai bellowed and slammed his fist on the table. Ruined. All ruined. Eating it didn't count. The point was to *waste*. It wasn't wasteful to feed someone you wanted alive. "Spit it out, you idiot!"

Harper stared at him like he'd never seen him before.

*"NOW!"*

Harper grabbed a napkin and pushed the food out with his tongue. Nikolai snatched it from him and strode toward the nearest wastebasket. Even the urge to consume the half-chewed food was overwhelming. His hand shook as he held it over the bin and refused to relinquish its prize. Disgusted with his own visceral reaction, he redoubled his efforts to control himself. One ... two ... three.

He dropped the napkin into the bin. It seemed to plummet in slow motion, and part of him wanted to snatch it back. He forced himself to watch. There, gone. He turned resolutely away.

That settled it. From now on he'd sacrifice a portion of food at every meal. He *would* master this. He was Nikolai Fedorov, talented Magi, and he would never go hungry again.

# ABOUT VAL NEIL

Val Neil was diagnosed with autism at the age of forty-one and couldn't be happier to have her weirdness professionally validated. She lives in California with her ADHDer spouse, three children (two neurodiverse and one undecided), a normal number of dogs, and an abnormal number of birds. Her debut novel, Dark Apprentice, follows Nikolai after he leaves the Academy and features two neurodiverse protagonists.

**Find out more about Val at:**
valneil.com

facebook.com/valneilauthor

twitter.com/ValNeilAuthor

instagram.com/valneilauthor

amazon.com/Val-Neil/e/B08YD8LC31

# SPIN CYCLE BY JAY RENEE LAWRENCE

The first hopeful buzz came during the morning huddle as my manager droned on about something to do with innovation and disembowelment. I peeked at my phone under the table.

*Sorry I haven't responded,* the message read. And with another quick buzz, *I didn't mean to worry you, Oksana. I'm ok.*

Two lines of text after five full days of unanswered messages from my side. It was the longest we'd gone without speaking since we met and it scared me.

Three dots appeared and I waited for his reply. Moments passed, and the dots disappeared and reappeared several times as my friend searched for the right words.

*It's just been hard,* was all he'd managed.

There were so many things I wanted to say. I wanted to tell him that it was totally understandable. That so many in our circle had gone through similar pain. But, I also knew that in moments when the past rears its ugly head, solidarity is a dull sort of comfort.

I started with, *I'm here for you, and so is everyone else.*

This got me no reply and I feared that I'd lost my

chance, so I attempted to reel him in before the connection was lost, like a fish about to jump off the line.

*What are you up to today? I can skip out early and we can go to the Palm Court for a drink. Or, we could see the new historical drama about that superhero. You know, the one starring Dirk von Wunderbar.*

*Thanks, Oxy, but I can't. I've got laundry. Every cape I own is dirty and I have resorted to tying a bedsheet around my neck like a child. :)*

I looked at that colon and curved line and could feel how forced and fake it was. Whoever invented this method of short-handing emotions should have their entrails pulled out through their nose.

The topic of the staff meeting shifted to who would bring what to Dearil the Dreaded's going away party. He was not my favorite colleague as he regularly waved his red jacket at me, shouting "¡Olé!" and made "bull in the china shop" references. As if making bull jokes to a minotaur was original or funny. I offered to take charge of the decorations, imagining a big sign saying "Fuck off, Dearil," and turned my attention back to my phone.

*Hey, no problem,* I wrote back. *Are you coming to Manic's show on Saturday?*

Nothing.

I followed that up with, *I'm proud of him for embracing who he is and giving up villainy and all, but making us sit through amateur stand-up comedy sounds like a form of torture if you ask me. It does give me an excuse to wear my new nose ring though.*

*Can't, I've got a shift that night and it's too late to get it covered.*

*Call in sick*, I replied.

*I'd lose my job.*

*Oh, and that would be tragic. After all, serving Sloppy Jacks in a diner that looks like the set of a 1950s horror film is your calling.*

*Very funny. Do you want to pay my rent next month?*

More than once, I've encouraged Ghoul to find another job. I get that the market sucks right now, but being surrounded by such blatant moralist images can't be easy for someone who's struggled the way Ghoul has. I mean, there's a mural of an acid green amphibious-humanoid carrying away a hysterical blonde woman, to do who-knows-what with. It's offensive, really. I'm surprised the place is still in business.

As much as the two of us have bantered about the subject in the past, though, the message sounded a bit more critical than I'd meant it to. I tried backpedaling and asked, *What's your schedule look like over the next few days then?* And I watched my phone for the text bubble, but it never came.

After lunch, I sent another message. *Hey, I'm worried about you. Have you talked to anyone?*

Nothing.

When four o'clock came with no response, I packed up early, stuffed myself into my Ford Taurus, and drove to Studio City with my horns sticking out of the sun roof. That smiley face he sent haunted me, and I needed to make sure that my friend was okay.

Ghoul has always been reserved. In all the years we'd been friends, he spoke very little of his past or his family. What I did know was that Ghoul was adopted at a young age and grew up in one of those states that like their monsters ugly and their heroes muscly, with dimpled butt cheeks squeezed into Lycra. Not that there's anything wrong with either of those things, in my opinion, but there's no tolerance for stepping outside the nicely drawn boundaries of who should be "good" and who should be "evil." From what I understand, it's one of those places that send what they consider to be confused young villains to camps that "Scare-The-Good-Away." This was particularly problematic, given that Ghoul, a flesh-eating, undead demon, identified as a hero.

On the way to Ghoul's place, I stopped into the trendy bakery that does a "pastry of the month" and donates all sales to a particular charity. That month's charity was some ocean clean-up initiative, which I could get behind, so I grabbed a few cannoli as a peace offering for intruding on his space. Then I hit traffic on the 101 thanks to some machismo villain trying to break into the industry by blowing up the downtown turnpike right before rush hour. Jackass.

For years, Ghoul hid his heroic side from his new family. Unfortunately, his mom found Spectacular Sam comics and a copy of Twilight under a rock in his cave, resulting in his banishment from the house and estrangement from the family. He was seventeen and had been living with those people for ten or so years which, really, is the worst time for something like that to have happened. After trust was built, but before the fear of abandonment faded. After the insecurity of puberty, but before maturity could give him the mental tools needed to maintain perspective and safeguard his spirit.

Ghoul dropped out of school for fear of the persecution he'd surely face once his secret was out and hadn't seen his parents or his hometown since. From what I've gathered, he spent the first few months roaming from place to place, finding work where he could and sleeping in his car—all the while making his way west until he landed in Los Angeles. Things got better for him after he joined our group. The

Fluid Fellows, we called ourselves. Manuel Manic, the evil
dentist turned comedian, was the newest edition. Then
there were the Bark Brothers, twin werewolves who were
working to change the stigma surrounding their condition.
There was also Pauline, the French sorceress who was gifted
with dark magic but was as sweet as pie and great with kids.
And, of course, Ghoul and me. As a bi-moral creature, I was
the only one of us who had evil leanings, but my friends
accepted me for who I am. We were all close and had each
other's backs.

It was at one of our monthly potlucks, just as my killer
lemon chicken was being spooned onto our plates, that
Ghoul received the call. He watched his phone sing and
buzz across the table, each of us falling silent at the look of
shock on his face. When the phone stilled, he told us in a
shaky voice that it was his mother. None of us had heard
from Ghoul since that night.

I passed the laundromat parking lot but didn't see his
car, so I made my way to his apartment complex a few
blocks away. The television was blaring through his apartment door. I knocked loud enough to be heard without
breaking the thing off its hinges and when he answered a
few moments later, I knew I'd made the right decision to
come. Ghoul was wearing nothing more than a pair of
basketball shorts, and his normally gaunt body was looking
even more sickly than usual. His small, white eyes were half
concealed under heavy lids and rimmed in shadow. He
looked like a very sad piranha with his exposed, needle-like
teeth jutting out from his pronounced overbite.

"Oh good, I caught you before you left. You look like
shit." I smiled and shoved my way into his apartment.

"What are you doing here?"

"Decided to skip out early anyway. Satanic Steve's been

driving me nuts with his séancing. I swear, he does it every time he works on an Excel spreadsheet. Hah. As if the dead are going to help him balance the budget for that sinking ship of a company. I don't even think he realizes he does it, but it creeps me out."

As I spoke, I assessed the room. Despite the familiar pale blue walls with bright coral accents, the apartment had a strange, stale smell, as though it were in desperate need of an open window and a break from its inhabitant. It was several degrees colder inside, and the curtains were closed against the afternoon sun. A plate of bare chicken bones lay on the coffee table amidst a general assortment of shit. The only thing I saw that offered any hope was the mesh hamper next to the front door filled with a heap of colored cloth, crumpled in the discarded sort of way unique to dirty clothes. He'd at least had the intention of washing them.

"I figured we could hang out while you do your laundry."

"You want to do laundry with me?" His skepticism told me I wasn't fooling anybody.

"Laundry sucks. What kind of friend would I be if I let you suffer alone?" I shrugged and added, "Besides, I've got nothing going on tonight, and look, I bought cannoli." I brandished the little pink box.

"Are you giving me a choice?" he asked. But I saw a trace of gratitude in his tired smile.

"Nope, come on. I'll drive." With my free hand, I grabbed the mesh hamper and effortlessly slung it over my shoulder.

"Can I at least have five minutes to get ready?"

I parked my haunches on the sofa and put my hooves up amongst the junk on the table while he dressed and concealed what he deemed to be his more monstrous features with some contacts and a set of dentures. The dentures made him sound a little like a child on Halloween with plastic vampire fangs, but it made him feel less self-conscious. Finally, he stuffed his clawed feet into a pair of Ugg boots and said, "Fine, let's go."

"Turn the TV off, you animal. It wastes electricity," I teased. I was relieved to have successfully gotten him out of the house.

The Super Suds' patrons were a mix of normals, off-duty heroes, and a ghost hovering in front of the detergent dispenser. The heroes looked completely unfazed, while the normals eyed us cautiously as we blocked their only exit. It was a reaction we'd gotten used to as monsters, but it would always sting.

"A minotaur and a ghoul walk into a laundromat. It should be the start of a joke, right?" I said to Ghoul with a chuckle, though my booming voice carried throughout the whirring room and eased the tension and people went back to reading their magazines and folding their underwear.

"Tough crowd. Is it always this packed?"

"Well, it's the only place in the neighborhood. Come on, I see a free washer."

Ghoul stuffed what should be two loads, separated by texture, or at least by color into the only available machine. The one everyone else avoided due to the dingy rim of petrified soap caked on so thick that the lid barely closed.

Once the water started to flow, we went to the plastic chairs that sat like ducks in a row on a metal beam.

"Why do they need to screw these things into the floor? Do they really think people want to steal them?" I scoffed. The chair cracked under my weight, which was embarrassing but we both had a laugh. The moment of lightness passed quickly and our laughter was replaced by a silence filled by the sounds. Sounds of water sloshing, air blowing, and a small child whining about boredom and wanting something from the vending machine.

"So, how've you been?" I finally asked. I have always been a rip-off-the-Band-Aid type.

"I don't really know. Fine I guess."

"I take it you never returned your mom's call?"

"What would I say? I mean, they made it pretty clear that I would never be welcomed back."

"Well—" I started.

"I mean, what the hell?" he exclaimed, causing a few nearby normals to flinch. "'We didn't raise you to be an abomination,'" he said in a deeper voice than his own. "The worst part is that they aren't even my real parents. They supposedly chose me. They brought me in and promised to love me. Maybe that's why it was so easy to get rid of me, once I broke their rules." He paused, then added, "They should have just left me in that graveyard."

I didn't know what to say. My friend's shoulders hunched from the weight of painful memories, and I placed my giant hand on him as gently as possible to avoid adding further pressure. My heart ached for him, but I could only imagine how difficult it all must have been. My parents had always been supportive of my bi-morality. They were equally as thrilled when I covered my horns in flowers and smeared nail polish on my hooves, declaring myself the fairy godmother that would make all of Cinderella's dreams come true, as they were when I staged executions for my dolls with my miniature war hammer as Oksana the Conqueror.

The hammer, forged centuries ago, passed from calf to calf much the same way a vintage dollhouse is inherited — as a plaything and an instructive tool.

I hoped warmth was radiating through my palm.

"I know why she called. I looked at her Mugbook..." he trailed off.

"And?"

"My brother died. Went and got hit by a train he was trying to heist. Probably misread the timetable. He wasn't exactly an evil genius."

"Oh shit. I'm sorry to hear that." I wasn't sure if it was the right sentiment, considering the circumstances, but what else was I supposed to say?

"It's fine. I mean, I dunno. We weren't close or anything and he terrorized me growing up." He stared ahead at the wall of dryers spinning clothes and was quiet for a few moments.

"Sorry, I didn't mean to dump all of that on you," he said.

"Dude, no need to apologize."

"It just brought up a lot of feelings. I thought I was past this, you know?" He sighed and buried his face in his claws. "I've done the therapy thing. I mean, I've accepted who I am and I barely think about them anymore. I'm happy."

Just then, as if to punctuate the intensity of Ghoul's statement, there was a banging of flesh on metal. A seemingly normal young woman was attacking the change machine and shouting, "What the hell. Stupid thing ate my money again." The commotion caught the attention of the super and he donned a charming smile as he rose to help the damsel in distress, but Ghoul was faster. He dashed across the tiles, his basketball shorts jingling with lifesaving quarters.

The alarmed young woman gave a shriek and backed against the machine she'd been beating as Ghoul approached her. I tensed, ready to charge, as the super's grin turned to a grimace and he prepared to spring into action.

Thankfully, everyone relaxed as Ghoul pulled out a fistful of quarters and said in a soothing voice, "Here. I have plenty."

The girl stood frozen, looking at the undead creature before her, whose skin was nearly the same color as the coins in his claws. But he flashed his pearly dentures and tucked his chin to his chest like a shy child and the girl softened.

"Thank you," she ventured, holding out her hand so Ghoul could drop them into her small palm. There was no way she would willingly put herself in danger of being snatched.

"No problem," he said as he dropped all the quarters and walked back to the plastic chair next to me.

"That was kind of you," I said with a mocking smile.

"Um, do you have four quarters? I just realized that I gave her all of mine and I need some for the dryer," he whispered to me.

"I got you covered. I've got a ton of change in the cup holder of my car."

"Cool, I owe you one."

"It's a dollar. If you never pay me back, I swear I won't disown you." The words left my mouth before I realized what I was saying. "Oh my god. I am so sorry."

"It's alright, Oxy. I'm not that fragile you know," Ghoul said, picking at the string of his shorts.

"So, you think your mom was calling you just to tell you?" I asked, trying to get the conversation back on track.

"Honestly, I have no idea. Maybe. I doubt she was calling to invite me to the funeral."

"How are you feeling about all this?" I asked, knowing it was an impossible question but one he'd needed to be asked.

"I feel sad. We may have never gotten along and I may hate the lot of them, but Kol didn't deserve to die."

"Kol?" I chuckled. I couldn't help myself.

"Kol the Colossal," Ghoul clarified with a chuckle. "And he was huge, let me tell you. Even as a child he was the size of a full grown man. That's the giant gene for you."

"I didn't know your parents were giants," I said.

"My dad was part giant, but it's a recessive gene so he wasn't nearly as large as my brother. Either way they were all way taller than me."

"Your brother didn't wear a loincloth, did he?"

"Na, but he did carry a club around with him like a giant caveman. He didn't even need it. He could grab my face and his fingers would wrap around my entire head. I'd have to bite the shit out of his hand till he let go."

"Maybe the club was compensating for something," I joked. I could feel that Ghoul was starting to unwind bit by bit the more he talked about his brother.

"My friends and I used to say the same thing. When they'd come over, we'd play a game where we took turns stealing it and hiding it around the house and watching while he blundered around trying to find it. We'd laugh when he smashed furniture or when he broke my mom's wedding china."

"Sounds a little evil of you," I teased.

"Nah, it was all good fun. And you should have seen that china set, it was appalling. All gilded and decorated with brown bats and dead flowers. I was doing the world a great service by ensuring their destruction."

Ghoul told me more stories of his brother. Of how he failed his driver's test so many times that he ended up knocking the instructor out. Or the time they got kicked out of the Olive Garden because Kol had put their endless soup, salad, and breadstick deal to the test, eating ten times what a normal person might in a sitting. I listened and laughed as my friend dug up childhood stories that had been buried beneath the layers of betrayal and hurt he'd experienced. After all, even the worst childhoods have at least a few pleasant memories.

When there were just a few minutes left on the wash cycle, I popped out to my car to grab the change and the forgotten cannoli that were melting in the back seat. Then I met Ghoul at a dryer and popped the coins in. Once the drum started spinning we sat back down and devoured the Italian pastries, licking up the sweet cream like uncivilized beasts and laughing as it dripped all over and clumped up the fur on the back of my fingers.

For a moment we were just two friends in a laundromat. Chowing down on sweets and watching the dryer toss Ghoul's socks and t-shirts and capes. Red falling on black and then covered by grays and whites. The fluidity of it was mesmerizing.

"Thanks for coming," Ghoul said as I crumpled the pink box.

"Hey no problem. You know how much I love mundane activities."

"Oh yes, they match your personality so well," he teased. It felt nice to fall back into our usual light banter.

"Next time, invite me over to clean your baseboards and we'll really have a good time," I volleyed and we chuckled.

"But seriously, sorry about ghosting you this past week."

"It's fine. Like I said, I was just worried about you. Don't do it again or I'll gut you like a fish. You know I still dabble in skinning."

"I will never understand how you can be so fluid with

your morality. One day you're tutoring underprivileged kids after school and the next you're keying people's cars."

"I only key cars that belong to people who park like dipshits. That's hardly a sin."

"Granted. But what about skinning people? That is definitely more on the evil side."

"Eh, they all usually deserve it too. I just never felt like the labels of good and evil fit me very well. I am attracted to both. Sometimes I really want to crush someone's skull with my hammer and sometimes I feel inclined to help push a stalled car to the gas station. Why can't I do both?" I shrugged and tossed my rust-colored mane.

"I wish I felt that way. That would have made it so much easier to fit in back home and they would've never kicked me out. Do you know how many times I wished I were more villainous? I used to look in the mirror and think, 'what's wrong with me?' I am hideous and undead and everyone will always see me as a monster, so why am I not one?"

"Because you're not. Fuck the mirror and fuck what people say you should be. You are who you are and you feel how you feel. You shouldn't have to pretend to be someone else just to be accepted by close-minded people." I blew air out of my nostrils in a huff. "Besides, if you were anything but who you are, you woulda never moved here and we would never have met. And that would be a fucking tragedy." I elbowed him in the ribs and he curled away, rubbing the spot and wincing but also smiling.

"I'd certainly be in less danger of bruising."

This was by no means the first time we'd had this conversation. Variations have played out over the course of our friendship, especially earlier on when he'd just arrived in LA and was getting used to being openly heroic. Conversations like this are needed once in a while to reaffirm and sort through the shitpile that is life. And that is what friends are for, to offer this kind of cyclical support.

"So are you going to call her?"

"I don't know. I've thought about it. Almost did a few times, but I just don't know what I'd say. I am sad about Kol and all. And I do miss them sometimes, but what if we get into another fight? What if she asks if I'm still trying to be a hero?"

"Then you say, 'yeah I am.' And if it turns into a fight, you just hang up the phone. Do you think there's any chance she wants to reconcile?"

"No idea. But so what if she does? She lost one kid and it suddenly makes her miss the one she tossed out? How am I supposed to feel about that?"

"People are complicated," I say. "Look, I am not saying that it isn't a dick move, but maybe this has put some things into perspective for her. You'll never know unless you call her back. But, of course, this is all assuming that you even *want* any relationship with her."

"It sounds exhausting to be honest. I'm afraid that if she does want some kind of relationship, I'd have to constantly justify my lifestyle."

"I get that. Relationships are hard. My grandad's a hardcore evil minotaur and knows I bat for both teams, so holidays are a bit strained since he likes to drop disapproving comments every opportunity he gets. 'Oh, Oxy, I hope it's okay we're having turkey this Thanksgiving. I know how sensitive you can be. But don't worry, I'm sure your mom bought free range.' He can be an old prick."

"Hah, like all heroes are vegetarians. God, I swear people can be so obtuse."

"One time, he thought he was being funny and tied a pink bow to my war hammer as a joke. I left it on there to show that it didn't bother me one bit and the next time he came to visit, I tied it back on and answered the door with the hammer slung over my shoulder."

"What did he say?" Ghoul gasped.

"Not a damn thing. But his tail was swishing back and forth so fast and I knew he was totally pissed. It was great."

"Doesn't it bother you when he does stuff like that?"

"Of course it does, but it bothers me less now that I'm older. He comes from a different time and is set in his beliefs. I have an easier time not taking it personally now. When I was a teenager, though, we'd get into some pretty explosive fights about it."

"At least you had your parents to back you up," Ghoul pointed out. He'd met Mom and Dad many times and was as fond of them as they were of him.

"That's true, it does help to have allies."

"I've never had any allies."

"You have them now, you know."

"I know that. But it's not like you or the gang can be around if the call with my mom goes south."

"Why not? I could be there when you make the call if you want. I'll be there for moral support and if things seem like they're getting heated and you feel like you're being verbally attacked, I'll grab the phone and hang up on her for you."

"Maybe," Ghoul pondered. He was staring again at the wall of dryers, some stood still and empty while others spun. Each on a slightly different rotation. Some stuffed to the max with long running times and others separated out for quick and independent drys. Each one a little window into a life. Ghoul's dryer spun around daytime ware and various pieces of his heroic ensemble; red capes, gloves, and scarves with holes cut out for the eyes. Important symbols of his identity. Another dryer spun around an assortment of ratty-looking rags belonging to an aging man with wispy white hair and green coveralls that told the world that his name was Otto and that he worked for some cleaning service. The rags looked as old and worn out as he did but the heavy scent of bleach that came from the soaked pile when he transferred them from the washer made them seem clean enough. The dryer above Ghoul's appeared to be tossing around tiny, lilac baby clothes, but in fact they were uniforms belonging to that cleft-chinned super who'd nearly sprung into action and pulverized Ghoul. It's hard to believe that such tiny pieces of fabric could stretch to accommodate that girth, but skin-tight is in fashion these days.

"If I did call her..." Ghoul hesitated. "If she does want some kind of relationship, I still don't know what I'd say. I mean, I hardly want to admit to the fact that I'm a server at some gimmicky diner. Or that I'm still single. I don't want her thinking she was right about me."

"What do you mean, 'right about you'?" I asked.

"That I'll never make it as a hero, because I'm not really meant to be one."

"Well, the bull calls bullshit!" I say pointing at my horns. It's the kind of dad joke I hate, but at that point I was willing to say anything to make him laugh. "You know how I feel about Sloppy Jacks, but you work at that gimmicky diner because you have bills to pay. Might I remind you that you came here with nothing. No money, no connections, no plan. And look at you now. You've got nothing to be ashamed of. You're CPR certified, and you're taking classes at the JC. You may not be a full time hero, but you live your life like one. Which is more than I can say for some hot-shot superheroes I know. Those hypocrites don't lift a finger outside of work to help those in need. You, on the other hand, are the kind of person who would give blood if you had any in your body. You're one of the most heroic people I know," I proclaimed.

"Thanks for the pep talk, Oxy. Clothes are done," he sighed, pushing off his knees to get up and hunt for a wheeled basket.

My affirmations seemed to have had no effect. He sulked between the rows of machines, saying "excuse me" when he encountered the ghost who now hovered right in the middle of the aisle. The ghost ignored him and continued to flip through his People Magazine as though Ghoul were the transparent one, so Ghoul backtracked and went to the next aisle. I would've walked right through the guy, but my friend doesn't have a rude bone in his undead body. What I said to him was true. I knew, and so did every one of our friends, that Ghoul was a hero through and through. Someone who put the needs of others before his own and wanted to leave the world in a better state than he'd found it. But the hurt and confusion he felt was the deep kind that couldn't be fixed by cannoli and clean clothes.

He wandered through the laundromat like an unmoored ship — adrift in a sea of memories and existential questions. I felt for him. I may have had an easier time expressing my own morality growing up, but the feelings of guilt and uncertainty were still unpleasantly familiar. Like the taste of foil in the mouth. I wanted to take those feelings from him and destroy them. I imagined myself in Dearil the Dreadful's idiomatic china shop, smashing painful memories like grotesquely painted teacups.

Ghoul found the only free cart — the one with the bum wheel — and emptied his dryer. I met him at the folding table, leaning against it while I thought of what I should say next. My bullish humor was obviously not getting my point across, so I thought about changing tactics. But he cleared the silence before I had the chance.

"You're not going to offer to help me fold my boxer briefs, are you?" He joked.

"Na, that's all you. As you know, my kindness has limits."

He grabbed a fire hydrant-red cape and spread it flat on the table. I never thought red was his color, as it seemed to highlight the bluish-gray tinge of his rotting flesh, but it came into his life before I did and I knew better than to criticize him for it. The cape was more than an ordinary piece of clothing, it was an identifier. I would be bringing up the idea of rebranding at some point, though.

"Hey, what you said before, about me being a genuine hero. It means a lot to me, really. I just don't feel that way sometimes," he said, bringing one corner of the cape to another and creasing the fold. "Like, for example, if I were a better hero, I'd be able to easily forgive my family and call my mom back. But the truth is, I don't know if I want to forgive them. I am still angry and I don't really feel like they deserve it."

"Well, I think that's fair," I added over him.

"But forgiving them is the 'right thing to do,'" he added with air quotes.

"Oh, please. We both know the lines between right and wrong are sometimes pretty gray."

"Hah. Says the bi-moral minotaur."

I stamped my hoof in mock indignation, and we both had a laugh. But Ghoul's face quickly fell back to a frown. He had a demon on his back and he'd decided now was the time to get it off.

"I'm also afraid that if I do forgive her and put myself out there to fix our relationship, it'll just end with more hurt," he said to the table.

"Forgiveness is a tricky thing. How they treated you was wrong and you have every right to still be mad," I started, but paused to think of how to carefully put into words what I wanted to say. While I pondered, he pushed aside his folded cape and reached into the basket.

"Look," I ventured, "I'm no expert on this kind of thing, but I think forgiveness takes time. And sometimes it may never come at all, which is totally fine. But, if you do decide to forgive them, it'll be because you're ready, not because you feel like you have to. And, you know what, you can forgive your family for what they did without inviting them back into your life... You don't have to call her back if you don't want to," I finished.

"I know," he replied. "I'm just not sure what to do. I keep thinking... What if they've changed their mind about me?"

"Do you think that's likely?"

"Not really," he said quickly. Then he stared down at a pair of shorts he'd long finished folding and said in a quiet voice, "But, what if this is my only chance to be part of a family?"

It felt like I'd been punched in the gut. I wanted to grab him and hug him. I wanted to drive to wherever his family lived and tear them apart limb from limb for causing him so much pain.

"You have a family," I managed in a cracked voice.

Slightly embarrassed, he hurriedly grabbed more clothes and spread them out one by one. Grouping together socks, track pants, and various costume pieces. The pile of tumbled clothes was shrinking and the neat stacks were rising. I was running out of time.

"What I mean is," I pressed on. "Family means a lot of

different things, you know? But in the end, what it boils down to is love and support. And you may not have that from whoever brought you into the world, or from the people who adopted you. But you still have it. From me and from the rest of the Fluid Fellows."

"I know that," he said.

"Everyone's been worried about you, man. They all keep messaging me for updates." Ghoul cringed at this.

"I guess I've been a lousy friend lately," he said.

"You haven't," I protested. "You've been going through some heavy stuff, which we can all kinda relate to. We're worried but we also understand that everyone's got a right to deal with their shit however they deal with it."

"Or avoid dealing with it," he added sarcastically.

"Everyone tends to avoid their problems. My point is, you've got people who care. People who accept you and want you to be happy. So you don't need to feel pressured to fix a relationship just because you feel like this is your only chance at having a family. Because that's simply not true."

"You're right, I know that. I know I'm lucky to have you guys."

"Damn right you're lucky. We're awesome."

"I'll call in and take this Saturday off for Manic's show. If my manager's got a problem with it, I'll tell him to shove it."

"That's more like it. Look at you, being bad. I'm sure some comedy will do you good, and so will hanging out with the gang."

"Dammit," he exclaimed.

"What?"

"I hate it when there's one left over." He held up one last unmatched, red glove. The same color as his cape. We laughed together as he stuffed the folded clothes back into the mesh hamper, putting the lone glove on top.

By the time we left, the crowd of washers had thinned and the setting sun turned the smog-filled sky from pink to a blueish purple. Ghoul tossed his clean clothes in the back seat of my car and fell into the passenger seat.

"If you really mean it, I think I'll take you up on your offer and call her back with you around," he said, pulling his phone from his pocket.

"Why don't you take a few more days and we can do it before the show on Saturday? That way you'll have something to take your mind off things afterward."

"That's a good idea. Thanks, Oxy."

"Any time, brother," I replied with a cheeky wink as I turned the key.

## ABOUT JAY RENEE LAWRENCE

Jay Renee Lawrence was raised in California and currently lives in Berlin with her husband and rescue dog. Her upcoming release, *Tinseltown Toils* will be the first in a series of short story collections. Each anthology will feature a different city, era, and cast of villains dealing with real-world problems. Using dark humor and elements of magical realism, she casts a satirical and honest light on difficult social issues. Featuring characters such as Muckins the Sludge Monster, a down-and-out gelatinous schmuck going through a divorce, and Hillary, the first-time (human) mother struggling to bond with her newborn monster, Lawrence's stories are as hard hitting as they are humorous.

**Find out more about Jay at:**
jayreneelawrence.com

facebook.com/jayrenee.lawrence

instagram.com/theresourcefulwriter

# THE EXQUISITE TASTE OF A BOOK-AGED SKULL BY MARK LESLIE

"Alas, Great Uncle Nathan," Herb triumphantly stated, holding the pale orb on an extended arm a few feet from his face. "There is nothing quite like the exquisite taste of a book-aged skull." There wasn't the faintest hint of an echo, as his words were absorbed by the insulating effect of the packed bookshelves.

He moved his focus from the empty eye sockets of the skull he'd been holding to gaze in admiration at the book spines, occasionally broken by the pale ironic grin of a human skull. Twenty-three human skulls of die-hard life-long readers; housed on shelves alongside a prestigious collection of first edition books.

The result of a lifetime of collecting.

It had started off innocently enough, with just a single skull, long before it evolved into a collection.

And that first one was a very special skull, indeed.

When Herb considered the origin of his little obsession, it was startling how book collecting and skull collecting had snowballed from that one into what it had become. That odd weathered and cracked book; and how it had led to his unique experience with this particular skull he was holding in the middle of his secret basement library, in a pose he imagined might be reflective of Hamlet in the graveyard.

This skull was older, drier. And it was relatively light. Maybe two to two and a half pounds.

It hadn't always been light, of course. When he'd first received it, it had to have been at least twice the weight it now was.

"You'd be surprised," his Great Uncle Nathan had whispered to him across the table of an old Irish pub. "How much fat and liquid are in human bone. It can grease out for years." The old man had gone on to describe how skulls, as they aged, continued to dry, and became lighter.

Which was exactly what had happened to the skull he was now holding.

The skull had been a gift. From that same uncle. His Great Uncle Nathan. It was a strange gift, from a strange man. Of course, it wasn't just the gift itself that was weird, but also the way it had been gifted to him.

Uncle Nathan hadn't done anything normal.

Strange seemed to be his modus operandi.

This was the same uncle who had single-handedly turned Herb on to reading and a love of books in the first place. Completely out of the blue. Herb hadn't been interested in reading at all. Except maybe for those *Fightin' Army* comic books he had enjoyed. But he didn't really read those so much as browse through them to look at the drawings of army tanks and jeeps, and planes in action. The other comic books, the funny ones, the superhero ones, none of them had interested him. Nothing about reading had interested him, in fact; not until Uncle Nathan placed that book in his hands.

It was almost as if the book itself had had some sort of spell on him.

The strange old man's gift of that book hadn't merely introduced Herb to the love of reading, it had ushered him into what inevitably became a lifelong obsession. An all-consuming one that dominated Herb's professional and personal life.

Technically, the books were dominant in both his professional and personal life.

And even though the two were connected, the skulls never made it over onto the professional side – at least not as far as anyone else knew.

That fateful day where that first important book exchange occurred was as vibrant and bright to Herb now some fifty years later as it had been on that hot and windy August afternoon when he and his folks had spent a few days at his uncle's cottage.

"Of any of the books in my collection," Uncle Nathan had said, placing the worn and slightly tattered paperback copy of *The Unending Tale* by Michael Stoppe into Herb's eight-year-old hands. "This is the one I think you will truly love, Herbert."

Herb had just stared at the old man, confused and, to be honest, a little frightened. The elderly man had appeared, seemingly out of nowhere. Even at eight years old Herb was baffled by the fact that the old man, who didn't so much walk as shuffle his way about, could come up behind him without the boy hearing a single thing. Not the pull-drag sound of his slipper-covered feet on the hardwood floor of the cottage. Not the creak of those old floorboards that effectively announced, in no uncertain terms, the movement of anyone from anywhere inside the four-room cottage to anyone else inside. You simply couldn't take a single step without the anguished shriek of those weathered and rustic joints of wood protesting.

And yet, while Herb had been standing at the book-shelf – wondering why and how anyone would want to have anything that boring-looking taking up so much space; row after row of spines of books that lined the shelves from floor to ceiling – the man had somehow snuck up on him and placed one of his hands softly upon the boy's shoulder.

"Looking for something to read, Herbert?" Uncle Nathan had said in a voice that sounded like a ceramic mug of gravel and marbles being slowly stirred.

"Y-yes," Herb said, the lie coming out of his mouth before he'd even turned his head to look up at the old man.

"Good," the man said in a hoarse whisper, dragging out the pronunciation of the word as if it contained at least three, perhaps four syllables instead of one.

That's when the eldritch man – his grandmother's brother – slowly lifted his hand up to the top shelf, a spot that was still a couple of feet higher than Herb could reach, adeptly plucked a small hardcover book from the shelf, and placed it into the boy's hands.

"This is the best book ever," the man said in that same gravelly voice with a strength and conviction he had never before heard in another person. "It will introduce to you the power and magic that books can offer – the worlds, the possibilities, the wonders of the universe."

The book was old, weather worn, dry and cracked.

Herb briefly felt the cool and parched skin of his uncle's hand as it brushed against his own tender and now moist palms while handing it over to him. The feel of the book was as brittle and desiccated as the man's hands, almost as if it were an extension of the man's own skin.

At the time, Herb had no idea how accurate that observation truly was.

The memory of that pivotal moment in his life was still strong in Herb's mind. He dwelled on it often. The way the man had managed to sneak up on him while walking on a surface that never didn't creak. The serious tone in his voice, as if he were handling a volatile explosive. Because he later learned that the book had only been produced a couple of years earlier, and yet the copy his Great Uncle had handed to him had seemed ancient – hundreds of years old; like the old man himself.

At the time, though, he had been more fixed on the man's words and the way he described the book with such passion and conviction.

Herb looked up from the book and up at the old man's wrinkled and leathery face.

"This book," his uncle went on, and his eyes pinned Herb to the spot – he didn't think he could move one inch even if a handful of spiders were tossed onto the back of his neck and started crawling in all directions. "Could be the only book you ever need to read. Because it contains, within it, every single other book, every single other story ever told, ever to be told, or ever to even be imagined."

He raised one gnarled hand up to the side of his own face and tapped the side of his head near the temple.

"The only other vessel that can hold even more stories, even more magic, even more wonder, even more endless possibilities is this one. All that we know about the universe, all of the sciences, the philosophies, the literature, the music, the art that graces our world, was first imagined within this sphere of bone.

"Books have been, and will likely remain, the most efficient way to capture and relay all of those things from generation to generation. But never forget, Herbert, that they were made possible because of the infinite universes that exist inside of our skulls."

Herb looked down at the book, then back up at his uncle.

"Never forget that," the old man said, again tapping on the side of his head.

That same head which had been delivered to him by courier, without the hair, flesh, muscles, or eyes, fifteen years later. It had come in a beautiful and stylish hat box, with a brief hand-written note from his uncle.

The same skull Herb held in his hands now, as he reflected on that day.

The way the man had spoken about that book, as if it were some sort of religious artefact, compelled Herb to want to immediately crack the cover and begin to read it; to see what secrets and treasures it held. He hadn't even baulked at the fact that there were very few illustrations in it.

And he'd read the book in almost a single sitting. Technically, it had been three sittings, but to Herb it felt like a single sitting with two frustrating interruptions: one of them agonizingly long.

He'd shuffled over to the armchair in the corner of the main cottage area and started reading the book. He stopped only when his mother called him for dinner. And, immediately after excusing himself from the table he returned to that chair, and the book, and didn't stop again until the adults were turning out the lights and ushering him off to bed. Because the cottage was so small, and there weren't doors to the room, he hadn't been able to sneak off to get the flashlight to read the book, and so, instead, he willed himself to sleep so he wouldn't have to lie in agony thinking about the book that he just wanted to keep reading. And when the first hint of morning sunlight came, enough that he could make out the words on the page, he popped out of bed, grabbed the book, and sat with it again until he had finished it.

"It was amazing, Uncle Nathan," Herb had said, standing at the old man's side while the elderly gentleman sat on the stool at his desk in the taxidermy workshop attached to the front entrance of the cottage.

"I knew you would like it," the man had said without stopping the puttering he was doing.

"What should I read next?"

"All of it."

"All of it?"

"Yes." The old man continued to talk without once turning his head to regard his nephew. "Now that you've had a taste of what a book can truly be, or the magic and all the possibilities that a single book can possess, you have unlocked the potential to see the greatness of any book, no matter who has written it, no matter what it is about."

"Any book?"

"Any book. All the books. Fill your head with as many books as you can in your lifetime. Absorb them all, regardless of the content. And the secrets of the universe will be yours."

And that was how it began.

Herb's love of reading was something he carried all through school and his career. His parents were astonished to see his grades dramatically improve when he had returned to school less than a month after Uncle Nathan had implanted this love of reading and books into the child. And his grades kept getting better the more he worked at increasing his reading. He ended up progressing so quickly that he skipped a grade.

"You are expanding your mind." The static of the phone line lent Uncle Nathan's gravely and hoarse old man voice an additional eeriness to it. Herb stood in the kitchen, the phone held to his ear in one hand, his other hand clutching the curly cord, all while leaning forward as if that would help him hear his uncle's words more clearly.

"With every single book you are increasing your brain's capacity, not just for knowledge and imagination, but for empathy, for compassion. Books make you a better, more well-rounded person, Herbert. Go forth and read. Fill that skull of yours." Herb could see the man tapping at the side of his head as he continued. "Fill this glorious vessel with as many of the books as you can, young man."

And Herb had done so.

But he not only read more books, he kept reporting to his uncle how he was progressing.

Though he only saw the old man on average about three times a year; during Christmas, at Easter, and during the summer break, whenever Herb and his parents visited Uncle Nathan's cottage, they spoke on the phone and wrote one another regularly.

Most of the talk between the two was about the greatness of books. And the greatness of the human mind, the imagination, the untapped potential that only books properly unlocked.

Herb read every book he could get his hands on. He dedicated his life to books. He started working at an independently owned bookstore when he was still in high school, and continued to work there all through college where he studied, aptly enough, English Literature. He had already read most of the works they were studying in the class, so he used that time to devour other books from the same authors, or the same time periods. By the time he had graduated college, he was the assistant manager of the store, and the day Uncle Nathan had taken the long train ride into the city where Herb worked to visit him at the bookstore had been one of the proudest moments of Herb's life.

But it had also been a bit unnerving, too. Uncle Nathan had looked far more decrepit, weathered and ancient than Herb's earliest recollection of the man. When Uncle Nathan had shuffled in through the front door of the bookstore, Herb had two rapid-fire thoughts on his short walk to greet him. One, that he looked almost like a zombie, except for the life still evident in the man's eyes as he gazed around the shop, not yet having spotted Herb. Two, that perhaps the man already had died a few hours, a few days, or even a few weeks ago, but the message about that termination hadn't quite made it all the way to the man's brain.

"Uncle Nathan!" Herb said as he approached the man.

"Herbert, my boy. So good to see you." The voice sounded like it was pushing up through the loose gravel recently tossed onto a fresh grave. "Look at this marvelous place you work. So much hope, so much wonder, so much marvel in a shop like this."

"I couldn't agree more."

"It was Cicero who said that a room without books is like a body without a soul."

Herb nodded.

"What then," the old man asked, "is a head without books?"

Herb didn't get a chance to answer. He had been called, via the store's intercom, to the cash desk to key in a manager code override. He excused himself to go attend to the need, but when he returned less than three minutes later he could have sworn that his uncle, who had moved deeper into the store and was carousing the shelves, was standing straighter and at least a quarter of a foot taller. He was moving a bit more quickly now too. And there was a much richer brightness in his eyes as well as a warm hue to his face that hadn't been present when he'd first walked in. He looked more alive, more vibrant. Herb wondered if it might have been a trick of the light, but then the man said something under his breath that drove the realization of the transformation home.

"So many books I haven't yet consumed." And he paused, tilting his head up like a dog sniffing the air. "Oh yes, I can sense them calling to me."

Being in the presence of new books to read was like a sort of nourishment to the man's very essence.

Later that same day, his eyes still bright and frisky, Uncle Nathan explained a theory he had been working on over dinner at Anderson's Pub.

"It's like this bourbon barrel-aged stout," he'd said, holding the glass filled with dark, thick liquid in front of his face. "This uniquely rich and delicious drink is created because of the transmission of flavor between the liquid and the vessel that holds it. At first, the bourbon itself soaks flavor in from the various chemical compounds present in the wood. These are the lactones, which provide floral elements, the phenolic aldehydes, which create vanilla, and the simple sugars, which make a caramel taste. But then, those same barrels, which helped to remove the harshness of the alcohol while adding unique flavor to the ageing bourbon, are used by beer breweries. And when they age a beer in the barrel, the flavor that was produced within the barrel is absorbed and part of the barrel themselves. And that essence is what infuses itself into the beer, creating this unique flavor."

He tilted the glass to his lips and took a long slow drink.

"Ahh, delicious. Now, you see, the human skull is like the wood of these oak barrels. Bones absorb liquids. And, as you well know, books are flowing with knowledge, inspiration, imagination, wonder. The ideas the books hold are quite fluid. They have flowed from the writer to the page, and from the page to your mind. And from your mind, those same elements are absorbed by the bone that contains the brain.

"Our heads are like those aged bourbon barrels.

"So imagine if we could be similarly infused with knowledge the way that beer can be infused with the flavors from the bourbon they once stored."

The theory had come back to Herb in a flash not two years later as he had stood holding Uncle Nathan's skull after pulling it out of the hat box it had been shipped in, and reading the hand-written note that had been enclosed with it.

*Take this skull and drink from it. This is my lifetime of reading and knowledge, which has been given unto you.*

That's all the note said.

No other explanation.

But Herb had known.

Later that night, he had taken the skull out, retrieved that weathered old copy of *The Unending Tale* and sat with those two items and a bottle of bourbon. He poured a little bit of the whisky into the skull, held upside down, like a bowl, and let it sit there for several minutes before sipping it.

He hadn't felt anything other than the bite of the liquor.

But when he woke the next morning, he felt more vibrant, more alive, and with a head filled with stories, ideas, and thoughts he couldn't recall having had before. Almost as if he had absorbed or imbibed something from the very marrow of his dead uncle's skull.

It had been like that life-altering experience of first discovering that classic young adult novel by Michael Stoppe.

So he continued the ritual. Nightly. He alternated between trying different whiskies, various stouts; as well as letting the liquor sit in the skull more than just a few minutes. The experience was on par with his introduction to the wonders of books and reading.

And he continued to do both. He would sip from the skull every night while enjoying reading some new book he had never experienced before.

The illumination was exponential.

After a few months, however, the effect lessened. He tried using stronger forms of alcohol, letting the drink sit in the skull for several days; but over time, the resulting high was muted.

His uncle's brain was drying out; in all senses of that word. Herb had already absorbed all of what he could from it.

But he knew what he had to do.

Find another skull, from a die-hard reader who was invested in and passionate about books. A book lover who couldn't get enough. Someone like his Uncle Nathan whose very skull would be, like those bourbon barrels, ripe with the knowledge and experience and wonder of the books the brain it had housed had consumed. A skull that had absorbed the very essence of that knowledge and reading.

It took him four months to navigate his way to finding an appropriate skull to fulfil his needs. It hadn't been easy, but he'd been managing a small antiquarian offshoot of his regular bookshop for well over a year by that point and had been accustomed to hardcore and in-depth research in scouring hard to find material for his high-end book collecting clients.

Sourcing black market skulls of deceased scholars wasn't all that much different; except for the legalities, and costs, of course.

The effect of the first skull he had managed to get his hands on wasn't nearly as effective as his uncle's skull had been.

Neither had the second one he had acquired.

Both of the skulls had been from exceptionally well-read scholars and academics. Older folks who had dedicated their lives to reading and books and knowledge. But their skulls hadn't been fresh enough. They had been too dried out. There wasn't much flavor of knowledge left in them for Herb to absorb. It had been like trying to read the faded words on an old text that had been bleached by too much exposure to sunlight.

There wasn't much of a choice if he wanted to reach the same high, transcend to the same places he had with Uncle Nathan's skull. Because his skull had been just a few weeks old by the time it had arrived at Herb's.

Herb had chosen an elderly person, a retired librarian, someone not only already close to the end of their life, but who had been diagnosed with cancer and given a slim chance of surviving.

He saw it as a perfect opportunity. A mercy killing to help prevent the man from suffering, combined with a fresh sharing of the knowledge-infused skull.

Drinking from this skull, just days fresh from the kill, was like some next-level drug. Despite this particular librarian's reading being nowhere near the same as Uncle

Nathan's, the freshness of the juices that flowed from his skull more than made up for it.

Like any addiction – although, to be honest, this was not like any other addiction; it was an awakening of the spirit, of the soul, of the mind like nothing Herb had guessed anyone could properly understand – he couldn't stop himself if he tried. He just needed more; constantly.

He was careful, though, and bided his time between fresh acquisitions. He fancied himself like a master brewer. Being patient – or at least as patient as he could be, considering the depths and lows when he wasn't able to absorb from a reader's skull – and trying to bide his time between kills. He was also careful to space out the fresh kills with skulls acquired through legal and illegal channels. It was like spacing out drinking two different finely and perfectly aged craft beers with a Coors or Miller Lite. Having the latter two satisfied the basic impulse to consume a beer, but the levity was mild and short-lived compared to a beer created with compassion and craftsmanship.

As the years and decades passed, his collection grew. His secret library of first editions and reader skulls would have been the envy of anyone with the wherewithal to properly understand the depths and breadths of such an accomplished collection.

He stood with his Uncle Nathan's skull in his hand while regarding the shelves before him. "And this also," he said, quoting the first line of dialogue from an old Conrad novel, "has been one of the dark places of the earth."

Gently placing his uncle's skull back onto the shelf beside that copy of *The Unending Tale*, he realized that was the issue.

Nobody would properly understand. At least not until

he was able to infuse the same wonder, wisdom, and awakeness to his own protégé, the way his uncle had in him.

As he lifted his hand off of his uncle's skull and looked at it, he realized that his own leathered, dried and cracked old man's hands were the same as Uncle Nathan's had been that fateful August afternoon.

It was time.

The next morning, in the bookstore Herb owned – the one he had named *Best Book Ever* in honor of that first book his Uncle Nathan had handed to him – Herb regarded the young book clerk he had hired six months earlier. She was standing at the wall across from the cash desk in front of the small antiquarian section of shelves in the store, seemingly in awe of the historic texts before her. Julie, a recent college English Literature graduate, had been the most passionate young book lover Herb had ever hired. Her thirst for new books to read, her delight in discussing great books with customers had reminded Herb of his own magical journey.

Yes, she would be perfect.

Herb slowly approached her, realizing that, despite the arthritis in his knees, and the overall aching of his lower back and joints, he was able to move quickly and quietly, almost in a predatory fashion.

"This," he said as he arrived at her back, and watched as she started, not having heard him sneak up behind her. "Is the best book ever."

As she turned to look at him, he continued, holding out a copy of *The Unending Tale* by Michael Stoppe. "I know that you already appreciate and understand the special calling of being a life-long book lover. I can smell it in your bones. But this book will re-introduce to you, in a whole new way, the power and magic that books can offer – the worlds, the possibilities, the wonders of the universe. Of any of the books in this store, this is the one I think you will truly love, Julie."

Julie smiled at him as she accepted the old weathered book into her hands.

Herb detected an almost perceptible deeper acceptance also taking place.

He felt the tingling of satisfaction that he had found the one who would not only be able to eventually absorb his entire lifetime of reading, but take it to exceptional new levels.

"C'mon," he said. "Let's close up early and go grab a drink at the pub down the street. They have a new barrel-aged bourbon stout on tap."

"Oh, I love barrel-aged."

That special and dark gleam in her eyes suggested that she would be – like him, obsessed to the marrow.

# ABOUT MARK LESLIE

Like the main character in this story, Mark Leslie collects books and skulls. Although the skulls in his own personal library are ceramic, plastic, clay, metal, and fabric – or so he likes to let the world believe. A life-long book nerd, Mark has long been drawn to the macabre in his writing. He is the author of more than two dozen books that include horror, speculative fiction, thrillers, and true ghost story explorations.

**Find out more about Mark at:**
www.markleslie.ca

twitter.com/markleslie
instagram.com/markleslielefebvre
youtube.com/markleslielefebvre

# THE FOLLOWER BY J. EMBER HINTZ

A decade passed since Clay Dennen last set foot in Wynnville, or rather the shithole bar that didn't check IDs when he and his fraternity brothers slummed it on Thursday nights. The place still reeked of urine and stale beer. Why the estate attorney insisted on meeting there instead of the property in question was unclear.

The man adjusted his glasses along the steep slope of his nose and slid a final document across the sticky table for Clay to sign. He glanced over the statement from the Department of Historic Resources.

"I was told the property wasn't on the historic register," Clay said, "that I can do whatever I want to the place? If I can't complete the renovations and start turning a profit before the end of the year, I'm screwed." Clay leaned back against the vinyl bench and ran a hand through his thinning hair. "I quit my job and sank my entire life savings into this. I can't afford any setbacks or surprises."

"The site marker on your new property doesn't convey protected status. This document is merely an acknowledgment that the sign belongs to the Commonwealth of Virginia and unauthorized removal is a Class 6 felony."

Clay let out an impatient sigh as he read the form, which included a photo of the site marker plaque.

*Marker 2749. Trial of Cora Pugh.*

*The trial of Cora Pugh is one of the few well-documented charges of witchcraft in Virginia. The sixteen-year-old girl was accused of bewitching a pox fever on the farming settlement. Allegations grew as more settlers fell ill and died, including her own family. In the absence of evidence, other than her immunity to the plague, the judge decided she would be tested by dunking. Early colonists believed water was a pure element and would not abide a witch to sink beneath its depths. On December 18, 1726, the girl's hands were bound to her feet, and she was thrown into the icy Wynne River. Pugh sank to the bottom, a sign of innocence, and nearly drowned before being pulled out and set free. Seven years later, when the pox fever returned, accusations against the young woman resurfaced, and the grieving townsfolk could not be persuaded to wait for another trial. On February 13, 1733, Cora Pugh was dragged from her bed and hanged from a beech tree outside her home.*

Clay's eyes narrowed on the attorney who was clutching his briefcase, as if ready to bolt as soon as he procured the signed paper.

"So, I *don't* need approval from the historical society to renovate the building?" Clay asked.

"They have no interest in the property, Mr. Dennen. You are free to make whatever changes you see fit or raze it to the ground if you like. No one will protest."

The corner of Clay's mouth curved into a smile as he signed the paper and exchanged it for a ring of keys.

A full moon painted shadows on the pavement by the time Clay finished with the lawyer and headed across town to inspect his hasty investment. The abandoned church, built in the gothic revival style, stood atop Pugh's Hill overlooking Wynnville's ruddy brick buildings and downtown waterfront. A broken beacon of stucco and stained glass surrounded by brambles and knee-high weeds. Square and octagonal towers stretched toward the sky at the north and south corners, respectively.

Clay's friends told him he was an impulsive fool when he purchased the dilapidated building at auction, sight unseen. He outbid the only other interested party—a green energy start-up interested in turning the property into a solar farm. Now that the citizens of Wynnville had voted to bring a casino to town, the church was Clay's chance to escape his dead-end job serving prune juice in highball glasses to retired resort residents. A chance to make some money of his own and finally put his degree in hospitality to good use after wasting five years as a concierge at a high-end assisted living facility.

It took everything he had to buy the property, including the funds from the sale of his condo and the money in his investment portfolio. A portfolio he built by taking out life insurance policies on a select few of his decrepit clients, eliciting their signatures under false pretenses and listing himself as the beneficiary. He had just enough to purchase the church and finance its resurrection into a kitsch Airbnb for the masses of urbanites who would flock to the soon-to-be southern gambling mecca.

Clay parked behind the church next to a small cemetery. During his college days in Wynnville, he'd heard tales of unusual phenomena surrounding the church. Stories told by drunk pledges sent into the graveyard at midnight to piss on headstones. Some claimed to see a dark figure lurking around the old beech tree. Others woke the next afternoon with mysterious cuts on their bodies.

The Follower. That's what the townies called it. A ghost that followed intruders home and took revenge on those who dared desecrate its resting place. Nothing more than an urban legend if you asked Clay. The cuts came from the overgrown hedge that surrounded the graveyard. Thorns as long and sharp as cat claws. He'd earned his own scrapes tumbling through those same bushes, but he'd only had the nerve to piss on the tree inside the cemetery. When he came across the auction listing, it brought back fond memories of his fraternity days and the one time in his life when he'd felt grounded—part of something greater than himself.

Clay Dennen didn't believe in ghosts, gods, or any other such nonsense. He believed what he could see with his own two eyes, and what he saw beneath the church's peeling paint, was opportunity.

The stench of rot and mildew choked the air from his lungs as he shoved open the rectory door and peered into a spacious office. A hefty ring of keys dangled from one hand as he turned on his cell phone flashlight with the other and walked from room to room. Local superstitions be damned. The property had terrific bones.

An addition at the back housed a dozen classrooms destined to be guest suites. The kitchen and meeting hall would be renovated into a communal space. The sanctuary, with its vaulted beams, arched doorways, and vibrant stained glass, would take on new life as a rentable event venue—just as soon as he cleared away decades of grime and bat shit.

Breath lodged in his throat as a pair of glowing green eyes stared at him from the pulpit. The raccoon blinked, taking him in—an unexpected intruder come to disturb its inner sanctum.

"Skat!" Clay shook his keys at the animal, and it skittered into the darkness. He made a mental note to call an exterminator first thing in the morning to deal with the raccoon and whatever the hell else was living there, rent-free. At least it explained the scent of death that clung to the place like a stubborn grease stain.

Clay jiggled the keys every few steps, announcing his presence to any other vermin that might lurk in the shadows. A buzzing sound drew his attention to the narthex at the front of the church. Light from his phone revealed a spiral staircase curving up to the second floor and north tower. His palm slid along a wooden railing worn smooth by a hundred and fifty years of righteous hands.

Something gummy stuck to his fingers. "Fucking guano," he said, grumbling to himself as he wiped the bat shit off on a denim-clad thigh. He continued to climb the creaking steps and passed through a pocket of cool air that electrified the hair on his arms. The buzzing sound grew louder as he reached the second floor. With neck craned, he pointed his light into the hollow spire that soared above the north tower.

Something darted past his head, setting his heart to race. He swatted at it as he stumbled back toward the steps. There was movement inside the spire. A pendulous black shape took form, blotting out the pale paper wasp nests hanging from the ironwork.

"Shit." Clay darted down a narrow hall. The surrounding air vibrated with an angry hum as he threw himself through an arched door, slamming it shut behind him. He spun around, spraying light into every corner with his phone, lungs straining against his ribs.

The room was empty, aside from a cluster of candles and melted wax sitting in the center of a sloppy pentagram chalked on the wooden planks beneath his feet. Five photos cut from a yearbook sat at the apex of each star point. Clay read the words scrawled on the floor aloud. *"I beseech thee, goddess of night, and offer these names for you to smite when you rise to avenge your plight."* Clay rolled his eyes as he slumped against the window and pressed his forehead to the glass to catch his breath. He glanced down at the parking lot that bordered the weedy graveyard.

Someone was there. A woman with hands cupped around her face as she peered into his SUV. He'd left his wallet in the center console. Had he locked the doors? He couldn't remember. His fingers sought the key fob in his pocket and pressed the automatic lock button. The head-lights flashed a reassuring response.

The woman—homeless by the look of her filthy bare feet and stringy hair that clung to her face and neck—twisted toward him, head cocked at an odd angle. She stared up at him the same way the raccoon had.

Clay rapped on the window. "Get away from there. This is private property."

She hissed at him with all the grace of an alley cat before retreating into the shadow of the giant beech tree.

"Raccoons, bats, wasps, and now thieving homeless squatters. How many more pests do I need to evict?"

He waited an hour after the buzzing quieted before he dared open the door and sneak down the hall. The old building creaked and moaned with each step, protesting his weight. He exited the way he came in, locking the rectory office door behind him.

The scent of rot clung to his skin and clothing, following him to the hotel. Even after a shower, the faint stench lingered in his nose.

))　（（

Curious glances tracked Clay as he entered the R & D Diner, an old passenger rail car turned breakfast grill the hotel clerk had recommended. He took a seat at the bar.

A rotund man filled the space between the counter and sizzling grill behind him. He rubbed a towel over his sweaty bald head as he took Clay's order.

"Black coffee and corned beef hash and eggs, please."

Whispers filled the air, but Clay ignored them and busied himself on his phone, searching for an exterminator. There were six listed in Wynnville—only one with a name he recognized. A national chain. He pulled a notepad from his back pocket and scrawled down the name and number.

The sweaty cook plopped a plate of eggs and a mug of black sludge in front of him. "You that fella done bought the old church up on Pugh's Hill? You a preacher or something?"

Clay smirked at the irony. "I'm in hospitality," he said. "The plan is to resurrect the old beast to her former glory and open an Airbnb."

The cook's deadpan expression told Clay the man didn't follow what he was saying.

"Like a mini hotel or bed-and-breakfast."

"I know what an Airbnb is, boy." The cook's gaze slid to the angry scratch on the back of Clay's hand.

Clay pushed the superstitious tales told by townies and drunk frat boys from his mind. "I fell trying to outrun a swarm of wasps." He held up his injured hand. "Damn place is full of territorial pests."

The man raised an eyebrow as he peered at the notepad next to Clay's plate. "You'll be wantin' a different kind of exterminator. Ain't no poison or mechanical trap gonna rid that place of its damned infestation."

The diner quieted. Every face focused on Clay Dennen.

Spider feet crawled down his spine again. "What kind of exterminator do you recommend?"

"The kind you ain't gonna find in them white pages." The man blotted sweat from his gleaming dome of a skull and returned his attention to the grill.

A hand clasped Clay's shoulder, sending a sharp prickling sensation down his arm. He swiveled around to a set of cloudy blue eyes and the wrinkled face of an elderly woman. Her girth balanced on the thin wooden cane in her left hand. "Carry yourself on down to Horsefeathers bar. Ask for Molly Crone. She'll be the one you're looking for. Be sure to tell her Odemaris sent you." The old woman gave him a curt nod before floating out of the diner, the skirt of her house dress swaying above thick ankles and fuzzy pink slippers.

Clay had no intention of doing any such thing. He needed a professional. A licensed and bonded contractor. Not some bartender who moonlighted in pest control. He sipped his coffee, bitter with a gritty, metallic aftertaste that brought to mind the muddy river water that ran behind the diner. Stomach now sour, he pushed his eggs away, called the exterminator, and set up an appointment for the next day.

) ◯ (

Half a dozen wheelbarrows and shovels sat on the front lawn along with a rusted dumpster. The demolition crew he'd hired, however, was nowhere in sight.

He called the contractor.

"Look, the southwest crew won't do it." The man's graveled voice scraped along Clay's nerves like a rusted rake. "They refuse to set foot on the site. I might be able to pull a few guys off a demo job in Richmond and send them down on Monday, but it's gonna cost you. We got travel expenses to cover."

He clenched the phone in his fist. "I'm not paying extra because you can't staff the damn job."

"You want a new crew down there on Monday or not?" the contractor said, his voice clipped.

Clay resisted the urge to chuck his phone across the parking lot. He was on a tight budget and even tighter schedule. The renovation had to be complete before the casino opened at the end of the year. "Fine. Just get them down here. No more excuses or delays, or I'll find another contractor."

After he hung up, Clay rolled the sleeves of his dress shirt up to the elbow before grabbing a shovel and wheelbarrow and heading inside. Clay Dennen wasn't afraid of anything, least of all getting his hands dirty.

The worst of the mess was in the sanctuary, which smelled more atrocious in the heat of day. Clay pried open a few windows in the rectory, but the once vibrant worship hall was a stifling box of decayed animal carcasses and fecal matter. He donned goggles and a dust mask that did little to filter the rotting stench and set to work shoveling shit into piles.

As morning melted into afternoon, sweat soaked through his dress shirt and jeans. He'd cleared most of the room and started pulling up the green carpet covering the center aisle. His nerves hummed with excitement as he peeled back the frayed edges. Blue mosaic tile ran from a mural depicting the Wynn River behind the empty baptismal pool and flowed through the middle of the sanctuary.

"Not very subtle, is it?" A craggy voice startled him from behind.

He whipped around to find a middle-aged woman with salt and pepper hair piled on top of her head like a wind-blown nest. She held a lit cigarette between boney fingers. Black leggings and an oversized blazer shoved over sharp elbows emphasized her overall skeletal appearance.

"The zealots that built this place had a real hard-on for the cleansing waters of salvation. Just pissed her off, if you ask me. You'd do well to cover it back up."

Clay pulled off his mask and goggles before running a hand through his damp hair. "I'm sorry, ma'am, but you can't smoke in here."

She took a final drag from the cigarette before dropping it on the dust-covered tile and crushing it beneath the pointed toe of her leopard print pump. "Name's Mol Crone. Word is you're in the market for someone with a particular set of skills."

"Unless you brought me five men looking for a few weeks of honest work, I'm not interested in whatever it is you're peddling. So, if you'll excuse me, I have a lot more to get done before sundown."

She propped a narrow hip against the end of a pew. "So, you know about Cora and the curse, then?"

"My lawyer informed me of the property's historical significance." Clay crossed his arms. The stink of his armpits mingled with the lingering cigarette smoke and odor of rot that seemed to be seeping from the walls.

"Did he inform you that the first rector, William H. Higgins, died under mysterious circumstances six months after the church opened its doors in 1871? They found his body arched over a pew. Back broken. Lungs full of river water." She reached into the floppy leather bag hanging from her shoulder as she glanced up at the balcony. "Some folks say he jumped. Others say it was murder. Case was never solved. He was the great-grandson of Arthur H. Higgins, the man who led the mob that pulled Cora Pugh from her bed the night she died."

"If you're trying to scare me off with tales of witches, ghosts, and curses, you can stop right there because I'm not a believer. There's nothing in this world that can deter me from turning this place into a successful business."

"I'm not trying to scare you, Mr. Dennen. Just a friendly warning." Mol stood; her figure too thin to cast a shadow on the watery tile despite the angle of late afternoon light falling through the window behind her. "If anything *unusual* happens and you need to talk, you can find me here." She handed him a black business card and swept toward the open doors at the narthex, the soft click of her heels echoing through the sanctuary like laughter.

Clay glanced at the card. A gold foil Pegasus, wings spread wide, shimmered on the front. A single word on the back. Horsefeathers. No number. No address. He rolled his eyes and stuffed it into his back pocket before hauling another load of carpet to the dumpster.

) ● (

The following day, Clay woke with abrasions on his hands and arms. He lamented not wearing gloves the day before. Carpet demo was rough on the knuckles and exposed skin. The power and water were scheduled to come on, so he skipped the diner and headed straight to the hardware store for a pack of light bulbs. He could squeeze in a few extra hours of work now that the church had light.

Much to his satisfaction, the exterminators showed up on time. They set live traps for the raccoons, kill traps for the rats, and got to work fogging the north tower and removing the dead wasps in their nests. Since it was illegal to exterminate bats, the technician recommended a sonic device to drive them out and a temporary net over the eaves allowing them to escape but not return.

While the exterminators worked, Clay took an inventory of the furniture and equipment separating what he wanted to keep from the trash. By midday, sweat stained his t-shirt and rolled down his ass crack beneath a loose-fitting set of boxers and coveralls. He escaped the thick air to eat his lunch under the shade of the gray beech tree. Guilt gnawed at his gut as he studied the cracked and kicked-over headstones. He could have them re-cast, rip out the overgrown hedge, and replace it with a tall iron fence. Clay was a business owner now. He couldn't have fraternity boys sneaking around his property and disturbing his guests.

He leaned against the gnarled tree trunk. The sore muscles in his back and shoulders relaxed as he gave in to the weight of his eyelids. Lost somewhere between detached awareness and a dream, the cemetery and church disappeared. He was still lying beneath the tree, but he was no longer alone.

"Clayton Dennen." Her garbled voice broke over his name, like water slipping over rocks in a stream. She cocked her head to the side in a curious posture. Soft brown eyes studied him from behind feathered lashes. Her pale skin mimicked by the odd linen dress she wore. The oversized garment hung from her body like a choir robe, hiding her feet behind the hem. Sun glinted off the golden waves that fell over her shoulders and down her back.

He shuffled to his feet. "Do I know you?" Clay tried to place her face. In her early to mid-twenties, if he had to guess. An old college conquest? There were too many parties and bourbon-blurred nights to remember everyone he'd fucked. Still, there was something familiar in the way her head lolled above her neck. Something that sat like a lead brick in his stomach.

The young woman's gaze floated over the crumbling headstones and weedy grass. "This used to be a beautiful garden," she said with a wistful sigh. "The hollyhocks and foxglove withered after mother passed, but I managed to keep beans, corn and peppers well enough. How I miss plunging my hands into the soil. Now I plant *other* things to sustain me."

Clay squared his shoulders and shook off the apprehension creeping along his spine. "This is private property now and you should leave."

The corner of her mouth twitched, as if torn between an irritated scowl and an amused smile. Her lips settled into a thin line. "You are not like the others," she said. "No false piety to cover the darkness."

He backed against the tree as she stalked toward him. "What others?"

The woman moved too fast for him to react. She appeared in front of him. Their faces inches apart. Clammy fingers grasped his chin in a tight grip. He tried to pull away, to shove her off, but every muscle in his body froze. Her putrid breath stole the air from his lungs as her tongue darted out and drug across his cheek, marking him with her scent. The stench of rot engulfed him as she spoke. "I hope you enjoy resting in my shade."

Clay woke gasping for air. The limb above his head swayed and groaned as if supporting a heavy weight. He left his half-eaten sub and soft drink behind as he bolted from the cemetery and made a note to have the branch cut down before it fell on someone.

The exterminators finished late in the afternoon. Clay pushed the dream from his mind and cursed Mol Crone for planting all that crap about witches and murder inside his head. He tried to focus on cleaning out the pastor's study instead. It was the least ravaged room in the building, and he was in desperate need of an office to oversee the renovation. The plaster ceiling needed patching, but the teak paneled walls were in near-perfect condition. Rusty filing cabinets went into the dumpster, along with a yellowed computer monitor and a dot matrix printer. The mid-century desk and swivel chair were keepers.

After a thorough once-over with a shop vac and mop, the room was livable. He opened the storage closet and found half a dozen boxes of old records; tax filings, printed sermons, and leather-bound congregation registers. His hands went for the one labeled CEMETERY.

Dust particles danced in a beam of light as he crossed the room and dropped the box on his new desk with a thud. Inside, he found nineteen dossiers containing photos and newspaper clippings—a file for all but one of the cemetery's inhabitants. Most included notes written in the same jagged script, scratched down by someone with an unsteady hand.

Clay read an article on the mysterious death of William H. Higgins, and it was as Mol Crone had described. Gruesome. Unsolved.

He thumbed through the rest of the folders and found similar cases. Each person tied to the church—all dying under unusual circumstances. A painter working on the bell tower struck by lightning on a clear day in 1915. The deacon who set himself on fire while burning leaves in his front yard in 1964. A Bible school teacher who died in her sleep in 1943. An apparent heart attack, according to the coroner, who couldn't account for the welts on her arms and legs that appeared to have been inflicted by the green switch clutched in her fist.

An idea percolated in Clay's mind. Ghost tours were a popular tourist racket, and the box of macabre history was a marketing gold mine. He'd need a few actors, of course, theater students from his alma mater who would work for tips and resume-building experience.

As he picked through the folders, his fingers paused on a name. Odemaris Crone.

A photo slid from the back and fluttered to the floor as he lifted the file. Clay groaned, feeling every sore muscle as he bent to pick it up. A familiar set of cloudy blue eyes stared back at him. Someone had scrawled the words, *Odie, in the new kitchen, April 1979*, in the white space beneath the photo.

The old woman stood in front of the deep triple sink that still lived in the church's social annex kitchen. She wore fuzzy pink slippers and leaned on a wooden cane that bowed under her weight.

He threw the photo into the box like a hot coal. A coincidence, he told himself—the name and likeness to the woman from the diner. She would have been a young woman in 1979. A relative, perhaps?

Clay jumped at a shrill screech that came from the sanctuary. Heart pounding, he grabbed the mop handle and inched down the hall. Metal clanged, and the shrieks turned into sharp desperate barks.

A caged raccoon arched its back as Clay approached. Live traps were a humane way to catch and dispose of the beasts, the exterminator had explained. All Clay needed to do was call, and they'd be there first thing in the morning to retrieve the animal and take it to the lab to be euthanized.

The thought made Clay cringe. Angry wasps and ugly rats were one thing. The raccoon, with its masked face and human-like hands, looked innocent. Maybe it was the macabre box he'd sifted through, the photo of the cloudy-eyed woman, or the dream he refused to admit had shaken him, but Clay Dennen had enough of death for one day and couldn't bear the thought of killing the thing.

"Let's make a deal, little trash panda. If you promise not to come back, I'll let you go out by the lake. How's that sound?"

The creature stood on its hind legs and hissed at him.

Clay donned a pair of work gloves and loaded the cage into his SUV. The animal whimpered as he drove to a wooded area twenty minutes outside of town. He set the trap on the ground at the edge of the road and disengaged the lock. The raccoon waddled out and escaped into the underbrush.

Streaks of pink and orange stained the sky as the sun sank behind the trees. Something Mol said about him being smart for wanting to get out of the church before nightfall made the hairs on the back of his neck stand at attention.

He still didn't believe in witches, ghosts, or curses, but he was beginning to understand why locals were leery of the church. Even he got a creepy vibe going through that box of death. A vibe he planned to capitalize on. Local superstitions, tourists' imaginations, and that treasure trove of historical data would substantiate whatever story he spun.

As he rounded a sharp curve, his headlights fell upon a woman standing in the road. Clay didn't have time to slam on the breaks. Nausea pressed at the back of his throat as he braced for impact.

There was no scream. No fleshy thud.

His SUV went right through her. To be accurate, *she* went through his SUV. Her body didn't flinch as it passed through the hood and engine block. She just glared at him with those cloudy blue eyes, the wrinkled skin around them littered with blood-red pinpricks.

Clay's foot found the break. The SUV skidded to a stop. He kept a white-knuckle grip on the wheel as he forced himself to glance in the rearview mirror.

The road was empty.

☽ ○ ☾

The bar on River Street wasn't hard to find. Clay threw back three shots of tequila while he waited for Mol Crone to emerge from the back room.

"Mol's real good at helping folks connect with loved ones after they pass," the bartender said. "Charges seventy-five bucks a pop, but she's the best psychic in town. You can't choose who you get to talk to, though. Only person ever showed up for me is my mamma to lecture me on why I haven't gotten married or given her any grandbabies to watch over."

After an hour and a half of listening to the bartender

drone on about her dead mother, Mol motioned Clay back with a boney finger. He followed her down a dark hallway to a light-filled office. Soft elevator music floated through the air, and lavender-scented mist rose from a diffuser in the corner, softening the stale scent of cigarettes.

Mol took in his perplexed expression. "What did you expect? Candles and a crystal ball?"

"A beaded curtain, at least," Clay admitted.

"I'm a professional medium, Mr. Dennan. Not a circus side show."

"Who's Odemaris?" He asked, getting right to it.

Mol motioned for him to take a seat on the seafoam loveseat. "Odie was my grandmother," she said as she settled into a cream leather armchair. "Loved her job at the church. Organized the weekly spaghetti supper and Sunday socials for the congregation. Fed stray cats and the homeless from the vestry kitchen. Choked to death on a hot dog at the fourth of July picnic at Mill Pond Lake in 1985."

Clay leaned forward and lowered his voice. "I think I saw her ghost at the R & D diner yesterday, and again tonight, out by the lake."

"So, you're a believer now?"

"I can't deny what I saw with my own fucking eyes. Why is she haunting me?"

Mol lit a cigarette and slouched in the chair. "She's not haunting you. She's been following you and trying to warn you. Gotten any strange cuts or abrasions since setting foot on the property?"

"I'm in the middle of a renovation. I've got scrapes all over my damn arms."

"Like the one bleeding into your collar?"

Clay pulled the coverall collar away from his neck and

peered down at the red stain. He swiped two fingers across his throat and felt the stinging gash. "Shit."

"Odie's harmless. She only scratches deep when she's trying to scare someone off before Cora marks them. Cora's the one you need to worry about. Been seven years since she planted a new soul in that garden of hers out under the old beech tree."

"So... she really was a witch?"

"We are what the world makes us." The tip of Mol's cigarette glowed as she took a heavy drag and blew smoke from the side of her mouth.

"Can't you help her cross over or some shit? I'll pay, whatever the cost. Just tell me how to get rid of her."

"If you're smart, you'll board up that church, throw away the key and go back to wherever you came from."

"What if I torch it? The church, the tree, everything. Burn it down and build something else?"

"When Cora Pugh died, her spirit was imbued in the land. She is the tree, the roots, and the soil. The very bedrock beneath your church. Her soul will reside on that cursed patch of earth long after you and I are gone. You should leave. Soon. Once she reveals herself to you, once she's chosen, there isn't anywhere you can go or hide to escape your fate. Old Odie tried. Quit her job at the church. Refused to go anywhere near it. She was dead a week later."

"What if she doesn't choose me? What if she chooses someone else?"

"Cora's particular about her trophies. I tried telling that to your predecessor, Henry Crenshaw. Like you, he had grand plans for the church. Wanted to turn it into a history museum. In Wynnville. Can you believe that?" She shook her head and flicked ashes into a coffee mug on the table. "Came around asking me questions about old Odie. Said he was putting together information about everyone buried in the cemetery. Showed me his files and got pissy when I pointed out the pattern. Every seven years, another death. Didn't believe me when I told him it was Cora's way of taking her revenge on the town. Called me a small-minded anti-feminist. Told me Cora Pugh was innocent and didn't deserve to have her memory defiled. Mr. Crenshaw drove his Mini Cooper off a bridge the next day. Now, he's buried out there under the tree with the rest of her victims. I think it's the lies she's drawn to. Mr. Crenshaw tried to paint her as a saint. Grandma Odie, God love her, but she was a gossip. Spread truth and lies all over town thick as icing on a sheet cake."

Clay's mouth went dry as he thought about the life insurance policies he'd cashed in on behalf of his dead clients. Policies he got under false pretenses. Money he used to buy the church and finance the renovation.

"I don't know about you, Mr. Dennen, but I never met a person who didn't lie."

The way Clay saw it, he was already damned, and he wasn't the type to take his fate lying down or to give in to defeat. He emailed his lawyer and drove back to the church. In the parking lot, Clay pulled a flask from the glove box, took a bracing swallow, and walked into the witch's garden to wait for Cora Pugh beneath the beech tree. She'd come to him once before, in a dream. Mol confirmed what his gut already told him. He'd been chosen.

Clay woke at 3:00 AM to the sound of rustling leaves and squelching footsteps. Wet tendrils framed her face, and the filthy nightgown hung in tatters around her mud-streaked calves.

The homeless woman. The golden-haired maiden. The witch.

A cold sweat beaded up on his forehead as he crossed his ankles and leaned back against the gnarled tree. "I have a proposition for you," he said, keeping his tone light, refusing to betray the unsteady feeling in his bowels.

She cocked her head to the side. Could she scent his fear, he wondered?

"You assume this is a negotiation?" Her voice rushed over him like icy water, chilling him to the bone.

"Let me live and I'll give you something precious in return," Clay said. "Something you're not even aware you've lost."

Her cracked lips curled into a snarl. "I require nothing but your death to sustain me."

"You awaken every seven years to claim a life. Revenge for the one you lost. That's how you perpetuate the curse, right? The one you placed on the town and yourself."

"What is a curse but a promise?" Cora inched closer.

"A promise to kill innocent people?"

"Not innocent. Only those corrupted by darkness."

"We're all corrupted," Clay said, "and you're shit at cleaning up after yourself. Locals won't come near this place. I sent a message to my attorney this evening, bequeathing the property to the Commonwealth Green Energy Alliance. If you kill me, you'll wake up in seven years to a fenced-off solar farm and not a single soul to perpetuate the spell. What happens when the energy created here feeds the town of Wynnville instead of you?"

"Lies." The witch bared yellow teeth, spittle spraying from her mouth.

Clay resisted the urge to gag as the stench of rotting corpse engulfed him. "Interesting. I was told you could sniff out a lie. Guess they misinformed me."

She moved faster than his human eyes could track and yanked him to his feet with preternatural strength. Icy fingers clenched around his throat, crushing his windpipe.

"What is your offer?"

Clay's voice came out in a hoarse gasp, "A future, for the both of us."

) ☽ (

The sound of wet feet slapping against the mosaic tile drew Clay's attention as he headed to the kitchen with a half-empty bottle of champagne. The guests in room twelve discarded it on the pew, too busy mauling one another to notice it spill on the antique bench, where it left a mark on the wood.

"Welcome back," he said, greeting the young woman with a deferential bow.

"What have you for me this evening?" Her voice gurgled like a spring stream.

"A full congregation, ma'am. If I may make a suggestion, the man in room twelve is here for a trade conference, and the woman he's with is *not* his wife."

A sneer curled the corners of her mouth as she nodded to the host and headed toward the guest wing, the stench of death lingering in her wake.

# ABOUT J. EMBER HINTZ

J. Ember Hintz writes romance and supernatural fiction with a gothic twist. You'll meet murderous disembodied spirits, human clones, psychic aliens, and apathetic ancient gods in her worlds, but never a damsel in distress.

Her debut novel, THE ASH GARDENERS (August 2022) is a Daphne du Maurier Award for Excellence in Mystery/Suspense finalist.

She lives in coastal Virginia with her husband, children and the occasional ghost and when she's not breathing life into fictional characters, you can find her in the studio throwing paint at a canvas and hoping for the best.

**Find out more about J. Ember at:**
jemberhintz.com

facebook.com/NoDamselsAuthor
twitter.com/JEmberHintz
instagram.com/j.ember.hintz

# THE FEATHERS YOU WEAR BY
## MEGHAN J. DAHL

Shadowman sat in the back of the church waiting for the priest to finish his interminable sermon. A smattering of the congregation dotted the pews in front of him, most of them vaguely familiar from the routine spying he did when he arrived in any new village or town.

He listened, stone-faced with hackles prickling, to the preaching of Father Eagan, the pompous, narrow-faced priest at the podium. This was why he avoided churches. The hypocrisy made his skin itch. Love thy neighbor, but not those heathen ones. We're all God's children, but *those* children will burn in Hell. He blew out a breath and let his head fall back, shutting his eyes. He'd tried to amuse himself by admiring the architecture, but he'd seen thousands of churches in his extended life, and this one was middling at best. Even so, he'd studied every line of the stained glass windows, the carvings adorning the altar; he'd even counted the arches in the ceiling but STILL the father droned on.

But worst of all, Elena hadn't come.

He'd been here for hours. He'd arrived early, anxious,

like a fool. At what point did one grow old enough not to fall victim to the madness of love? Pretty fucking old, apparently. He'd thought himself well past the point of being caught by pretty faces. He'd seen over a millennium of birthdays, but still proven a fool.

She had insisted he wait for her in the church. She knew he loathed them, but it was the only place her father would allow her to go alone because the priest, that simpering pustule on the podium, was her uncle. Elena's father knew his hold on his daughter was slipping and he'd reacted savagely, clamping down on her remaining freedoms, a last ditch move to keep the control he'd exerted over her, to maintain the only place he felt powerful. Humans will do anything to keep their little kingdoms. Even raise violent hands to their grown daughters.

Shadowman had spent more than one night dreaming about his hands around the man's throat, his blood spattered on the walls like a grisly abstract painting. But she'd made him promise not to hurt anyone in this abysmal little town. So his art went unpainted. And justice unserved.

He ground his teeth.

Shadowman was convinced he must have aged yet another year in this church when the priest finally uttered the last "Amen," echoed by the scattered churchgoers. The devout were now gathering their things to leave, a quiet rustling of coats and shoes, but he stayed in his seat, unwilling to move, to accept that she'd decided not to leave with him tonight.

A young woman next to him in the long pew sneaked a glance at him. He recognized her from his spying around the village. A gossiping, sniping creature with some surprising skeletons of her own. Ellis, something. Margie? Marjorie? She slipped her glasses off her face, tucking them into her bag and adjusted her flowered dress as if nervous. As if she were gathering courage.

Oh bloody hell, she was going to speak to him.

"So lovely to see a new face at church!" she chirped.

Shadowman made a noncommittal noise.

"Are you new in town?" Her gaze was hopeful.

How new was new? He'd been here for months, though only Elena knew he existed. He preferred it that way.

"Passing through," he said finally. It was true. With her or without her, he was leaving tonight.

"Only the most faithful come to evening mass," Margie/Marjorie breathed.

"I am a true believer," he said, savoring the irony. He could hardly not be. The things he'd seen would curl the girl's hair without rollers. He was also ninety percent certain that God was fucking with him — again.

She clasped her hands together. "I can't wait to tell the others about you."

Time to cut this off. Give her something more interesting to tell "the others."

He smiled darkly and watched her flutter a little. Women often reacted to him this way. He was the quintessential tall, dark stranger, green-eyed and broad-shouldered. He stood out. It was why he'd been chosen — why he'd been made into the creature he was.

It would have been better if he'd been born ugly.

"I love our little church. Don't you?" She was babbling. "If I could, I'd stay here all the time. Do you feel that way too? About church?"

"Can I tell you a secret?" He smiled conspiratorially. She nodded, breathy in anticipation.

He leaned in close, lips inches from her ear. "I'd sooner burn it to the ground."

Her eyes widened, a shocked, short silence as she processed what he'd said. A moment longer as she realized he was serious. Then she snatched up her bag and half ran out of the church.

He leaned back into the uncomfortable pew, musing on the darkness seeping into his soul. Scaring young girls, even gossipy, miserable ones, was new for him. Perhaps he shouldn't have been so honest, but he was too moody for sidestepping.

Perhaps that was why Elena wasn't here. She'd seen him crossing lines, growing darker. He'd warned her often enough. Maybe she'd wondered if she was trading one kind of darkness for another.

Or maybe she'd realized she never loved him at all, but got caught up in how he'd rescued her, in the things he'd shown her no mortal could see. Why had he done that? He wasn't in the habit of getting into other people's affairs. Well, that wasn't strictly true. There were very specific activities that he interfered in whenever possible, but this wasn't that kind of situation. All he knew was that whenever he closed his eyes, he'd see her again, poised on the bridge rail in the blue dress that matched her wide, broken eyes. Seeking escape in the only way she believed she could.

He'd had hundreds of dalliances before, amusements to pass the time, but Elena was different. He loved her in a way he couldn't name, in a way that smacked of destiny and despite his disdain for the word, he'd been drawn in. In a thousand years, he'd never asked anyone to share his life, his strange existence, until now.

But it seemed she had decided against the idea.

He reached into his coat, pulled out a large, engraved flask, and took a deep swig, feeling the burn work its way through him. If only it could burn out the place where his heart used to be.

"How dare you bring the devil's drink into the house of God?"

Father Eagan stood in the aisle stiff with outrage, or perhaps it was just his collar. Shadowman felt a little outraged himself. Elena's uncle. The brother of the man he dreamed of killing. He felt venomous. He wanted to smash something, starting with this balding sack of fish guts.

Restraint was going to be difficult.

Shadowman took a deliberately lengthy swig of whiskey and studied the priest. "Would it please you, Father, if I gave up my 'devil's drink'?"

Father Eagan opened his mouth to answer, but Shadowman leaned over the side of the pew, turned the flask upside down and poured the whiskey out in wide circular swirls onto the red carpeted aisle. It made a pleasing pattern. Look at that, he got to make art after all.

The priest's mouth set in a peeved line. "You are godless, sir."

"Oh no, I assure you, I'm quite the opposite of that. In fact, I'd argue that out of the two of us, I'm the only one who truly believes in God."

"How dare you insinuate—"

"Do you fear for your immortal soul, Father?"

Father Eagan bristled, visibly trying to tamp down his irritation. "And why should I have any cause to fear?"

"Why indeed? Tell me, do you believe it is a sin to have knowledge of a crime but do nothing?"

"Of course. Evil triumphs when good men do nothing," Father Eagan quoted dryly. "Do you know something you wish to share?"

"I do indeed, Father. And it weighs on me greatly," Shadowman mocked, pressing a hand to his heart. "You see, I knew a man, outwardly pious, who preached (at length!) of kindness, tolerance and helping the needy—but abandoned his own motherless nieces to the whims of his violent brother."

Shadowman stood, his long, black coat unfurling around his legs. He towered over the diminutive priest.

Father Eagan's eyes narrowed. "Who are you?"

"A marvelous question—that I have no intention of answering."

"How do you—"

"I know many things about you. I know you disapproved of their mother, her *ethnic* heritage—"

"She was bad news. I didn't want her teaching the children any of her false religion."

"But she never had the chance, did she? Because she died at your brother's hand, and you helped conceal it, didn't you, Father?"

It had been a wild stab in the dark, but the shocked, panicky look on his face confirmed it. Humans were so predictable.

"I don't have to listen to this." Father Eagan turned and headed for the front doors.

Shadowman followed. "And then you abandoned the children to the man that murdered their mother. How do you sleep at night?"

Father Eagan yanked open the front doors and gestured curtly for him to leave. As if he'd go so easily.

"So we return to where we started," Shadowman continued. "If you truly believed in God, you would be more careful with your immortal soul—lest something like me take an interest in you."

"I am a man of the cloth," Father Eagan protested.

"Faith is not about the feathers you wear, Father. It's not about your clothing, your customs or how loudly you profess your beliefs in public. Good and evil are not defined by your race, gender, religion, or your taste in men or women. Good and evil lie in your actions."

The priest puffed himself up, trying to rally the situation. "I see. And you've appointed yourself my judge and jury, have you? And who will judge you then? Are you so squeaky clean?" he scoffed.

"Not in the slightest," Shadowman said, flicking a hand dismissively. "But I needn't worry since I'm no longer human..."

Father Eagan stared. "You're mad."

"Is that what you truly believe?"

"I believe you're a liar!"

"I never lie." It was what Elena said she loved most about him. *Sometimes you're good, sometimes you're bad, but you never, ever lie. And you always keep your promises.*

He'd inconveniently promised her not to hurt anyone in this backwater village. No one in his life had ever extracted so many damn promises out of him. The woman had a gift.

Uncertainty flickered across the priest's face. Shadowman bent close, close enough that the priest would feel his breath on his cheek. "You know it's true, Father. There's something *wrong* about me, you can feel it in your bones."

The father looked less angry now and a lot more afraid.

"Are you concerned for your immortal soul now?" Shadowman purred.

"I did nothing wrong," he stammered.

"Hmm. Let's examine that, shall we? When Elena grew up to look just like her mother, you saw how he tried to control her, didn't you? How she looked drawn? Moving tenderly, as if she had bruises?"

Father Eagan stuttered, his face pale. "Look, my brother may have his demons, but I—"

"Demons? Your brother doesn't have demons. *I* have demons. And I think it's time you met a real one so you know the difference."

"No! No, please, I—"

Was it terrible that he took pleasure in this part? His alter ego tugged at his edges, begging for release. Shadowman was happy to oblige.

He watched Father Eagan's face drain as his body grew larger and darker, growing, melding into a seamless, featureless shadow. Then he slipped sideways into the shade of the doorway and (from the priest's point of view) vanished. In reality, Shadowman slid along the shadows as one fluid entity, sliding, shifting, bending his form to fit in any size space until he found the hiding spot he wanted. Right behind Father Eagan.

The priest stood terrified, goggling at the space he had just occupied. In one swift movement, Shadowman stepped from a tiny crevice in the door, breathing heat down the priest's neck. "I'm watching you, Father. Take better care of your soul," he purred into his ear.

Father Eagan let out a strangled cry and bolted down the church steps, tripping on his robes in his haste.

Shadowman stood in the doorway, watching the priest scrambling and stumbling down the street, screaming incoherently about demons. He couldn't punish the man he wanted to punish but scaring the shit out of his brother was surprisingly satisfying. Maybe he would look out for Elena properly now.

Shadowman wasn't exactly a demon, of course. But he'd made his point.

Also, he *loved* to fuck with the clergy.

The screaming would draw attention, though. Someone would no doubt come to investigate soon. He didn't intend to be around. Shutting his eyes, he breathed deep into his core and pulled his shadow back into himself, wrestling back control from his alter ego, shuddering and flexing his hands as the constraints of corporeality settled back onto his shoulders like chains.

It was harder to change back now than it used to be. He didn't like to think too much about what that meant.

He took a deep breath of cool night air and felt an ache return to his chest. A blustery November breeze rippled the folds of his long coat and night dimmed as the moon slid behind a lacy net of clouds.

She wasn't coming.

It was probably the smarter choice. He'd certainly told her so. There was no going back, so she needed to be sure. But it still surprised him. He'd thought she would come.

And it hurt.

Sighing, he looked out at the empty night. Father Eagan was nowhere to be seen, but he could hear voices coming from the direction of the village's main street now.

He regarded his empty flask. It had been a shame to waste such good whiskey, but one never knew when one might need a decent accelerant. Gasoline was better, of course, but the first time he'd accidentally taken a sip of that had convinced him wasting a little whiskey now and then was better.

Ducking back into the church, he pulled a matchbox out of his long coat, struck one and tossed it onto the alcohol-soaked carpet and watched with a satisfied smile as it burst into flame. It bloomed all along his circular patterns and cozied up to the pews, licking up their sides, already darkening the wood.

He always liked to leave a signature.

At the bottom of the church steps, Shadowman paused. The moon drifted from its nest of clouds, illuminating the churchyard in a ghostly patchwork of silver and shadow. The temptation to slip like smoke into the darkness, to visit savage mischief on this miserable place and soothe the chasm opening up inside him swelled in his chest but with effort, he held himself in check. He'd kept his promise. He hadn't (physically) hurt anyone. Elena wouldn't be pleased about the fire—but she wouldn't be surprised either. He'd been wanting to burn the thing down since he got here.

A flicker of movement caught his eye.

"Was that my uncle running screaming down the street?" Her voice, dark and lilting like water in a forest stream, slid over his soul, igniting a fire that hummed inside him.

Elena moved toward him, emerging from a shadowy line of trees edging the churchyard. Her dress and boots peeked out from under a cherry red overcoat, hugged around her tall, willowy frame, a single bag looped over her shoulder. Long dark hair framed her heart-shaped face, eyebrows arched in gentle disapproval.

He reached her in three strides.

His hands tangled in her hair, breath fogging the air between them as he kissed her, deep and lingering until he felt it imprinted in the depths of his soul.

He brushed her hair back, revealing the face he so loved. "You came."

"You doubted?"

"You made me sit through that interminable sermon."

Her lips twitched. "Well, I could hardly make it easy for you. Leaving my whole life is certainly not easy for me." Her voice hitched slightly, betraying the depth of her fears despite her flippant tone. "Saying goodbye — putting an ending on everything I've ever known..." She dropped her gaze, face turned. Her eyes flicked to the church. "Are those flames??"

With gentle fingers, he turned her face back to him.

"Not an ending. A beginning," he said.

"A beginning," she echoed.

"Of something amazing."

She lifted her face to his. "Do you promise?"

That was a promise he had no trouble making.

# ABOUT MEGHAN J. DAHL

Meghan J. Dahl is a writer and artist living in the suburban wilds of British Columbia, Canada. She writes mainly contemporary fantasy with a smattering of non-fiction. She is currently finishing her first full-length novel so she can (finally) make space for the backlog of ideas piling up in her head.

**Find out more about Meghan at:**
meghanjdahl.com

twitter.com/MeghanJDahl
instagram.com/meghanjdahl

# THE WHITE HARVESTER BY MATT HOLLON

It was his voice that decided it. The kind of voice that no amount of rum could curb. It rose above the din of the smokey tavern—loud, boisterous, and laced with an unearned arrogance. Lapis had dealt with countless like this, and they were all the same—thinking they were God's gift when they weren't even Satan's shit. There was nothing better than hearing those oily voices slip into screams.

She narrowed her eyes at the man as he told anyone that would listen, in crass detail, about the mermaid he'd fucked. She knew it was a lie because if he really *had* fucked a mermaid, his bloated corpse would be at the bottom of the ocean and crabs would be picking the flesh off his bones. But instead he was here. Still talking. His crew clapped along like the trained seals they were. Why were men so loud?

She turned her attention away from her target. He wouldn't be going anywhere. She sipped her dark rum and tried not to gag on the stale haze of tobacco and urine settling on every grimy surface like ash. She longed for the smell of salt and gunpowder, for the sun to beat down on her bronze skin as she paced along the deck of The White Harvester. She longed for the sea.

But the crew needed time on land—to drink, to fuck, and to drink again. Truthfully, they did plenty of both on the sea as well, but whatever made them happy. It was better to have a happy crew. Unhappy crews led to mutinies, mutinies led to dead crews, and dead crews were pretty fucking useless, though her darling Teach was a fan. It was easier this way.

Across the bar, opposite Dumbass-The-Mermaid-Fucker, her first mate Lily was about to break a man's nose. Her stunning icicle eyes had that look to them. Sure enough, the man must have said something stupid because she smashed a bottle over his head, sending glass, beer, and blood splattering across the filthy floor. Not quite a broken nose, but a concussion was close enough.

The unconscious man's friends were either loyal or stupid because a handful of them rose from their stools and rushed toward Lily. She spread her sun-kissed arms wide, accepting the challenge.

Lapis sighed and shot her drink down. The corner of her mouth turned up in a smirk. Perfect. She rose from her corner booth and glided past the slack-mouthed imbeciles watching Lily fight. Other members of Lapis's crew, along with anyone else looking for a face to punch, were pulled into the brawl's gravity. Before long, the entire side of the tavern was caught in a tangled mass of violence. Lapis glanced over her shoulder at her target. For once, he had stopped talking. He looked over the crowd, likely trying to see if the fight would give him a chance to impress anyone. Too easy.

The sound of twinkling gold rose from her belt, hitting her ears over the yells and shattering glass. She smiled down at the medallions. "Patience, loves," she whispered. "When I'm ready."

She waded through the scrum, no one paying her any mind. Her poor crew, it seemed this was the first brawl for many of them, their lips already splitting, teeth splintering. She swallowed a sigh. If only learning to be a Harvester wasn't so deadly. It took talent to not get killed, but it took not getting killed to develop talent. A rather corpse-ridden paradox, really. Better to end this early before she had to recruit more fools.

A bare-chested man with hairy arms attempted to put Lily in a headlock. He was shit at doing so, allowing her enough room to maneuver her head and clamp her teeth into his forearm. Blood squirted and the man yelped. She kicked her leg back like a mule, directly into his groin. Before he could mourn his ruptured manhood, she'd slammed her fist into his jaw, crumpling him. He lay moaning on the ground. She spat his blood back onto him. "I don't know what you're crying about, not like you had any balls to begin with."

A man between Lapis and Lily pulled a flintlock from his belt and aimed at her.

Lapis closed the distance in an instant, unsheathing her pearl dagger, and resheathing it in the back of his neck. The blade's tip scraped against his chin, blood bubbling down the handle, soaking her hand. "Poor choice," she cooed in his ear, before pulling the blade free and letting his body fall to the ground.

Lily rolled her eyes, placing her hands on her hips. "You bitch. I had him."

Lapis walked past the stunned onlookers, the dead man putting a damper on their fighting spirit, and grabbed her

Lily, giving her an impassioned kiss. "We have a target," she breathed.

She pulled away and addressed the crowd. "Let the hole in his neck serve as a reminder of what happens when you try to kill a Harvester. Now if you'll excuse us..."

"You're the captain of The White Harvester?" an awestruck woman asked.

"Charmed," Lapis said with a smile.

Her target, seeing his opportunity, had lumbered over. He looked ridiculous. Garish gold, half of it fake, adorned his sunburned hands. His face, equally blistered, was shrouded by a large, clownfish-orange beard, braided as if by a toddler. "I've never heard of you," he said.

"It's alright, love. No one has heard of you."

His chapped lip curled, revealing his rotting teeth. "I'm Coal, Captain of Hellfire."

Such a ridiculous name. "Is hellfire burning on coal these days? I'd no idea."

Some lanky man with greasy blond hair slithered to Coal. "Captain, I've heard of her before. They say she lives in a cove of demons, her gold forged in the fires of Hell."

"If that were true, I'd think the Captain of Hellfire would be aware of it, no?" Lapis asked innocently. "I am but a lowly captain, taking what the sea provides and protecting her crew. I know nothing of cursed gold." The medallions on her belt rattled angrily to her.

Coal's blue eyes narrowed for a moment. "You talk a lot for a lowly captain."

"In my experience the better captains talk less. You, on the other hand, talk enough for all the lowly captains of the world. But I suppose not all of us can be so blessed as to fuck a mermaid. Now, if you'll excuse my crew and me, we must be getting out of this stench that you're so generously contributing to."

She turned, leaving Coal to decipher the insult, and pressed her way out into the sun. She didn't bother to see if her crew followed. If they didn't, she didn't want them.

Within a few paces, Lily was at her ear. "Coal is the target, yes?"

"Aye."

Her pink lips grinned. "Lovely." She reached back and tied her long white-blonde hair into a ponytail. "Hope they put up more of a fight than the fuckers in the bar."

Lapis smiled to herself. "Sometimes I think you lust for violence more than me."

"On the contrary, Captain. I lust for you *because* I lust for violence."

Before long, they had reached the docks, her crew following behind her. The White Harvester's snowy hull soon came into view, whale bones adorning it. Her sails, matte black, featured golden coins, floating placidly in a pool of freshly spilled blood. They loaded onto the deck and Lily began shouting orders. Within minutes, they were pressing against the waves, leaving the stench of land behind.

Salty wind blew through Lapis's dark brown hair, the hot air caressing her skin. She slid her fingers down the helm's smooth wood, steering them toward her cove.

Calloused hands traced gently down her exposed shoulders, the nails giving the faintest hint of a scratch. "*Let the hole in his neck serve as a reminder of what happens when you try and kill a Harvester,*" Lily mocked, wrapping her arms around Lapis's waist. She rested her head against Lapis's neck. "How many Harvesters have I killed? Where's the hole in my neck?"

Lapis gave her lips a soft peck. "You can get away with more than most, love. Besides, I had to offer a challenge."

"You could've simply said he had a krill cock."

"Something I imagine he's heard before. Men like Coal want nothing but attention. He'll follow, seeking glory that is far beyond him. Poor thing."

"And embarrassing him in front of his crew..." Lily smirked.

"Simply setting my hook." She grinned. "And it was good fun."

The sun had barely moved across the azure sky when a ship emerged from the horizon behind them. It sliced through the sea, quickly gaining ground. Lapis arched an eyebrow. Perhaps she'd take this ship as her own, it was certainly fast enough to be useful. Though, if she acquired it, *Hellfire* would certainly need a remodel. Black hull with pure black sails? How macabre. How bland. Maybe she'd introduce some purples and reds, anything to give it some flair.

But she was getting ahead of herself. "Harvesters! Let's pick up the pace a bit, shall we? It seems Coal has had his feelings hurt." They sprang into inefficient action, grasping at ropes and trying to look capable. Lily left her side to command the crew.

Her medallions whispered from her belt. "Be patient, my darlings. Not much longer."

An irritated screech sliced through the bustle of her crew. Several of them jumped—the newer members, those not yet used to Teach. Skeletal wings spread from atop the crow's nest, painting a silhouette across the mast. He leapt from his perch and soared down, circling above the shaking crew before finding home on her shoulder, his bleached talons gently digging into her flesh. His empty eyes looked into hers expectantly.

"Did the noise wake you, baby?"

He clicked his beak angrily.

"Goodness, you too? Just be patient, love. You've lived a thousand years and yet you can't wait thirty minutes? Honestly, why do I even bring you along?"

A small flame erupted in Teach's empty eye sockets, his exposed ribs heaving with disdain.

"Oh hush, you know I'm only joking."

She gazed out over her desperate crew. Lily barked orders, herding the crew to their stations with ferocity. "Lily, darling?"

Lily looked over her shoulder, her eyes squinting in the sun. "Yes, my love?"

"Do get them to hurry. I'd hate for many of them to die. Crew members are so hard to find."

"Well, maybe it wouldn't be so bad if some of these fuckers died. Maybe we could replace them with some sailors who actually know what they're doing!" The crew winced at her screams.

"Cut them some slack, dear. They're new. Teach will take me ashore. Coal will follow. The rest are yours."

Lily grinned. "I'll have the crew mop the blood when I'm finished. I know how you hate a dirty ship."

"I expect nothing less." She smiled back. "Teach, I need you, love."

Her loyal albatross spread his twelve-foot wings and she grinned when she saw a young man flinch. Teach picked her up in his jagged talons and, with one flap of his great wings, carried her up into the blue, a puddle of night slipping through the sunshine. Shadows fluttered, carrying her faster than any vessel man or god could make. Only a devil could move this fast.

He deposited her onto the familiar jagged shore.

"Thank you, sweetheart."

He gave a deathly hiss in return before nuzzling his skull into her shoulder.

"My, my, how sweet we're being. Don't worry, I'll have a treat for you soon enough."

Teach gave a delighted wail before soaring off once again. She watched him for a bit before turning on her heel and sauntering into her cove.

Eons of water and salt had carved her vault deep into the heart of the sandstone cliffs. She strolled inside, glancing over pile after pile of worthless gold, warm sunshine trickling in through the ceiling's occasional collapse. She'd give them the chance to take as much as they could carry before they'd even lay eyes on her. But of course, they wouldn't take the opportunity. Men were so predictable.

She strolled deeper into the heart of her cave, where her more valuable treasures lay. Gems the size of skulls, trinkets both blessed and cursed, vials of sea dragon venom, blades sharp enough to cut souls, sands from the end of the Earth. She ignored them all and plopped down upon her carved damp stone just beneath a hole in the high ceiling, angelic sunshine pouring over her. She gazed out at her shadowed vault. These were the treasures the men would want, but really, they too, were worthless. Remnants of some forgotten year, valuable only for their dust. Nothing to the medallions clinking from her belt. They whispered to her again, louder this time.

She ran her fingers across their metallic surface, unfastening them before clasping each of them between fingers and bringing them to her lips. "Soon, my lovelies. It will be but a moment."

Sure enough, five stinking men burst into the cavern, their cutlasses and pistols drawn. Lapis tried her best to look frightened, but fuck were they making it difficult. Coal puffed out his chest like a blowfish trying not to be eaten by a shark. "You offended me back there. I don't like to be offended." He pointed his blade at her. "But we have you now, bitch."

Goddamnit. This facade would be impossible to uphold. She sighed at their snickers. "I apologize. I really didn't think I was telling you anything you weren't aware of. What is it that you want from me?"

"Don't play dumb," Coal spat. "You know we're after your cursed gold."

"You passed plenty of perfectly holy gold on your way here. Surely that would be more desirable, no?"

"Real pirates care for glory more than coin." He grinned, his algae-colored teeth turning her stomach.

*Real pirates.* She raised her hands, medallions still glittering between her fingers. "Apologies. I'm fairly new to this whole piracy thing. Don't know the code and all that."

"Shame you won't get the chance to learn," Coal's first mate, the lanky gullshit, sneered.

"What, you're not going to kill me, are you?" She mocked a look of horror.

"Only after we're done with you," Coal said. "I'm going to make you beg for mercy as I slice you into pieces."

"Oh no, please don't," she said in a flat voice. She tossed the medallions over their heads, the coins clattering across the stone. "Here. Take my cursed gold."

Coal watched the medallions soar over his head before turning back to her. "Think we'll take you first."

"If you insist, but the gold may be a more pressing issue."

Coal and his crew gazed at her with open mouths. Behind them, the medallions began to rattle.

Time to reap.

Coal sneered. "The gold will still be there after you're dealt with."

Lapis arched an eyebrow. "I wouldn't be so sure."

Coal had time to blink at her before a sword pierced his chest. He looked down at the soaked steel before collapsing to the ground.

His crew stared in horror. Not at their dead captain, but at her legion, all of them stood at attention, their ghostly hues lighting the cove. Her treasure. Her harvest.

The men flung themselves to their knees. "Please!" sobbed the lanky one. "Don't kill us. Whatever you are, we'll serve you."

"Oh there'll be no need for that, darling." Lapis gave her sweetest smile.

The man's eyebrows knitted together in confusion.

"You see, I already have a crew."

She clapped her hands once and her captains went to work, turning the crew into meat, their dead steel cleaving through warm flesh. Their screams bounced around the stone for a moment before, at last, the men had been silenced, save for their blood dribbling over the now tarnished coins.

The spirits of the medallions glared back at her, their features drawn with eternal resentment.

"Oh, don't look at me like that, I could've killed them without you."

She stepped over the corpses to Coal, the blood flowing from his mouth clashing horribly with the fiery orange of his beard. She pulled a dagger from her belt and jammed it into his chest, punching through sinew and bone. After a few seconds of carving, she plunged her hand into the hot cavity, feeling around for her treasure.

*There.*

She dug her nails into the slick surface and ripped out his leaking heart.

She held it out in front of her, her face splitting into a grin. "Welcome to the crew," she cooed before squeezing. The flesh gave, squirting between her fingers. She clenched her hand tighter and tighter until she felt a hard core pressing against her palm. Smiling still, she opened her fist, revealing a blood-soaked gold medallion. She brought it to her mouth and kissed it, and the taste of meat and metal kissed her back.

She looked the new treasure over before tossing it to the ground. The ghostly vestige of Coal sprang from the medallion, solemn. Loyal. "Welcome to the afterlife, darling."

She scooped the scarlet coins from the ground and fastened them back to her belt. Already, they had begun to drink the blood they'd spilled, returning them to their golden purity. The spirits vanished, waiting to be called upon by their master once more.

She turned her attention to the empty bodies strewn about the weathered rock. She put bloodstained fingers to her mouth and whistled.

"Teach, sweetheart! Mummy has a treat for you."

# ABOUT MATT HOLLON

Matt Hollon is a published short story writer and soon-to-be novelist with a taste for sharp-tongued protagonists and a splash of magic here and there. Raised between the cornfields of Ohio, he splits his time between crafting adventure-filled fantasies and acting as a regular contributor to Samantha L Nasset's writing-centric YouTube channel. When he isn't typing away at his manuscript, you can find him trying his hand at new recipes, scarfing the results down, and occasionally being stalked by his darling cat.

**Find out more about Matt at:**

# WHEN THE CIRCUS CAME TO TOWN
## BY J A MORTIMORE

It would be wrong to say that the Grand Library at Chatris Arbor had never seen such a gathering, but the crowd that spilled in when the doors opened was the equal of any in its past. As well as most of the town's movers and shakers, tourists had come from far and wide. For once, their interest was not in the best collection of books and scrolls in the country, but instead the focus of attention was the crown jewels of Freeland, safely displayed on black velvet in a glass dome at the very center of the massive atrium. Fashionably clad men and women could be seen pushing and shoving to be the first to exclaim over the glittering array. The choker with its massive faceted emerald was accompanied by a pair of matching earrings, but it was the crown with its diamond-encrusted spikes that elicited the loudest cries of admiration. A bevy of security men glowered at anybody who got too close, and it was rumored the best spellcasters in town had warded the glass dome.

"Fuck me, this is boring." Ria Matthews hid a yawn behind her hand.

"Dull as dishwater," her fellow librarian Marian agreed. "And my feet hurt."

Ria gave the older woman a sympathetic look. They were stationed at the locked doors of the room in which the library's collection of grimoires were padlocked to a series of podiums, their assignment to ensure no curious tourist attempted to access the hazardous collection. Other librarians were guarding other doors, or acting as greeters. "How long d'you think it'll be before things settle down and we can go back to work?"

"The mayor has to make his little speech first."

"Oh god, I'd forgotten about that. I hope he doesn't bugger up his lines like he did at the rehearsal."

Marian nudged her. "Straighten up and smile — and watch your language! The head librarian's looking this way and you've already had two demerits this week."

"Must I?" Ria scowled.

"I see your best buddy Jordan is briefing the security guy and his mages."

"So he should — he's the sheriff. And he's not my best anything."

"He'd like to be." Marian smirked. "He's always hanging around you. He might be worth a night's..." She broke off, a flash of color in the atrium catching her attention. "Oh my, who's the hottie in the plumed hat?"

Ria glanced in the direction indicated and her eyes widened. "Cassidy Morganstern!"

"*The* Cassidy Morganstern? Look sharp, he's headed this way!" Marian patted her bob of hair self-consciously.

"You're a respectably married woman," Ria reminded her friend.

"A girl can look, can't she?"

"Hush!" Ria suspected her face was flaming as Cassidy reached them, doffed his plumed hat and executed a flamboyant bow.

"Kariann Matthews — my goodness, you haven't changed a bit!"

Ria would have liked to say that Cassidy hadn't either, but that wouldn't have been strictly true. The best-looking boy in her class had always had the kind of charisma that caused damp panties — now, grown up, he exuded sex appeal at a truly extraordinary level. "It's just Ria now." Oh god, had her voice squeaked?

"And you... work here?" He raised an eyebrow. "Somehow I imagined you running your own bookshop by now. Does your father still sell the best fish in town?"

"Fresh caught every day," she parroted automatically. "Yes, I work here. And you — are you still with the, uh, same outfit?"

"Naturally."

It had been a scandal of truly colossal magnitude when the eldest son of the wealthiest merchants in town had run off to join the circus. Ria caught herself glancing anxiously around, wondering if his parents were anywhere in the room. "Are you here to see the crown jewels?"

He smiled. "Of course — I was headed that way when I spotted you and couldn't resist coming over to say hello." He lifted an eyebrow. "If you wouldn't mind waiting, I'll go and check out the sparklers — and then I'd like to ask you a favor."

"My goodness." Marian fanned herself with one hand as he strolled away. "That man's charisma is dangerous."

Ria opened her mouth to reply, but closed it again as Sheriff Jordan pushed his way through the crowd. "What did he want with you?" he demanded. "I'd prefer it if you stayed away from him. He's trouble."

"He always was," Ria agreed. She resisted the temptation to add that at least somebody she'd grown up with had been entertaining. Jordan, who both she and Cassidy had been at school with, had always been pleasant enough, but was incredibly straitlaced. It had surprised no one when the mayor picked him to be the town sheriff. "As to what he wanted," she continued, rallying a little, "he's an old school friend, he was just paying his respects."

"He didn't speak to me." Jordan took off his cap and smoothed down his ruffled blond hair. "He's probably here for the jewels," he fretted. He was a short man with a tendency to pudginess, and Ria caught herself musing that he didn't compare favorably against Cassidy's whipcord, dark-haired good looks.

"To look at them, you mean?" Marian enquired.

Jordan scowled. "To steal them! Everywhere that circus of his goes, things go missing. Nobody's managed to catch him at it yet, but I'm going to make sure this time he's put behind bars where he belongs. So I need to know, Ria, what he said to you. Every word, please."

"Fuck off," Ria said pleasantly, enjoying the way he flinched at her profanity. "He was just saying hello. And he wanted to ask me a favor."

"What favor?"

Ria shrugged. "I expect he'll tell me later." Cassidy had reached the podium and appeared to be examining the security precautions. She wondered if he really was a jewel thief or whether Jordan was just jealous of his charisma.

"I've changed my mind." Jordan folded his arms. "You're a sharp cookie — I'd like you to keep an eye on him. When you've wheedled his plans of out him, come and tell me. I'm sure there'll be a suitable reward."

He smirked at her, and Ria wondered, not for the first time, whether she should admit to him that she just didn't find him attractive. On the other hand, nobody else had ever shown any interest in her.

"Ooh!" Marian sniggered as he strode away. "A reward, eh? I'm thinking he hasn't realized it's not your eyes you want to keep on Cassidy Morganstern!"

"Chance would be a fine thing."

"Look sexy — he's on his way back." Marian took a step back to give Ria the impression of privacy while still in earshot.

Cassidy unleashed a grin that caused Ria to realize that damp panties were not a thing of her adolescent past. She shifted a little uncomfortably. "Pretty, aren't they?" she said.

Cassidy actually looked down her modest cleavage before meeting her eyes. "Very pretty... the royal family must be desperate for publicity, allowing those treasures to be toured all over the country. Do they get a cut of the door takings?"

"I have no idea," Ria said.

"Are you glued to that spot for the rest of the day? Do they still keep the grimoires in there? I remember we used to bet each other we couldn't get in there."

"And nobody ever won the bet," Ria agreed. "Although these days I work in there," she added.

"Mm. I saw Jordan talking to you — how by all that's good did that goon manage to end up sheriff? Did he tell you to keep an eye on me?"

"Maybe."

"You're not seeing him, are you?"

"Fuck, no! Although," Ria allowed, "he has hinted from time to time that he might be interested."

"Is the Broken Wheel still the best restaurant in town?"

"Uh — I believe so?" Ria, confused by the sudden change of subject, was unwilling to admit she couldn't afford to eat there.

"Excellent. I'd hate to disappoint the sheriff. It will give me great pleasure if you would consent to join me for dinner this evening... and after that, I'll take you to see my circus."

"Your circus?"

"Oh, didn't I mention that? Yes, I own it now." He gave her an exaggerated wink and then turned to face the throng, holding his plumed hat high. "Ladies and gentlemen, lords and ladies! Tonight, for your delectation, for one performance only, the Great Circus of Freeland invites you to be teased, tantalized and thrilled! We have acrobats! We have a glorious team of matched horses! We have jugglers and clowns! See our aerialists walk the wires and fly! Come along for the best evening's entertainment in the kingdom!"

As he moved away, Marian moved back to Ria's side. "My panties are wet," she sighed.

"Mine too."

～

Wearing her best — actually, her only — decent frock, Ria presented herself at the entrance to the Broken Wheel at eighteen bells sharp. The doorman — who knew whose daughter she was — looked down his nose at her, but begrudgingly admitted that Ringmaster Morganstern was awaiting her within.

Ringmaster, huh? Ria was hiding a smirk as the doorman handed her off to the head waiter, who escorted her obsequiously to a table in a shadowed booth. Cassidy, clad from head to foot in black, rose to his feet to greet her, and waved her into the seat across the table from him. "I took the liberty of ordering a selection of dishes," he said.

Ria was glad she wasn't hungry, as the Broken Wheel's idea of a satisfying meal appeared to be a couple of slivers of fish artfully draped at the center of a swirl of tartare on a wooden platter. It took her a moment to realize the platter had little spokes, one of which was missing. Very droll.

She sampled one of the dishes, and let Cassidy talk. He had always been good at that, and he didn't disappoint her now. How exactly he'd gone from tag-along to circus owner Ria was not — on this occasion, at least — to learn, but she enjoyed his slightly scurrilous tales of life on the road. She was just thinking she'd got away with not talking about herself when he said, "Enough about me — do you like working at the library?"

She paused with her fork halfway to her mouth, a shrimp dangling precariously over her cleavage, and then shrugged. "Not really, but it keeps the roof over my head."

"You don't want more... excitement in life? To travel, perhaps?"

Ria shrugged. "Fuck, no — I couldn't take my books with me. I like my excitement... vicarious. Being a librarian gives me access to more books, too... and it means I don't have to live with my parents."

"The fishmongers." He nodded. She guessed he remembered the way the other children had teased her, claiming she smelled of fish — which, in fairness, it was difficult to avoid when your whole house reeked of the day's catch.

He'd been one of the only kids who'd defended her. "So," he continued, "you rent a house?"

She nearly choked on her mouthful of food, coughing into her hand. When she'd recovered, she said, "I guess when you grow up in the biggest house in town you have no idea what rentals cost. I live in the room over the butcher's stables. It's warm and dry and has plenty of bookshelves."

"The important things in life."

"You think I'm funny, don't you? I can't imagine why you wanted to have dinner with me..."

"Ria, Ria... I am not laughing at you." He put a hand over hers on the table, and despite her best intentions she couldn't help the frisson of pleasure his touch gave her. "There aren't many people in this town I want to spend any time with. We had some fun together when we were kids. Frankly, I wouldn't have brought the circus to Chatris Arbor if it wasn't for the crown jewels. We go where the crowds are."

The crowds, or the swag? Ria frowned. "Your parents..."

"Disowned me years ago. They were at the opening yesterday. They ignored me."

Ria felt a pang of sympathy for him. His hand was still resting on hers, and she put her other hand over his. "I'm sorry."

"I made my bed. And as it happens, I always thought you were... attractive." He turned his head as the bells tolled the hour, giving her fingers a gentle squeeze before he extracted his hand from between hers. "Time we were on our way. Next stop, the big top!"

～

Ria remembered the circus. She'd been with Cassidy, all those years ago, the night he decided he'd found his vocation. She'd never understood what had appealed to him — her memory was of tawdry, fake sideshows, peeling paint and faded artwork, tarnished glitter, and an almost overwhelming smell of animal feces and human body odor. If Cassidy hadn't invited her, she wouldn't have bothered attending the show.

The circus was set up in the large park close by the Grand Library. As they emerged from the buildings that edged it, Ria's eyes widened. Instead of the huddle of phony sideshows and sad-looking caged animals, brightly colored pennants flew from a myriad of poles, surrounding the biggest tent she had ever laid eyes on. It was striped red and white, twinkling lights encircling the join between sides and top, and there was a steady stream of townsfolk, talking and laughing, headed toward the well-lit entrance. A group of giggling girls spotted Cassidy and surrounded him, teasing him with hints of what they might do if he just looked their way during the performance. He smiled, his eyes making promises, but said nothing as he guided Ria past them. To one side a big man wearing a leotard over a black bodysuit stood frowning, arms folded, beside a smaller tent flap.

"You're late."

"Leo, Miss Matthews is my guest tonight. Ria, Leo is our strongman."

"Hello," Ria said.

Apparently hearing Cassidy's voice, a girl popped out from the tent and handed him a bright scarlet coat, which he donned over his black clothing. The coat was heavily embroidered with gold thread which caught and reflected the lights.

Ria blinked. "You're part of the show?"

He laughed. "I'm the ringmaster; of course I'm part of the show. Follow me — tonight you'll have the best seat in the house."

The inside of the tent smelled not of the crowd that thronged the tiered seating, but rather of vanilla and musk. Ria looked around at the beautifully decorated tent poles, and at the clean sawdust that coated the floor of the marquee. Overhead, poles and wires confirmed his promise of aerialists.

"You've made a few changes," she said as Cassidy led her up some steps and into an otherwise empty garlanded box.

"For the better, I trust?"

"I would say so, yes. What did you do with all the side shows?"

"I let them go. They were pretty much all fakes. I employed a couple of jobbing mages to enhance the show instead. It's a pity there are no good magicians anymore," he sighed, leaning on the side of the box as she took her seat. "Think of the crowds I could draw if I had an illusionist on the books." He straightened. "Well, the show will be starting shortly. I hope you enjoy it — and don't forget to keep an eye on me." He blew her a kiss and then strode down into the ring, his feet scuffing up little puffs of sawdust as he walked. Musicians blew a fanfare.

There was a podium at the center of the ring, and it was from there that he ran the performance, his voice ringing out, introducing the show with promises of amazement and delight. The rapt audience cheered the team of white horses that pranced around the ring, scantily clad girls posing on their backs before springing athletically from mount to mount. As the horses weaved in and out of one another, one girl caught a dangling rope and clambered up it to hang upside down from a swing. Bright lights swirled and twinkled on falls of glitter around her as she twirled. Ria looked for but couldn't spot the magicians Cassidy had mentioned who she guessed to be responsible for the effects.

The horses were followed by a team of jugglers, and a pair of tightrope walkers clad in sparkling black outfits who teetered along their wires, drawing gasps from the audience before springing into their real routine, a balancing act that looked miraculous to the cheering onlookers. The musicians continued to play appropriate music — quiet notes in minor keys accompanied the precarious swaying and triumphant chords greeted each success.

A girl came by and sold Ria a tray of something crunchy smothered with caramel sauce and sprinkled with chocolate which was eaten with a wooden spatula. She was busy trying to eat it without dripping it down herself when the lights dimmed to imitate flickering candlelight. Shapes throwing frightening, distorted shadows ran out into the ring. One moment Ria was gasping along with the rest of the audience, and then laughing as the lights went up and she saw that the shadows belonged to a troop of brightly clad clowns, carrying the props for their show — a small tunnel, a metal contraption whose purpose eluded her, and hand carts filled with mysterious objects.

Cassidy, atop his podium, introduced them as the fabulous Fantollini family, and stood, arms folded, as they capered around the ring, performing pratfalls and cartwheels, and popping in and out of the tunnel to perform tricks on one another. Ria found herself laughing along with the rest of the audience when one of them tried to push the ringmaster from his stand. He turned to remonstrate with the clown, and several others gathered near one of the carts, reaching in and producing what Ria realized were plates piled high with a creamy substance. The clowns pointed to

their plates, and then mimed an appeal to the audience —
should they rescue their friend?

Cassidy turned, reacted to their play, and leapt athletically down from the podium. They set out in pursuit of him
— round and round the ring he ran, dodging their props,
while the audience cheered him on. At one point, one of the
musicians dropped a cymbal, distracting the clowns.
Cassidy dived into the clowns' tunnel, and they pantomimed
looking everywhere for him until one of them mimed realization. The clowns split into two groups and staked out
both ends of the tunnel, so that when Cassidy tried to
emerge he was showered with cream pies. He stood, his
whole visage obscured by white goo, and one of the clowns
ran around him with a rope, tying him up.

This was obviously part of the show, and Ria was
laughing so hard there were tears running down her face.
The clowns conferred, miming argument, and then towed
their "captive" toward the metal contraption. One of them
turned on a tap and water began to cascade from the top
into a catchment tray at the base. They edged Cassidy, still
apparently blinded by cream pie, toward the makeshift
shower, presumably to clean him up — but as he was
pushed under the jets, the naughtiest clown bent over and
pressed a switch. The jets of water changed to jets of foam,
which completely covered the clowns' hapless victim. The
clown mimed laughter, and the others chased him around
the ring while all that could be seen of Cassidy was his red
and gold coat. One of the clowns leapt onto the ringmaster's
podium and began to mime an introduction to the next act,
while the others continued to pursue the naughty one.

The ring filled with acts pretending to be confused by
the replacement ringmaster's waving hands. A pair of
contortionists tangled; a fire eater spewed streams of flame

toward the audience; the horses reappeared and circled the ring, weaving around the small mountain of foam, trailing streamers of bubbles in their wake. Spotlights zagged unevenly around the ring, alternately hiding and exposing the chaos.

Finally the clowns caught up to their "bad" member and made him turn off the foam. One of them picked up a bucket of water and threw it over Cassidy, who emerged, spluttering, from the froth. He folded his arms, glaring, and the clowns fled the ring. The crowd cheered as Cassidy, his hair dripping wet, clambered back onto the podium. The acrobats cartwheeled into the ring to clear up the remaining debris, and the clowns ran one last circuit, waving to the crowd and threatening the front row with cream pies, which they eventually threw at one another.

The rest of the show was fabulous, the aerialists performing amazing leaps and catches, Leo the strongman anchoring an entire pyramid of acrobats, and the horses making one last, triumphant circuit of the ring. Ria realized she hadn't enjoyed herself this much in years.

When it was finally over, she expected Cassidy to disappear backstage, but he took his bows and then walked up to the box where she was sitting. While his hair and clothing had mostly dried out from his soaking, he still had smears of cream on his jacket and trousers.

"So," he said, sitting down as the audience filed out of the tent. "What did you think of my circus?"

"It's fabulous," she said honestly. "I really enjoyed it. I liked the fact you allowed the clowns to use you as their stooge. All that cream and foam must be pretty unpleasant, though!"

"I'm used to it," he said. "May I walk you home?"

"If you want to."

He gave her a look from under his long dark eyelashes. "Oh, I do," he purred.

~

Ria couldn't think of anything to say as they walked back through the town. Cassidy had taken off his bright jacket and, without it, few of the townspeople heading for their own homes paid him any attention. As they neared the butcher's, he took her hand, and she swallowed nervously.

"Well," he said, "I hope you're going to invite me in."

"For a nightcap?" she hazarded. This had to be the point where he bade her goodnight — she didn't dare hope for a kiss, however much she might want one — and went off to commit his robbery.

He laughed. "That wasn't quite what I had in mind," he murmured. "After all, you're supposed to be keeping an eye on me, and if I was going to steal those jewels this would be the most likely time, wouldn't it? I expect Jordan wants to catch me in the act. I was thinking there's a different sort of act I'd quite like to be caught in..."

Ria stopped at the base of the rickety stairs that led up to her door and turned to look at him. He gazed down at her, a decided twinkle in his dark eyes. "Erm, are you suggesting...?"

"I was hoping you'd invite me to stay the night," he said. "You appreciate, of course, that I'm not planning to stick around... but I thought we might have some fun before I disappear again."

"Yes," she said, and then amended hurriedly, "I mean, yes, I know you're not going to stick around."

The corner of his mouth quirked. "Good," he said. "I wouldn't want you to be under any misapprehension." He raised an eyebrow. "Of course, if you're worried about your reputation...?

"Seriously?" Ria laughed. "Having you spend the night is only going to enhance that!"

She led the way up the outside stairs to the door of the small room she occupied. She half expected Cassidy to laugh at the stacks of books — she'd long since run out of shelves — that were piled everywhere, but he just looked around and nodded.

"I can't give you your heart's desire," he said. "You already have it — it's to be surrounded by books. But perhaps I can appeal to other desires you might have?"

Well hallelujah, Ria thought to herself, and smiled.

Cassidy didn't disappoint, and neither did he rush anything. He captured her mouth, sucking her lips and pushing his tongue between them until she parted them. He wrapped her in his arms, drawing her against him, and she realized without surprise that her panties weren't just damp; they were wringing wet. She pressed herself closer, abandoning any claim to naivety. So what if they only had one night together? She planned to make the most of it.

So, it seemed, did Cassidy. "My goodness, sweet Ria," he murmured to her as he slowly peeled her out of her dress. "You grew up very nicely... very nicely indeed." He paid homage to her breasts, kissing and licking them until she was gasping.

Ria's expectation of a quick coit after which Cassidy disappeared into the night was the only part of her that ended up disappointed. The ringmaster played her expertly, teasing her, keeping her on the edge and not letting up when her first orgasm took her, nor the second, or ... well, she lost count. Eventually, blinking, she murmured, "Is it me, or is it getting light?"

"I guess I've been here all night, then."

"Yes, and..."

Someone hammered on the door and she sat bolt upright with a gasp.

"Ria? Ria, wake up!"

"Jordan." Ria giggled, pulled a sheet around herself and went to open the door. The sheriff stood on the top step, looking disheveled and anxious. The sun was just lifting over the horizon. "Yes?"

"I'm sorry to wake you so early, but there's been an attempted robbery and I wanted to check whether..."

Jordan broke off with a gasp as Cassidy, completely naked, came to stand behind Ria. "Attempted?" he said. "Well, you must've scared the thieves off, then."

Ria found herself wanting to laugh at the horrified expression on Jordan's face. He tugged her out of the door. "You — you sullied yourself with this man?"

"I had sex with him, yes." She tugged the sheet more firmly around herself, shivering in the chill air.

"How could you, with this — this..."

"Expert," Ria grinned, folding her arms. "Very, very satisfying expert! You're just upset because he was with me all night and you can't pin your attempted robbery on him."

"How can you be sure? He could have slipped out while you were asleep..."

"Sleep?" Ria yawned widely. "What makes you think we wasted any of the night sleeping?"

Jordan glowered at her. "The head librarian is calling in all the staff," he said. "You'd better get dressed and get over there." He turned and stomped off down the stairs, nearly putting his foot through one of the boards, which was in need of replacing.

"I think he was annoyed." Cassidy put his arms around

Ria from behind and kissed the back of her neck. "One more for the road?"

"I'm supposed to ... oh, if you insist!"

Marian looked Ria up and down. "I'd ask what took you so long, but since you look pretty pleased with yourself, I think I can guess. Cassidy?"

"I couldn't possibly say," Ria said.

"Well, if you can't, Jordan certainly can. I think he's complained to everybody here that his prime suspect has a cast iron alibi!"

"Well, something was cast iron," Ria grinned.

The two women sidled past the group of security men standing around the crown jewels. They lay, sparkling, on their black velvet. The sheriff's team of mages were wandering around the atrium pulling on their beards and scratching their foreheads, apparently at a loss.

"So what exactly happened?" Ria asked.

"Somebody tried to turn off the protective dome, and it set all the library alarms off," Marian said. "Apparently the noise scared the thieves off. I wonder who it can have been."

"Not Cassidy," Ria said confidently. "I never took my eyes off him all night."

"Maybe it was someone else from the circus," Marian said. "From what I've been able to pick up, nobody has a clue how the thieves got in, or who they were. And as they didn't get away with anything, I guess we'll..."

The head librarian stepped into their path. "Gossiping, ladies? I need you to check every inch of your section of the library." He glowered at Ria, looked her up and down, sniffed, and strode off.

"Jordan!" Ria grumped.

Marian unlocked the three locks that fastened the door to the grimoire room, and murmured the password before pushing the door open. The two women stood in the doorway and looked around. Nothing appeared to have been disturbed — the tomes sat, or in one case writhed, on their podia, padlocks firmly in place. After a moment, Marian walked down the room, examining each shelf and podium for anything out of place. Halfway, she came to a sudden halt, and turned to look at Ria.

"Come and stand here," she said.

"Why?" Ria joined her friend and looked around herself, expecting to find something moved or missing. When nothing was, she began to relax, and then stiffened in sudden alarm, her head turning toward one particular book. "The tome of mysteries isn't begging us to open it." She frowned at the book, apparently still chained firmly to its podium, and then went across to it and wiped a careful finger along the surface of the red leather cover. "No dust. Well, fuck me sideways with a banana, someone's stolen it — look, the chain's been snapped clean through!"

"This must've been what they were after all along," Marian said slowly. "They couldn't have snatched it on the way out... I'm guessing they set off the alarms on the crown jewels as a distraction. It may be just as well you've given Cassidy an alibi, or Jordan would probably have arrested him on suspicion!"

Ria shook her head. She remembered how Cassidy had walked up to them at the reception, when they'd been standing by the door, and joked about how they'd never succeeded in getting inside the room when they were children. But how could it have been him? She hadn't taken her eyes off him once.

Except...

Later, alone in her room, Ria thought about the circus performers who'd been clad in black — the strongman, some of the riders, two of the aerialists... and, under that fancy coat, Cassidy. Cassidy who had used her, she realized, as his alibi. He'd made sure she thought he'd never left her sight... but anybody could have been under the cream pies and foam. She tried to decide whether the clowns' act would have given him the time to attempt the theft, and concluded that it just might have. She'd been had, she thought.

She looked at her crumpled bedding, and a smile crept across her face. Oh yes, she'd been had all right — and she wouldn't have missed a minute of that amazing night. She thought about telling Jordan her suspicions... but hell, she could just be imagining it, couldn't she? Just as she had all those years ago when he'd told her he was leaving with the circus, she had to let Cassidy fly free.

A month had passed. The crown jewels were back with the royal family, and there had been no sign anywhere of the tome. Life at the library went back to what passed for normal — Ria had several more demerits for swearing and disrespecting her superior, but couldn't afford to tell him where to stick his job. Besides, she liked working with Marian.

"There's a man here to see you." The director glowered at Ria. "I hope you're not dragging our reputation further through the mud, Miss Matthews."

Puzzled, Ria followed him into the atrium. She returned to the grimoire room half an hour later looking bemused, a roll of vellum in her hand.

"He's fired you," Marian guessed. "Or someone's charged you with indecent exposure."

"It wasn't me who was naked," Ria said distractedly.

"So...?"

"Oh." Ria waved the scroll. "It seems I'm the proud owner of Cyril's bookshop."

"What?"

"Apparently the old git decided to retire and has signed the property over to me."

"Why, because you were his best customer?" Marian shook her head. "I think you have a different benefactor to thank for this largess. Just how much d'you think Cassidy got for that grimoire?"

"Well, fuck!" Ria said, and started to laugh.

Cyril's bookstore was in the twists, a bow-fronted store that reeked of old paper. Ria stood in the doorway and inhaled with delight — the scent of adventure, just the way she liked it. She had no idea how Cassidy could have persuaded Cyril to sign the place over to her. In fact, she didn't really believe he had until she opened the cash drawer behind the sales counter and found, nestling in black velvet, a very familiar pair of emerald earrings.

Well, fuck me, she thought — had Cassidy stolen the jewels after all? She picked up one earring tentatively. Was this the real thing, or a replica? She should hand these over to Jordan... except, no, that wasn't going to happen. Cassidy might have played them all — but he'd more than adequately rewarded her for her unwitting assistance with his crime. He had, despite claiming he couldn't, managed to give her her heart's desire.

She couldn't wear the earrings in public — but sometimes, at night, alone in her bedroom above the shop, she'd slip them on and stand in front of the mirror wondering what —if anything — would happen the next time the circus came to town.

# ABOUT J A MORTIMORE

J A Mortimore is legendary, but isn't admitting what for. She started writing fiction at a young age and has never stopped. She has run UK fan clubs for Star Trek and the A-Team and written in a number of fandoms, predominantly pre-internet. Now retired, she writes space opera novels with romance, and lives in Gloucestershire with two friends, a number of cats and far too many books. She is an expert procrastinator, but plans to start self-publishing her novels in 2022.

**Find out more about J A at:**
jamortimore.co.uk

 instagram.com/judithmortimore

CPSIA information can be obtained
at www.ICGtesting.com
Printed in the USA
LVHW112000050422
715401LV00006B/299

9 781913 236892